BREAKING POINT

Also by Freddie P. Peters:

In the HENRY CROWNE PAYING THE PRICE series

INSURGENT

COLLAP$E

NO TURNING BACK

SPY SHADOWS

HENRY CROWNE PAYING THE PRICE BOOKS 1-3

IMPOSTER IN CHIEF

In the NANCY WU CRIME THRILLER series

BLOOD DRAGON

Dear Reader,

I'm thrilled you've chosen BREAKING POINT Book 2 in the HENRY CROWNE PAYING THE PRICE series.

Think about getting access for FREE to the exclusive Prequel to the HENRY CROWNE PAYING THE PRICE series: INSURGENT.

Go to freddieppeters.com/breaking-point

BREAKING POINT

FREDDIE P. PETERS

HENRY CROWNE PAYING THE PRICE BOOK 2

Breaking Point

www.freddieppeters.com

ISBN: 978-1-9999811-3-6

Cover design by Ryan O'Hara.

Typesetting by Danny Lyle.

This is entirely a work of fiction. Names, characters, businesses, places, events and incidents are either the products of the author's imagination or used in a fictitious manner. Any resemblance to actual persons, living or dead, or actual events or localities is purely coincidental.

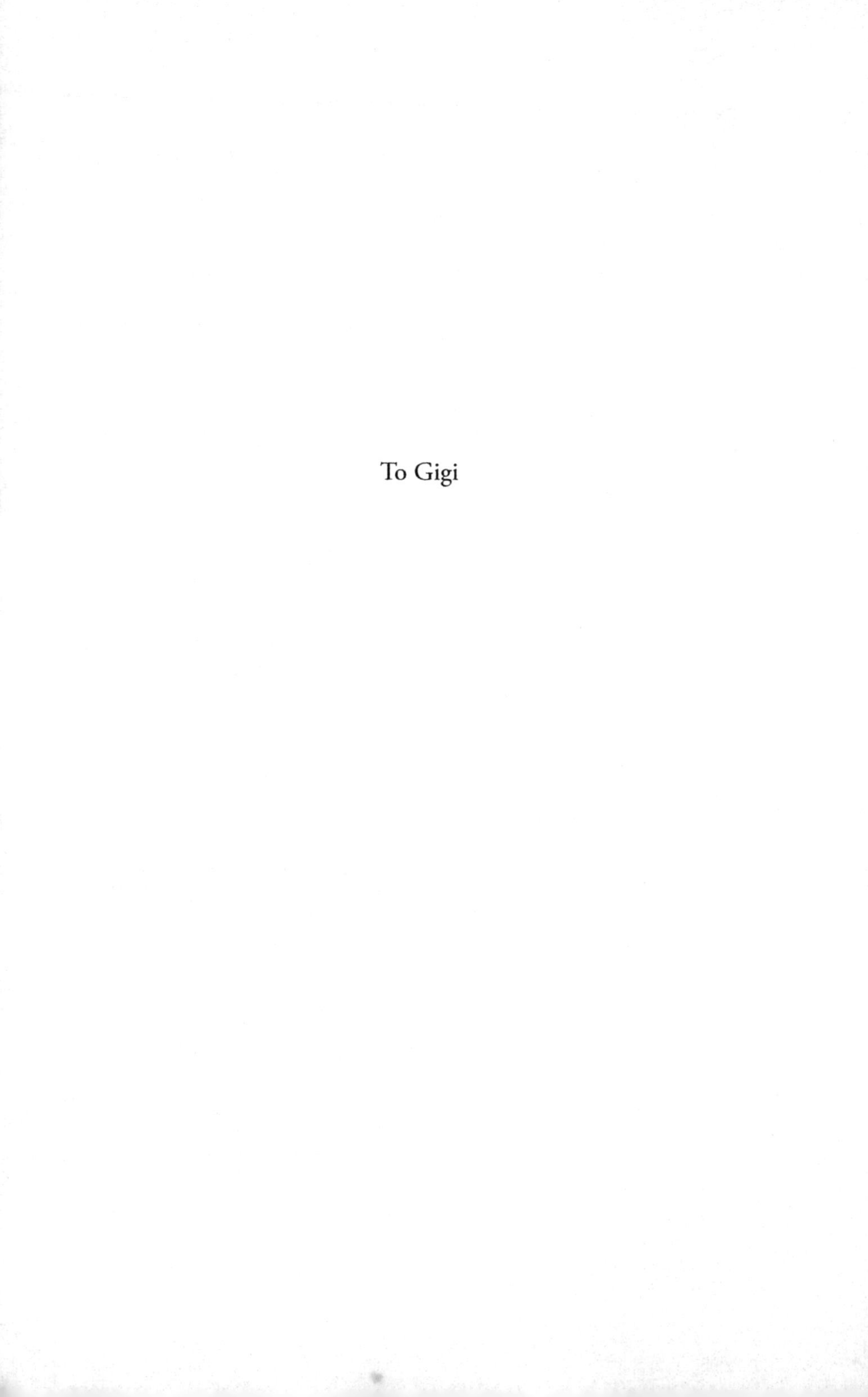

To Gigi

Chapter One

The room stood up and erupted into applause. Nancy joined them, crossed the platform and clasped Edwina's hand warmly. She grinned at her friend. Yes, Edwina had delivered a trailblazing speech that had provoked a robust Q&A session. Edwina could soon be joining the most powerful women in the world, tipped to become the next Governor of the Bank of England. Edwina had discussed the offer with Nancy, in confidence.

The Women in Enterprise Conference had become the highlight in the calendar of professional women striving to make their mark not only in international investment banking but also now in the whole of the UK industry.

The conference theme was the reworking of an old chestnut 'How women break the glass ceiling?'. But the developing financial crisis had given it a new twist... Would all this have happened had women been at the helm? To give the debate more bite, high- profile men had been invited. The panel was well constructed, a mix of captains of industry and bankers.

Nancy, the newly appointed Chair of Women in Enterprise, had agreed to act as moderator. The atmosphere had been electric as senior ladies in the audience had taken a gloves-off approach and the gentlemen were having none of it.

"One final question... one."

A sea of hands shot up, waving, snapping, eager to attract Nancy's attention.

"The FT will have a last say tonight... Pauline, go ahead please."

"A question for Edwina. Christine Lagarde is the Managing Director of the International Monetary Fund; Janet Yellen is almost certainly going to be appointed by Obama as Head of the Federal Reserve. Is the Bank of England ready for a woman at the helm?"

Edwina stood up again, moving back to the lectern at a slow deliberate pace.

"Any institution, private or public must consider the best outcome for what it needs to deliver. Talent will be found in a pool of diverse people and the most forward-looking organisations will not shy away from it." A roar of approvals interrupted. "I know what you are asking me, Pauline – indirectly. I have only this answer – *may the best of us win*."

How clever, Nancy thought. *An answer that will inspire the women,* appease the men and say nothing about her, quite simply brilliant.

Nancy had been a high-profile barrister practising criminal law, then became the youngest ever appointed Queen's Counsel at the age of thirty- five. For a very long time she had thought talent should prevail. But the latest report on lack of progress in female status had pushed her to advocate for set quotas for women at all levels of the corporate structure.

Edwina had concluded the debate with a final flash of genius. The voice of a woman who could inspire by her exemplary career alone.

"Thank you," Nancy said. "Thank you for the extraordinary show of support." She was broadly smiling at the crowd and turned to Edwina with a nod. "It has been an exceptional event. I must again thank the participants for the quality of their intervention and for the quality of the audience input."

The room erupted once more.

"I know, I know," said Nancy whilst trying to appease the gathered people by gesturing with both hands. "Please, you know it is not completely over. We still have drinks – much-needed – waiting for us next door. You can strike up a conversation with our guests. Do be gentle with some of them!"

The room broke into laughter and the men in the audience took it in good humour. When the panellist were returning their clip-microphones to the staff. Edwina approached Nancy.

"I think it's in the bag,"

Edwina said.

"It certainly is. Did Gabriel work with you on this? I detect a forceful yet compromising approach in your speech."

"Yes, Gabs helped me with my spiel... No, I was referring to the governor's job. Osborne spoke to me about *the* appointment."

Nancy grinned. "Oh, I see. We must catch up. I am excited for you."

"We must catch up indeed, but here's not the place. Let's do lunch."

"Do let's – utterly delighted for you, Eddie."

Nancy moved away and started circulating amongst a crowd of women gathered on the roof terrace of the tall building at Nbrl Poultry. In the City. She was mobbed by a group of enthusiastic young lawyers eager to speak about her experience as a QC. She finally moved on and was about to join one of the panellists, CEO of a notorious airline, when someone grabbed her arm.

"Do you really believe in that bullshit of yours?" a voice slurred. The large man was standing too close for comfort. He swayed slightly, moved backward. His small beady eyes narrowed in a vengeful squint. "And who do I have the pleasure of speaking to?" replied Nancy whilst slowly removing his hand from her arm.

"Gary Cook, former head of trading at GL Investment – got the boot, courtesy of one of your bloody females."

"I doubt any of these females are mine as you put it," replied Nancy.

"Yeah right, but you – you and your little friend up there on the stage are not whiter than white; you lot are trying to say you are better than blokes on the trading floor. That's bollocks and I can prove it...'cos I've got something to share." Gary's heavy jaw had clenched so hard a muscle in his neck leaped out. He had not finished yet.

"I say, how clever of you. Not whiter than white – with my Chinese ancestry that is going to be rather certain."

"Gary Cook," exclaimed a voice from behind Nancy. "Great to see you again."

Gary stopped in his tracks. Gabriel's unexpected welcome confused him.. The well-groomed young man interposed himself effortlessly between Gary and Nancy who slowly retreated. There was no point in making a scene. Gary was a loser who should not be humoured. Nancy could hear the smooth-talking Gabriel holding the man's anger, absorbing it until it had subsided completely. Edwina had chosen well: Gabriel Steel was an impressive right-hand man. He manoeuvred Gary towards a more secluded part of the roof terrace, called for more drinks.

Nancy was not sure Gary needed more champagne, but no doubt Gabriel would move him gradually towards the exit and Gary would eventually take the hint. A small tremor of revulsion ran through Nancy's body. She had not recognised Gary's old and bitter face to start with.

She rubbed her hand against her dress but she needed more than that to wash away the stickiness of Gary's feel.

She entered the ladies' room briskly, lathered her hands with sandalwood-scented soap and ran cold water over them, watching the foam disappear down the plug hole. An apt image of the place where Gary ought to end up one day. She retraced her steps but before turning into the corridor someone grabbed her shoulder. Edwina was standing close to her.

"Just had an email from George Osborne's PA. Final meeting in a couple of days' time," Edwina whispered. "Perhaps a little coaching may be warranted?"

"I somehow feel the student has surpassed the master," Nancy murmured, smiling. "But of course, I am there for you if you feel the need."

"Very much so." Edwina squeezed Nancy's shoulder gently and let go at the sound of voices coming their way.

Both women emerged from the corridor separately and as she reappeared Nancy found herself mobbed once more by a group of enthusiastic women… the banking industry had to change its ways.

One of the young women mentioned the name Henry Crowne. She must have done her homework on Nancy. Nancy answered the question with a frosty look. She would not be discussing Henry at this conference or anywhere else for that matter. Then a whirlpool of other queries swept her away, away from Gary and Henry.

There was only a small group of people left by now and Nancy was about to say her goodbyes when two uniformed officers walked through the elevator doors alighting directly onto the terrace.

One of the officers bent his head towards his shoulder radio set. "Yes, I am on the roof now. There are a few people still up here."

A disembodied voice replied. Nancy thought she heard the instructions *keep them there.*

"Sorry ladies, I am PC Barrett, and this is PC Leonard. We have a jumper..."

The women who hadn't left yet, looked at each other incredulous.

"I mean someone has jumped from the roof terrace. Dead I am afraid..." PC Barrett asked to see the guest list and the young security guard who had checked guests' names at the door produced it in an instant. PC Barrett turned away from the crowd and towards his shoulder radio, sheltering his voice.

"Yep, got it there. Yep... Gary Cook."

Nancy had turned away, still all ears. She shuddered; Gary had jumped – *impossible.* What Nancy recalled of Gary did not fit the profile of a man who would ever become desperate enough to take his own life.

* * *

Henry's back muscles screamed and yet he kept going.

"One hundred and ninety-seven, ninety-eight, ninety-nine, two hundred. Shit!" puffed Henry as he rolled back onto the mat. He was nearly at the end of his routine in HMP Belmarsh gym. He needed to start stretching but he lay there for another minute. A small luxury in a place devoid of the comfort he once knew.

He closed his eyes and a face appeared He sat up slowly, eyes still closed. Was Liam also exercising in the prison in which he was? Northern Ireland Maghaberry was a tough place, a tough place for a tough boy. Liam would survive it but what of Bobby?

Anger gripped Henry again. He stood up abruptly and started stretching.

"Let go – just let go," he said softly, applying pressure to release the pain. His muscles ached. He eased off the stretch a little.

The question had haunted Henry for months. Could Liam have done anything differently? Could his best friend have chosen Henry rather than his brother Bobby?

But Bobby had barricaded himself with a hostage in an office in Dublin. The police in Dublin would never have spared the life of Bobby, a dissident IRA operative, a man for whom decommissioning had no meaning. Bobby wasn't ready to give up the fight, not now, not ever. There had to be a bargain and Henry was that bargain.

And what a deal he was. A financial superstar, a City banker who had not only contributed to the IRA's finances but also set up the money laundering structure that shielded the IRA's cash. Henry's stellar financial career masking his terrorist activities, how clever and daring – but how wrong.

"No – Liam had no choice," Henry murmured, wiping his face with a towel. No matter how many times Henry went through the logic of why Liam, his childhood friend, had chosen to tell the police about Henry's IRA involvement, the result remained the same. Henry's mind understood but his gut was still wrenched by the betrayal.

Yet, Henry had wanted to be chosen, like the brother he had always thought he was to Liam and Bobby O'Connor. And this yearning to belong had cost him everything. Beyond the sacrifice of his own career and hopes, he had also sacrificed lives, many lives, and for that he would pay.

Henry ran the towel over his hair. The standard prison cut had left very little of what had been a dense mane. He threw the towel over his shoulder, went into the changing rooms, stripped down and started showering.

He had been apprehensive of his life in prison to start with. Would he find a fate there only reserved for the bastard of a banker he was? Would he be molested, beaten up and humiliated? But the fear had not materialised, and it had faded away. He had learned to become unnoticeable amongst the Category A, most dangerous prisoners of Belmarsh.

Even in prison Henry had managed to land in the highest ranks amongst cons, deemed to pose most threat to the police and national security. He, the forever competitive banker, had been moved to a special unit within Belmarsh.

Henry was high-risk too. A knife might well go astray in the main prison and land in his back. On Nancy's advice he had played that card fully. He had been assigned to a block in which cons shared the same Cat A high-risk profile, except that there was no other bankers there. Or at least not yet.

"Hey, good set of press-ups, man."

"Thanks, Big K. I plan to get really fit in the next twenty-five years."

"Man, you get good muscle tone here, you get respect."

Henry nodded, grabbed his towel and got dressed quickly. He still didn't like to linger in the changing rooms. Another inmate had moved out of the showers too. Henry felt eyes on him, but when he looked up the man was facing the other way, going about his business.

Henry noticed two entwined faces tattooed on his back – strange, the faces looked similar. Big K had already got dressed and left but he would know who this was. Big K had been allocated the cell next to his and he had shown interest in Henry straightaway. Drugs were his domain, and the term money laundering had his undivided attention. Big K was someone who knew what it meant to do time and worth cultivating with a few snippets of info.

Henry rang the buzzer, the security guard opened the door and informed the next guard that Henry was on his way to his cell, running the gauntlet of the next four doors to cross.

At Belmarsh High Security Unit no two doors could be opened at the same time and Henry had learned to be patient with the procedure. Even the prison officers went through security checks when they entered for HMP Belmarsh HSU was the most secure prison in the UK.

"Thanks John," Henry said. The guard nodded and let Henry into Cell 14 on Wing Three. The door shut with the usual heavy clunk and Henry sat on his bed. He looked at his watch, 9:47am – only thirteen minutes to mail time.

He hoped for a letter from Nancy. It was too early for her to give news about her big night at Women in Enterprise Conference but she might feed him titbits on its preparation.

Once the post had been delivered, he would take down a heavy art book sitting sideways on his small bookshelf, from its thick spine he would retrieve his pride and joy, a small netsuke in the shape of a dog with pups.

It had become a comforting ritual to be reading a letter from the outside world whilst fingering this small object, a piece of art that did not belong to prison life.

Henry had allowed himself this luxury, a reminder that although he had to pay for his financial terrorism, he had also lost everything he had ever held dear – his father, his friends, his reputation.

* * *

Nancy was watching the news from a distance whilst opening her mail. She was half expecting to hear about Gary's death but perhaps it was a little too soon.

Nancy shuddered at the thought of what she had witnessed the night before. She had offered to go down with PC Leonard to identify the body lying on the pavement. She was after all a consultant with the Met. The thought of seeing Gary's skull smashed and shattered on the ground had made her stomach heave, but she had stilled herself and gone to identify the body. She had answered the police's questions as best she could, disturbed by the image that kept flashing in front of her eyes.

Escaping to the safety and calm of her apartment had done little to soothe her. She had not recognised him to start with. A twenty-five-year career in the City had destroyed the image of the man she had once met. Gary Cook was a name she knew well and had hoped never to hear again.

And yet here was Gary again. Nancy recalled Gary's face and his expression of surprise, not shock.

"No, this is ridiculous," she said and switched the TV off.

She recognised the old feeling of unease with surprise; it had settled quietly in the pit of her stomach and tightened the base of her neck. The stress from high-profile trials had left her when she had hung up her QC's gown and keep her wig well tucked in its box. When Henry had placed his fateful call four years ago, the world of crime had entered her life again.

Henry might not have chosen Nancy in the first instance. A high-profile barrister recommendation had not delivered the punch Henry had hoped for. He had called Nancy out of desperation. Still, she had not minded. Henry's complex case had been the challenge she had forgotten she missed Pritchard QC, a old acquaintance of Nancy, had represented Henry. She was part of the legal team, keeping a suitable distance from the front line of criminal law. She and Henry had grown close, an unlikely friendship on the surface, an obvious one for those who knew them both. She glanced at her watch, 10am. Henry should have received her latest letter by now and she hoped it would provide the link to the outside world he needed.

The phone rang, interrupting Nancy's train of thought. She crossed the room, picked up the old 1930s ivory phone and gave a simple hello. "Nancy, good to hear that you are around. It's Jonathan, I mean Jonathan Pole."

"Jonathan, *mon chère ami*. How good to hear from you. Or should I say Inspector Pole?" exclaimed Nancy delighted to hear from the other man who had entered her life at the time of Henry's case.

"How did you know I was calling you in my formal capacity, *étonnant*?" Pole slipped into French. She enjoyed the way he reminded her of his own French ancestry.

"I did not. In fact, I was going to call you in your formal capacity – *les grands esprits se rencontrent*."

"*Absolument*: great minds think alike," replied Pole amused. "Now, are we talking about yesterday's incident?"

"You mean Mr Cook's unfortunate experiment with gravity?"

"The very one. I can't think of any other reason why you might call. I have not gone through a red light or exceeded the speed limit I promise."

"I don't do traffic. Well, not yet anyway although I am sure our new Superintendent, Marsh would gladly have me reassigned."

"Surely, he could not do this to one of the best DCIs in London, the one who holds the highest rate of crime resolution in the Met.?"

Pole was blushing at the other end of the phone; Nancy heard it in his voice and she enjoyed the effect.

"Jonathan – accept a compliment from a friend, will you?"

"Gratefully accepted, *ma chère*. How about coffee to discuss the jumper?"

"Splendid idea. The usual place, say eleven?"

"Inns of Court, at eleven."

Chapter Two

The mail was late, something Henry had become accustomed to. Yet today it frustrated him. Anger, his lifelong companion, was stirring up again. Henry had learned to deny it the power it once had but today the waiting was intolerable.

He could not risk unearthing his small treasure until Johnny had knocked at his door in his raspy sort of way with the mail, and Henry had responded with his usual "I'm busy". A silly answer but one that gave him the sense that he still owned his life.

He stood up, breathed deeply, exhaled – letting the burn in his throat slowly extinguish. He reached his small desk in one step. He was still amazed at how much he had piled into the diminutive space of his cell: a table, a tiny bookshelf for the books he was currently reading, a chair that could accommodate his tall and now muscular body. The pile of correspondence, his most treasured possession even above the netsuke, was neatly arranged on the desk. He lifted the letters slowly to reach for Nancy's first. He sat on the chair, drawing the letter from its envelope with careful fingers.

Henry, mon ami,
This letter took me a while. I realised I had not put pen to paper for such a long time. I do not mean emails or texts. I mean actual writing, the act of my hand on paper, the slight hesitation that precedes putting down what cannot be erased. Mais enfin la voici.

A sketch of it came on the day I left you behind. The heavy doors closing on you brought a chill to my heart. So, it felt right I should reach out, maybe even necessary. And I have come to realise that a good letter must divulge something intimate about its writer, so I will start with my own news. I have decided to reconnect with my previous life, the one I thought I had left forever behind. Don't be alarmed and think I am recanting after talking so much about giving up the rat race. I have found an unexpected use for my old talent, my new-found bohemian style joined up with the impeccable training of this legal mind – well, you have seen the result!

Of course, you may already have gathered that I received a little nudge. It came in the shape of our mutual friend Mr. P. I want... no. I need to plunge into the City once more, but this time on my own terms. A final test, maybe? Time will tell. To be completely honest, the gentleman in question attracts my interest terribly. There you are. How about this for a confession – ha!

I think I should finish swiftly, and now that my letter lies in front of me I hope it will be the first of many. Please reply, for I know that coming to terms with the act of terror you lived through and the deceit you endured will bring you resolve. But for today I simply say I understand. The rest is up to you.

A très vite
Nancy

The colour of the paper had started to fade. It was slightly crumpled at the top and a splash of water had blurred a couple of words. Nancy's letter had been a lifeline when it first arrived three and a half years ago. It had provided a small glimmer of light in that most desperate of moments. He had so wanted to do the right thing, to show he could be a better man.

"Henry Crowne, notorious banker and IRA operative, seeks to atone for his mistakes," murmured Henry. Alone in his cell, he had first thought he would go mad. His mind, so accustomed to the intense activity that the trading floor demanded, could not cope with idleness.

He had slowly managed to quieten the constant churn of thoughts and found that silence was a friend. Breaking that silence with words uttered aloud gave a sentence so much more weight, and instead of sending him over the edge, this practise had ground him. He could not deny that the shock of conviction had been immense, but he would survive. Just the way he had in Belfast. Just the way he had on the trading floor of GL. He would survive and set himself free.

Henry folded the letter lovingly and replaced it at the bottom of the pile of correspondence. Today, his restless mind moved to the hot topic whispered amongst the other cons on his wing, the latest arrival – Ronnie Kray. Henry had thought it a joke. Could someone seriously be called Ronnie Kray, borrowing the name of the notorious 1960s criminal? But it was true and Big K had advised Henry against making fun of Ronnie when Henry managed to catch up with him before bang-up time started.

"Man, this guy has a reputation for being a crackpot, a real nutjob – thinks the Krays were the best thing since sliced bread, actually before sliced bread," Big K had said with an air of conspiracy followed by a chuckle.

"Is he the guy with two faces tattooed on his back?" Henry asked.

Big K's chuckling face grew serious. "Not sure, why?"

"Saw a guy in the showers with a strange tat on his back but the weird thing – the faces were similar, and the Krays were identical twins if I remember right."

"Don't know, Man… was before my time." Big K considered Henry for a moment. "Did he look at you or did you look at him?"

"That's a bit of a technical question, mate – in the vastness of HMP Belmarsh showers I'm not sure who saw who." Henry had found it hard to suppress a smile.

"I mean it, Man, you don't want this guy to notice you." Big K had run his massive hand over his shaven head. This mass of muscle was uneasy at the thought of Kray. Henry had taken note.

The much-awaited knock came at his door and Henry had to exercise superhuman control not to rush to answer.

"I'm busy." Henry replied.

"Letter for Mr Crowne."

Henry reached his door in one step. The same con distributing the mail daily was at the door of his cell.

* * *

Nancy walked in and saw Inspector Pole bent over a low table at the most comfortable end of the cafe. Nancy moved slowly, observing Pole arranging the cups of tea and coffee together with their favourite pastries. Nancy smiled at this display of thoughtful attention. She made some intentional noise with the heel of her shoes. Pole straightened up more quickly than he would have wanted. He too was all smiles.

"Nancy, *très heureux de vous revoir.*"

"*Moi de même* Jonathan," said Nancy undoing the belt of her orange trench coat. She was wearing one of her colourful dresses that Pole loved, its pattern inspired by a Sonia Delauney design he had seen at a Tate exhibition they had visited together. Nancy noticed Pole's appreciative look.

"I know, I know. How did I manage to wear the black attire of a barrister for most of my career?" said Nancy with a wry smile.

"And did you find a way?" asked Pole amused.

"Very much so. You should have seen the colour of my bags."

Pole raised a quizzical eyebrow. "Bags. I see. Could a young woman raised in France not do better than that?"

Nancy blushed slightly and laughed in turn. "OK. You got me there."

They both sank into the deep leather chairs and enjoyed a leisurely conversation. Pole had nearly finished his coffee by the time Nancy put down her own cup.

"What is the story so far with Gary Cook?" Nancy asked.

" Some more unpleasant business coming out of the City."

Nancy averted her eyes for a moment. "It was a shock. I have seen some pretty bad things in my time as QC, but it has been a while – strange or perhaps good that I have left all this behind."

"Have you? I thought you were still in touch with Henry and – are you not looking at some other cases?"

"How do you know? I thought the Arts were not in your jurisdiction."

Pole nodded. "*Peut-être pas mais* – it is that of my good friend Eugene Grandel."

"Eugene, such a gossip. How does he manage to keep the case on track, I just don't know?"

"He manages all right. He just can't help revealing all he knows to his good friend Pole."

"Working with Eugene is fun, I must admit. Fake pieces of art that even the best dealers think are worth millions; Russian oligarchs fighting over the valuation of horrendously ugly contemporary pieces..."

"I get it," said Pole. "Blood on the street no longer appeals – I am miffed."

"For you, I will make an exception."

"That's very kind of you, Nancy but I also think it is because Gary Cook's death troubles you."

"There is indeed more to it I fear," said Nancy putting her hands together in a reflective way. "Everybody assumes it is suicide. But did you see the way the body fell?"

"He landed on his back."

"I think it is odd. I can't quite put my finger on it."

"It may be that the fall was partly intentional, partly accidental, in which case the body might have fallen backward. He was trying to save himself and couldn't."

"Perhaps," said Nancy stirring slowly what was left of her tea. "The SOCO team checked. There was no sign of struggle." Nancy sat back, thinking through the implication.

"The pathologist has requested an extensive toxicology report," Pole carried on.

"But the report won't be ready for a while, will it?"

"Very true; he stank of alcohol, pupils were a little too dilated."

"Alcohol and possibly drugs. A bad combination. And a strange combination for a conference."

"Or a way to get into the right frame of mind," said Pole. Nancy finished her tea and replaced the cup slowly in its saucer. "Still not convinced," said Pole.

"Did you see the expression on his face, more surprise than horror or resignation?"

"Not enough to give me a new lead. You know something I should?"

"Well, Gary Cook might have been sacked from GL after the merger was announced but he was a tough boy..." Nancy let the sentence hang.

"I'm all ears and this will stay between us for the time being," said Pole reassuringly.

"That's fine Jonathan. I will tell you and frankly it no longer bothers me as much as it once did."

Pole leaned forward in an encouraging fashion.

"What did this bad boy do to have such a lasting impact on you?"

* * *

The lunch had gone well.

How much could Chinese people eat? Staggering, Brett wondered as he was nursing his Cognac. The waiter had produced brandies and cigars of quality, Brett Allner-Smith had insisted. He would never concede that such upper- class refinements could be enjoyed in equal measure by foreigners, but he had learned to be more circumspect in expressing his opinion after his involvement in the Crowne case.

His open resentment of Henry as a collector not worthy of the name had attracted the police's attention, bringing them too close to his illegal business. Something he could ill afford. His MI6 minder, Steve, had been very clear. He was free, even encouraged to do business in the Middle East as long as he did not create too many ripples back in the UK.

The pictures of several artefacts were circulating around the table again. The quality of what was on offer was outstanding. Only a war-torn country could produce such exceptional looting opportunities. Too bad for the idiots who could not preserve their national treasures. The Americans could do little about it. It was hard enough to stop Iraq from imploding.

The pillage of Iraqi treasures had started well before the 2003 conflict, and it had now become a full-blown business. The black market was inundated with pieces from all the main antique sites: Babylon, Nimrud, Ummu and Ur. Brett had developed a network of knowledgeable looters who would never fail to produce large and rare pieces. And today he knew that what was on offer was simply unique.

Brett cleared his voice and resumed his sales pitch. "Allow me, please, to take you once more through the amazing array of pieces available to you."

The translator bent down and whispered into Mr Chong's ear. Mr Chong replied, and the translator addressed Brett in a low voice. "Mr Chong would be delighted to hear about the pieces once more. He would of course want to ensure provenance."

Mr Chong's leathery face had become animated over food. He had commented enthusiastically about the quality of the meal; stories of other banquets celebrating business deals had followed, interrupted by loud laughter, and resounding burps and slurps. Brett had become accustomed to the etiquette surrounding such meals, but the show of power still irked him.

Imbecile, thought Brett. *These have been looted. He would certainly not be going back to Iraq to ask Baghdad's Museum for a certificate of authenticity.*

"Absolutely," said Brett with the most honest face he could muster. "I can most certainly provide an ample description of the site of provenance."

Again, the translator bent towards Mr Chong and whispered in his ear. Chong gave a short nod, his face closed to scrutiny. It was time to do business.

"The most exclusive piece is this 3500 BC gold jar of Sumerian origin. Baghdad's museum is searching for it, but I am able to procure the object for you instead."

The translator did his duty. Chong's face remained unmoved. Brett's long experience as an art dealer had taught him to read the signs. This magnate of the gambling trade in Macau would buy and pay the price no matter how much negotiating he did first.

* * *

Edwina's thoughts drifted to Gary Cook's demise again. Gary's death hadn't made the news. Nothing in the *FT*, a small article in the *Evening Standard* on page 20. Banker-bashing was at its height, but more important matters had taken precedence. Sky News and the BBC were too busy speculating on the appointment of the next Bank of England Governor. Edwina James-Jones put the paper down and finished her espresso, two shots, no sugar – strong and bitter, just the way the battle to reach the top tasted.

She looked at her watch, 8:27am. In exactly three minutes her phone would ring, and Mervyn-The-Oracle-King would summon her. She knew full well that the nickname The Oracle had been coined for Alan Greenspan, and perhaps applying it to her boss was not entirely appropriate. But was it not what all central banks' governors aspired to be?

8:29am. Edwina finished her espresso, crushed the cup and threw it into the wastepaper basket in one perfect arch. In one minute, she would be told that The Oracle was expecting her with the latest status report on the crisis. Today's topic would be red- hot – at what level would LIBOR become dangerous for the banking system?

So much depended on the interest rate: mortgages, financial instruments, the bond market... LIBOR was traditionally fixed by a number of banks that submitted the level at which they each were prepared to lend money to one another. But lending had been distorted by the financial crisis and banks had stopped trusting each other. If interbank lending did not resume, the entire banking system would collapse.

Edwina had started her career on the trading desk of one of the largest UK banks. She had become the first woman head trader and subsequently head of capital markets. "Too ambitious for her own good, a political animal, a cock-sucking bitch" – terms of endearment often used by her male colleagues. She smiled; there would be no glass ceiling for Edwina Maude Mary James-Jones.

The phone rang.

"I'm on my way," said Edwina without waiting for an invitation. She took a look at the pile of documents she and Gabriel had prepared.

She moved out of her office and stopped briefly in front of Gabriel's desk. "A bloody good job if I may say so myself." Edwina smiled, tapping her number two on the shoulder. "Where would I be without you, Gabs?"

"In the same position, Eddie," Gabriel responded with an amused smile.

"You're just too modest for your own good."

"Yeah, yeah, just go and get them." Gabriel waved her off to her meeting.

Edwina opened her handbag and pulled out a small mirror. She applied a dab of rouge to her lips, brushed her blonde hair and checked the reflection in the window. She was ready to do battle with the Monetary Policy Committee. Grabbing the pile of documents she needed, she turned once more towards Gabriel.

"Anything new I need to be aware of?"

"Nope, all in good shape. And nothing on Gary Cook either."

"A surprising but welcome omission from the papers."

"Not completely surprising. I made a few calls to some of my contacts in the press."

"And what will they want in return?" asked Edwina.

"Nothing you're not going to like. Now, to your meeting please or else you will be late," said Gabriel waving her away.

Edwina headed off with a small pang of excitement in her chest. She was walking a straight line to becoming the new Governor of the Bank of England.

* * *

Henry had meticulously organised the desk, in the corner of the small cell.. A brown file was squeezed between a pencil holder and a discreet box of biscuits. Henry had finally been allowed small privileges. He had tried to be content with them: one chocolate chip biscuit after lunch and one shortbread in the evening.

Henry's universe had shrunk from the entire world to a cell barely big enough to swing the proverbial cat. Outside HSU inmates resorted regularly to self-harm or even suicide. And he had contemplated both.

His mind had drifted. Away from the new letter he had received from Nancy. Fresh correspondence still unsettled him, reminding him of the world he once knew. He laid the letter on the desk. He had started composing a reply and was nearing the end. It would almost certainly be read before it reached its recipient. He could not indulge in deep honesty, but Nancy knew him well enough to understand his moods and thoughts.

Nancy, mon amie

Your letters are always a breath of fresh air that keep me sane in this place. But two letters less than twenty-four hours apart… this is pure joy!

Your latest one has also intrigued me. Something to get my brain going is most welcome as you know. I am still reading profusely but it is never enough. The course on philosophy would be interesting were it not for the level of the attendees. Of course I am a pain in the arse when it comes to intellectual pride but even the Cat. A prisoners can't spell their names – I am being a little flippant but not much. Even the crème de la crème of the worst baddies in HSU are hardly challenging. The lecturer is patient and of surprisingly good quality, still I AM BORED. I know, I know, I have said this so many times and we have spoken about it equally often. Contrary to popular belief, nothing, I mean nothing, happens in prison. Unless some poor sod decides to call it a day and meet his maker (which is not unusual) or some psycho decides to go on a rampage against nonces… I hear scraps of it. Since I earned the privilege to do time within HSU as a could-escape-so-better-keep- him-doubly-locked-up con, I have been kept away from real prison life.

But enough of my rambling, I am really surprised that Gary Cook's suicide did not attract press attention. I knew him, well enough I suppose. He was in Rates (meaning interest rates to the profane) and I used to speak to him regularly about those. I'd be lying if I didn't admit this brought back fond memories.

I spent all day pretending I could still be a banker: the complex products, the clients, writing deals – shit, that was FUN. But then I realised four years out of action, away from the trading floor is an eternity in the world of finance, even more so with the financial crisis. It's all over for me.

But mustn't digress, Gary was a typical Rates guy: aggressive, pig-headed, an East-End lad made good. He was bright and had the memory of an elephant. You did not want to be on the wrong side of Gary.

I remembered rumours circulating about his involvement in a financial scandal. I can't remember the details: it was another firm and way before my time. I am sure he got out of that one scot-free otherwise GL would never have hired him.

He did piss off a lot of people eventually, so no surprise he got the black bin bag treatment after the HXBK takeover of GL. I hope you are surprised. I have finally stopped calling it a merger.

Back to Gary, I'm amazed he committed suicide. He was not the type. I would have rather thought he had an ace up his sleeve. He must have known his time was up at GL. The likes of Gary always feel the wind turning and prepare accordingly.

Henry was struck by the memory of his own last day at GL, a mixture of pride and bitterness. A day so memorable he could still see it unfold before his eyes with absolute clarity.

He had been prime suspect in the Anthony Albert murder investigation, and as a consequence, banned from entering GL. A decision Douglas McCarthy, GL's CEO, had taken himself.

Henry's body tensed. He was back there as he managed to enter the bank and reach McCarthy's office. The old man was not expecting him.

"Doug, you motherfucker, you were surprised," Henry says aloud. "Although, granted, you sure held your own."

Henry kicks the door of the office open and challenges his CEO. His heart is racing now the way it was back then.

"Good afternoon, Douglas," Henry points a gun at his boss. He has grabbed it from a secret compartment in McCarthy's desk. Henry can still feel the ridges of the grip panel in his hand. McCarthy is stunned at Henry's knowledge of the weapon, and he wants it back.

"Don't try anything stupid Douglas, I didn't come here to kill you." Henry feels a strange blend of excitement and anticipation. McCarthy changes tack. Confrontation is not an option, neither is reasoning.

"How?" McCarthy asks, no longer hiding his amazement.

"You hired me because of the accuracy of my observations, Doug, and so I observed. The undisclosed documents, the hidden cache. I know all your dirty secrets."

McCarthy is about to move but Henry stops him "I know what you are trying to do, Doug, and time is of the essence."

"That's the name of the game, I guess." McCarthy shrugs.

A pinch of admiration for the old man runs through Henry. Under threat and still in control.

"Open the top drawer nearest to you." McCarthy does not flinch. "No."

"Suit yourself."

Henry lifts the gun and its discharge deafens them both. The sound resounds against the windows, shattering the wood in a burst of violence Henry has not experienced for decades. Fear and shock show for the second time in McCarthy's eyes, both men facing each other, on their guard. McCarthy moves first, desperation and rage overtaking him. Henry avoids the charge and McCarthy comes crashing down on the side of his desk. As he is about to turn back and resume his attack, Henry gives a single kick, hitting McCarthy in the face. The blow throws the old man flying across the room.

Henry grabs the file that McCarthy had concealed only a few hours ago.

"What are you going to do with it?" mumbles McCarthy, incapable of getting up.

"What you should have done, Douglas, had you had a shred of honesty in you," replies Henry.

Through a mouth full of blood, McCarthy starts laughing, stopping and starting through pain.

"You are not going to give me a lesson in ethics, are you Henry? Not you—"

Henry does not reply. He needs to get hold of David Cooper-James, HXBK's CEO, and dials his number.

McCarthy takes only a few seconds to realise what is about to happen. He summons his last ounce of strength and lunges forward one final time, straight into Henry's foot. Henry presses the mute button just in time. McCarthy's body curls up in the middle of the room, in a heap, motionless.

David Cooper-James is now on the phone and Henry tells him all he knows about GL's true financial position, delivering the fatal documents that confirm his revelation.

Henry shook his head, his mind returning to the cell he now occupied. The consequences of his conversation with HXBK's CEO he knew only too well.

McCarthy had been arrested the following day and GL taken over by HXBK only after the Treasury and the Bank of England had intervened. GL would not go the way Lehman Brothers had gone. The deal that was then negotiated for GL had been a bloody affair. The senior management of GL had taken the brunt of its consequences. Gone were their dreams of a reverse takeover. They would never be back in the driving seat.

Henry found he had clenched his fists, a man ready for a fight. He stood up, rolled his head around and simply stood tall for a moment. Those days were gone and would never come back.

He was in jail not because of the failed takeover or some fraudulent financial deals but because of his involvement with the IRA finances. Henry slowly bent forward to pick up the pen that had rolled onto the floor He had one final essential point to make to Nancy.

Chapter Three

The files were full of dust and unpleasant to handle but Nancy needed to take a look at the case again. One of the most crushing defeats she had ever known and Gary Cook had been at the centre of it. It had only taken twenty-four hours for the boxes to arrive from the secure warehouse in which they were stored. An express request had done the trick

Nancy had slipped into frayed jeans and an old King's College T-shirt, – a very casual dress code even for this keen gardener. She had called for the main boxes that contained the summary court papers as well as some of her personal notes. Half a dozen boxes were cluttering her hallway. She had gone through most of them looking for something, but she did not know quite what yet. A faded memory, a detail of the case kept pushing but remained at bay – a piece of information relevant to Gary's death was nagging Nancy.

She opened a heavy file; the smell of stale paper made her sneeze repeatedly. She rubbed her nose vigorously and found what she was looking for, Gary's lengthy statement. Fifteen had gone by but she could still remember how cocky he had been.

Nancy dialled Pole's number on her BlackBerry and turned the loudspeaker on.

"Pole."

"Jonathan, good morning, it's me. Do you have a minute?"

"*Bonjour* 'me' – and for you always," Pole said amused.

"*Bien sur, je n'en* ésperais *pas moins*. In particular as I have recovered some old files in which Gary Cook shows his true colours and what he was capable of as a trader. I told you I had some details for you last time we met and here they are."

"Is that so? Now you really have my complete attention."

Pole had learned not to underestimate Nancy's instinct. It had proven invaluable in the convoluted Henry Crowne affair.

"Yes, I have gone through a lot of documents this morning and finally found what I was looking for." Nancy held back.

"OK, don't keep me guessing; you know I can't take the pressure," said Pole.

"*Eh bien, mon cher* Jonathan. Just because it is you, of course."

"*Ma chère*, I am all ears."

"Let's start with a recap of the case." Nancy said, launching into her story.

The case had arisen a couple of years after the Big Bang. Nothing to do with the creation of the universe, but rather with a fundamental change in the way the stock market operated in London. A simplification of the Stock Exchange's rules transformed London into the greatest financial centre in the world. The change had altered the way market-makers – he people who bought and sold stocks – operated with exclusivity.

Before 1986 they had a monopoly for holding stocks and shares for sale, whilst brokers were allowed to match orders for clients. After 1986 the difference was abolished together with the transactions' commission market-makers were earning. As a result, a lot of the firms that lived off market-making were absorbed by UK or international banks. As part of that process, the accounts of those firms were scrutinised in depth.

"Gary's broking firm was part of the trail of acquisitions?" asked Pole.

"Precisely, he was a market-maker then, young enough, around twenty-six, but he had been in the job for nearly eight years. He knew what he was doing when it came to buy and sell shares. He never took an exam, not even O levels, but he was as sharp as sharp can be."

"That is mighty impressive, what background?"

"His father was a typical East-End boy, made a lot of money selling antiques."

Pole whistled and could not contain a laugh.

"I find myself in the middle of *Minder,* the old copper TV show suddenly. Was his father called Arthur Daley?"

"Not quite. But not far off... although Cook was a darn sight cleverer than Terry, Arthur Daley's mate," replied Nancy.

"I can't believe you watched that stuff," exclaimed Pole.

"And why the hell not? I tell you for a new girl like me, keen to know the ways of the world, it was the perfect intro into the world of petty crime."

"I suppose you started at the bottom like everyone else."

"You bet I did. I was a woman, and I was half-Asian. You can imagine the result. It was not that easy to be taken seriously as a barrister."

"Actually, I probably can't imagine. A story for another time, *peut-* être?"

"*Absolument* but going back to Gary. The case should have been much easier than it turned out to be. Gary's firm had been involved in taking large equity positions in a particular takeover. A classic case of insider trading."

"OK, so Gary had knowledge of the takeover before it became public and bought stocks in the company on his prop book."

"Spoken like a pro," teased Nancy. "This is what the prosecution contended. Nowadays most insiders end up in jail. The technology banks employ is there to catch them. Although you'd be surprised how many still try."

"You mean that in those days it was relying on the culprit eventually bragging about it."

"Partially yes, but not Gary."

"So not the typical cocky cor-blimey type of bloke?"

"Well, he sure had a thick Eastender accent, but he was in control. He had thought about it in the minutest details."

"What do you mean exactly?"

"I mean, he had envisaged being caught. He had not relied on the fact he would simply get away with it and that his fraudulent activity would not come to light. That made all the difference."

"And you lost the case?"

"I did – no matter how hard I tried to break his arguments he remained credible, never arrogant, showing just the right amount of anger an innocent man may show. The image of the typical low-class guy made good and who was unfairly accused."

"And he established reasonable doubt—"

"The little git did." Nancy grabbed the pen on the table and started doodling furiously on her newspaper.

"OK, so what does that tell us in the here and now? Maybe he was a reformed character. He was young, gave himself a fright. He got away with it once, that was enough..."

"Maybe, or rather I agree that for the last twenty years he seemed to have stayed out of trouble. But leopards don't change their spots. Then comes the financial crisis."

"You think that the old demons came back to haunt him and that he might have organised something dodgy because he was pushed by circumstances?" Pole asked.

"It is a possibility. And Gary was a bit of a lad, as most of them were in those days: a lot of booze, lap dancing clubs, and so on."

"So, Gary liked to party with the boys, very nineties or rather naughties of course. You must have checked whether he had confided in the lovely ladies of the various clubs he frequented."

Nancy laughed an uncomfortable laugh. "As a matter of fact, I did, or rather the prosecution did – not a pleasant task, but Gary never revealed anything material that I could use."

Pole stayed silent as though pondering. Nancy sensed that Pole was wavering.

"I know what you're thinking, Jonathan. You believe I don't like the guy and that it might make me biased. But by the time Gary arrived at the conference he was already completely drunk. There is no reason why I would want to make this case more complicated than it is."

"Apart from the fact that you would like to spend more time in the company of your favourite inspector."

"Jonathan Pole, you are flattering yourself."

"I am? What a shame I had managed to get two tickets for a Kodo concert at Sadler's Wells. I thought you might be—"

"Now you are talking," Nancy said with perhaps more enthusiasm than she would have wanted.

* * *

The meeting of the Monetary Policy Committee had been excruciatingly painful. Edwina was enraged by the dithering of some of its members and its lack of vision. She was advocating for another round of quantitative easing when another member was already asking for a rise in interest rates – seriously!

She entered Gabriel's office. He did not bother to lift his head. "That bad, was it?"

"Arggggh! I swear I am going to strangle one of them. Where on earth did they get their degrees in economics?"

"Wrong question," said Gabriel. "The real issue is what are they doing with that degree? Are they hiding behind the theory or are they capable of taking a pragmatic approach and embracing new ideas?"

"Well said," replied Edwina.

She sometimes wondered why Gabriel had never wanted to be in the front line himself. She had pondered at length about this and was still perplexed. Surely the scar on his face was not enough to dissuade him? He spoke seldom of the accident. She knew it had taken years of patience and surgery to achieve an appearance he could live with. But perhaps he was also a man who enjoyed the elaborate process of strategising, happy to leave someone else in charge of the advocacy. If so he had chosen a woman as his advocate, and Edwina had plenty of respect for a man of intellect who could make that decision.

"Do you think The Oracle will want to speak to you again about Quantitative Easing today?" asked Gabriel.

"After the meeting, definitely. Mervyn does not like intervention, but he knows it has to be done. A second round of QE will irk him though. I need to speak to the Yanks. Can you organise a call with Ben Bernanke's chief of staff, the delightful Rose?"

"Absolutely, I will get something set up on a secure line as soon as they have arrived in Washington. I will arrange it myself. The fewer people know the better."

"Right you are. Now, what's on the agenda for lunch, nothing I hope?"

"Free as a bird," replied Gabriel with a twinkle in his eyes.

Edwina wagged a finger at him and disappeared through the connecting door into her own office. She left the door open and started going through her emails.

She had begun the process of weeding outwhat was urgent when a niggling thought kept interfering with her concentration. Had Gary's death made the news yet? She opened Google and searched Gary Cook's name. Nothing. Gabriel had spoken to his contacts in the press. He had assured her it would be the end of the matter. She was so close to her goal, and she was damned if Gary Cook would come between her and the title of Governor.

Edwina had not seen Nancy since that dreadful night. She had looked shaken by Gary's death too. Perhaps she should check with Nancy, get what her take was on the matter, casually of course. Nancy was a good friend, a woman for whom female diversity was not self-promotion but a desire to see other females succeed, even exceed her own achievements. A rare quality.

Edwina picked up her Blackberry and called her friend.

"Nancy – Edwina here. How are you?"

"Fine, but still shaken, of course."

Edwina nodded. "Yes, me too, what a tragedy... Would you have time for an impromptu lunch?"

"An excellent idea... How about Moro on Exmouth Market?"

"Perfect, meet you there in half an hour... Looking forward."

"I am nipping out for a short while," Edwina told Gabriel as she walked out of her office. She was putting on her jacket and awkwardly handling her handbag with one hand. "Just a quick catch up with Nancy."

"Sure. What's her take on the event, if you don't mind me asking?"

"Not quite sure. I'll find out."

"She's such a great supporter of yours," Gabriel said with admiration.

"One of the few women who doesn't only talk the talk but also walks the walk. Did you know she was, and I believe still is, the youngest QC ever appointed?"

"Impressive."

"And she never mentioned it to me in all these years. I read it recently in the press. You remember the Henry Crowne affair?"

"Yes, I do. And you will be late if you don't leave now."

"Good point, till later. If The Oracle calls let me know, and I'll come back straightaway."

* * *

Moro in Exmouth Market was fully booked.

Nancy had called ahead as soon as she had finished her conversation with Eddie, and a friendly waitress had managed to squeeze them in.

Nancy was a regular who came too often for the staff not to find a place and, as always, they had managed a table *En Terrace.*

The sun was giving the pedestrian streets of Islington a Parisian feel. Nancy's Sorbonne days were long gone but the happy memories lingered. Paris had been an eye opener. The intellectual buzz surrounding the law faculty, the rebels that debated everything from politics to fashion at the Pantheon café had flung her mind open to all the possibilities that life presented.

On a sunny day Exmouth Market gave her the same feeling of freedom. It had changed so much in the past five years, nearly unrecognisable, changing at the pace Islington had.

Despite the financial crisis the restaurants were always full here. She wondered whether people were having fun to forget the trouble they were in or simply whilst they still could.

Nancy found Moro trendy. It was not the typical City restaurant despite its proximity to the Square Mile. Nancy quickly surveyed the inside of the restaurant before staff came to greet her. She recognised a couple of regulars: one a TV producer, the other a screenwriter. She had spoken to them in the past when they had all found themselves at the same art gallery preview. The small contemporary art gallery she was supporting had made the news with one of their up-and-coming artists. She waved and they waved back.

Nancy sat down, content with the cosy position of her table, and opened her *FT.* She had barely started the companies' section when a firm hand squeezed her shoulder.

"Hello Eddie. How are you?" said Nancy looking up and folding her *FT* neatly.

"Still fuming after a frustrating meeting at the shop. Hello Nancy. A spot of lunch with you is exactly what I need to calm down," Edwina replied with a perfect smile.

Nancy called Juan, the head waiter, and placed the order, letting him make recommendations and going with what he thought they should try...

Edwina pulled her BlackBerry out of her bag. She fidgeted with it until Nancy asked her what she would like to drink. Disappointingly Nancy followed Edwina with a bottle of sparking water.

Edwina made herself comfortable, unbuttoning the jacket of an impeccable light-blue suit. She rearranged the pearl jewellery she was wearing and untied the Hermes scarf that sat loosely around her neck. Edwina looked around, briefly inspecting her surroundings.

"How is John?" Nancy asked.

"My dear husband is well, busy. The London School of Economics is introducing a new curriculum and John is teaching it. The financial crisis has created a lot of interest in the Great Depression of 1930."

"And he is an expert in the field if I remember rightly."

"He is. John in the UK and Ben Bernanke, the head of the Federal Bank in the US. Sometimes I wonder whether he should be in my role," Edwina said unconvincingly.

"Eddie, you know you are in the right job and John is perfectly happy in his – otherwise you two would never have worked out," Nancy said, surprised at her friend's remark.

"I suppose that's true – still, the buggers at work are not making it easy for me."

"What do you expect? Janet Yellen is likely to get the top job because of Obama and replace Bernanke as head of the Fed but you've got a Conservative government to contend with."

"Osborne is more progressive than people think but unfortunately he is not the only one deciding."

"Which is why you need to keep at it, stick to your plan the way we discussed—" Nancy stopped abruptly as the tapas were being served. Juan produced plates and cutlery, arranged the food tastefully on the table and disappeared swiftly.

"And avoid any adverse publicity," Nancy finished.

"I know, the Gary Cook suicide is unfortunate – and very sad of course."

"Why do you mention it? I have read very little in the press about it and this has not marred the Women In Enterprise Conference."

"I suppose there is little compassion for a banker taking a dive from the terrace of a posh City restaurant." Edwina shrugged.

"Perhaps but I would have expected the press to like the fact that the said banker had taken a dive as you say. Still, I presume Gabriel has been on the case."

"He has. Cook had lost his job anyway. So maybe it is less interesting to crap on a banker who is no longer a banker."

Nancy was about to ask how she knew of Cook's redundancy but then thought better of it.

"Are you worried about the impact it could still have on the conference's success and indirectly on you as key speaker?" Nancy asked.

"Well, he was at the conference, and he was being a nuisance."

"Yes, I am aware, - he was arguing with me. I think he was extremely drunk or possibly worse."

Edwina paused her fork in mid-air as she was about to stab the last prawn on the dish.

"Not Gary, surely. How do you know that?"

"Well, I have many sources."

"I just don't want to be associated with yet another bad banker's tragedy. It won't play well on my CV." Edwina lay her cutlery across her plate. She seemed to have lost her appetite.

"Why would you be?" Nancy asked. "Are you not overreacting a little? Even if the press made a meal of it, the conference was an enormous success. ary's suicide can't undo that."

"You're right, I am probably overreacting. Another bad banker bites the dust – So what?"

Nancy smiled a reassuring smile.

"You are doing incredibly well. You know that don't you?"

"Yes, yes I do. I simply need to keep going and ignore the noise. Thanks for being a friend."

"Any time, it's always a pleasure. Now let's discuss your plan in detail."

Edwina had left their lunch with a spring in her step. Nancy smiled at the invigorating effect she had had on her friend. The weather was too good to return home. She fancied a brisk walk to the Barbican: a new show had just opened at The Curve Gallery she did not want to miss.

She would enjoy a cup of coffee at the pond afterwards. Her cotton dress felt comfortable despite its elegance. Nancy caught sight of herself in a shop window and approved. She rarely spent time in front of a mirror: a shop window would always do. She enjoyed fashion. Perhaps her time in Paris, even as an impoverished student, had left its mark. She had an eye for the beautifully made, the textures, the patterns. She appreciated craftsmanship, a taste she carried into art.

Nancy walked at a pace, still thinking about the lunch with Edwina. As ever she had enjoyed the company. But something had engaged the large cogs of her mind, a feeling, the start of an idea that would not leave her alone.

Why was Eddie worried? And why check on Gary Cook? She was busy enough as it was, Nancy wondered. There was no denying Edwina was concerned. Just an overreaction?

No, not her style. She was under a tremendous amount of pressure, the financial crisis, the QE schedule, the ghost of the Great Depression. She was a technical person, but she was also inventive, prepared to think out of the box. In fact, the crisis had brought her best qualities forward. It had been the differentiator between her and her male colleagues. Edwina had come up with new ideas and Mervyn had listened.

Nancy reached the Barbican and decided to get her cup of coffee first. She sat down at the far end of the pond and took out a small writing pad from her bag. She would do what she always excelled at doing, ask herself the tough questions. To be effective they had to be in black and white. She smoothed the page on which she was about to write and started on her list.

1-why has E checked the background of Gary, in particular his latest position at work?
2-why is E concerned about an event that does not directly implicate her?
3-why has Gabriel acted upon it?
4-what is the impact of me pursuing with Pole? 5-is it suicide?

Her last question struck her with more force now it was written down. She slowly stirred her cappuccino, the chocolate flower design gradually disappearing as the sugar melted in the middle of it. She stopped and took a sip. The taste of good coffee reminded her of the last time she had visited Henry. His obsession with quality coffee sad and yet all par for the course.

Henry had spoken at length of his latest interest. A book, *Gang of One* by Gary Mulgrew, a real-life account of the NatWest banker extradited to the US who had found himself in one of the most violent high-security prisons there.

"I have it so easy, Nancy. Mulgrew was lucky to survive and to have his sentence commuted so that he could come back to the UK, otherwise he would have died there."

"But why are you concerning yourself with what cannot happen to you?" Nancy had asked as she was sitting opposite Henry in the prison visiting parloir.

"Why not? Is it sad that it helps me to think it could have been worse?"

"But you know that if you carry on, try to rebuild your life the way you have done so far, you will not serve the full sentence."

"You mean twenty-five years rather than thirty?" Henry said spreading his long fingers on the table.

"I know it is not tomorrow. I won't deny it."

"The worst thing is… Nothing really good happens here. Nothing. I keep myself to myself. I am not amongst friends or even comrades. I have nothing to say to these guys. High-profile cons are less of a challenge than I thought. There is a lot of rambling going on."

"Isolation is also the sad part of the deal," Nancy said extending a friendly hand, reaching for him.

"I believed it was that for a long time. But it is more than that."

Nancy nodded encouragingly. There was little Henry would not speak to her about.

"Even thirty years won't give me redemption. How can I show I have changed?"

"Henry, the first important thing is for you to believe that you are redeemable. Do you believe that?"

"Maybe, yes – it's about what I have done and what I want to do to fix it. And from here I am powerless."

"You mean your link to the IRA?"

"You know the score, Nancy. For years I contributed to building up their finances. The funds that Liam was running for them, I constructed them. I put the mechanism in place to ensure no one could trace them."

Henry had stopped. He had never been as brutally honest. He had admitted it of course, but it had been a mere acknowledgement of the facts presented to him.

"You always wanted to belong to the family Liam and Bobby offered to you. Northern Ireland during The Troubles was not the place for a lonely lad of mixed background to grow up in. It was bad enough to have an Irish father and an English mother... but you also lost your father." Nancy reached Henry's hand briefly, wondering whether she'd said too much.

"I am not interested in excuses. I understand why I did it. I could have walked away. I had a brilliant job, a brilliant team and the past could have been left behind but I could not let go." Henry closed his eyes, the deep lines around his mouth arched in pain. "Whichever way I look at it, I helped kill people – a lot of people."

Nancy had remained silent. She needed the right words. "It's in the past."

"Perhaps, but it is not good enough. For the victim's families it is the present still and will always be."

"There is something else—"

Despite the intensity of the conversation Henry had managed a smile. "That is what I love about you Nancy. You always get to the nub of the matter."

Nancy had clasped his hand and squeezed gently. Henry had put his other hand over hers and squeezed back. She was his best friend.

"Yes, something else is troubling me—"

Nancy waited. She looked at the clock on the wall. Henry turned back to look at it too.

"It will take a bit more time than the five minutes we have left – next time."

"Are you sure?"

"I am sure." A prison officer looked in their direction and Henry withdrew his hands.

As Henry was pulling his hands away, she noticed that one of the inmates was observing them, a strange fellow sporting an unmistakably fifties' haircut. His visitor, a man of similar build, was still talking to him but he was not listening. He only moved his gaze away when his visitor turned around to check what was distracting his attention.

Henry noticed and glanced in the man's direction. "Ignore him, Nancy. He is a nutjob."

She nodded. Nancy noticed the violence in his glance; even from a distance she could feel the sharpness of its blade.

"And now for something a lot more mundane," Henry said. "How can I manage to make one of those lovely cappuccinos with a flower on top?"

"That is mighty technical. But I think you'll find that the special mix I got you should do the trick. You need to find a small piece of cardboard, cut the outline of the flower, place it on the cup and spread the chocolate over it. *Et voila.*"

"Prison is good at broadening my skills." Henry sighed.

Nancy had almost finished her coffee. A light breeze moved the pages of her newspaper gently. Perhaps she could indulge in another cup? The Barbican was pleasant enough and she was in no hurry.

Chapter Four

The little newspaper shop was crowded with sweets of all colours and flavours. Brett grabbed a burner phone and took a few notes out of his wallet to pay cash. The small podgy Indian man took his money hardly looking at him.

Good choice of shop, thought Brett. He had gone all the way to Mile End to purchase a couple of phones, dressed in what was the most inconspicuous clothing. His kind did not do jeans but some navy slacks together with the appropriate dress-down jacket would do the trick. He had managed to dig out an old jacket shapeless with age and kept for these occasions. Again, a clever choice.

Brett walked to the bus stop and waited for the number 205. The route would lead him back to Belgravia after a suitable number of changes. He might make the call on the way if he found a suitable spot.

He felt a vibration in his jacket pocket and hesitated. Mobile phones were lifted regularly in the area. He had seen it done a few feet away when he had last visited the place. Brett shrugged and picked up the phone. His MI6 minder was calling; so what if he lost his mobile?

"I'm not in a secure place," Brett said by way of introduction.

"You mean more dangerous than Iraq?"

"It feels as though I am there..." Brett looked around and the number of men wearing the traditional dishdashi and taquiya impressed him.

"If you're visiting Mile End you shouldn't be surprised.

"How do you know...?"

"Never mind that... any contact with the Middle East yet?"

"I need to speak to my Italian smuggler first. You know this is the routine." Brett batted back.

"Anything unusual, even if this looks insignificant, I need to know."

"Fine..." Brett killed the call as his bus was approaching.

Brett tried to remember where the next few stops would lead him; to the London's business district, the City for sure. He boarded, sat down and activated one of his phones. The screen lit up. He keyed in three numbers he had memorised: his Iraqi contact, his Chinese client, his Italian smuggler. The bus was approaching the City. Brett stood up and alighted at Liverpool Street station. He walked past the Andaz hotel towards Moorgate. The cafes, small restaurants and pubs were still full. The sun was shining and the terraces heaving with people.

"Is there even a crisis, I wonder?" Brett mumbled. His complaint was disingenuous he knew. His business in art dealing had never been better. Although he had to admit that contemporary art was taking the prize. Maybe he could change his tack.

A ridiculous idea, he knew – his heart would always be with the classics: the exceptional craft, the complexity and skill of the old Masters. But his pocket was always empty and the sums that contemporary art yielded astronomical. The latest Basel fair had earned its participants just short of one billion dollars. One billion dollars – unthinkable.

The flow of cars had stopped, and Brett crossed the street. He turned left and entered the Barbican Centre. The place was large enough for him to find a secluded spot to make the call. The brutal architecture offended his senses but somehow it suited the call he was about to place. It was already 2.30 PM; people would be leaving the pond area to go back to work. Excellent.

* * *

Nancy had just started on her second cup of coffee.. Her mind had moved to the work she'd completed before Edwina's call.

Nancy was working on the next Women in Enterprise event she was sponsoring but she was well advanced with the paper she would deliver. Her conversation with the founder of the newly created 30% Club promoting greater gender balance on FTSE100 boards had galvanised her thinking.

She raised her cup to her lips and swept the Barbican courtyard with her eyes, curious about the people who were enjoying the seclusion of the place. A tall, gangly man was making his way to the far end of the plaza. He seemed to be deliberately looking for a quieter spot.

Nancy watched him for a moment but a young man interrupted her, asking whether he could borrow the sugar dispenser on her table. Nancy nodded with a smile and returned to her thoughts.

The young art gallery she was supporting had turned the corner. The crisis had put pressure on their finances, but they had managed to survive with new commissions for their emerging artists. Charles Saatchi was rumoured to be taking an interest in the stunning photographs that were on display there, a politically loaded subject that the photographer had managed to render compelling, almost aesthetic: the *Spomeniks* of Eastern Europe.

The owner of the gallery was also expecting results from the Hong Kong Art Basel Fair during which they had started to connect with Chinese galleries and collectors. Nancy had been slow to respond to their enthusiasm for China. She was not yet ready for a foray into the country of her ancestors.

Her eyes crept up the building side to reach the large concrete blocks that formed the Barbican, a perfect example of the brutalist architecture that she could never quite understand. The sign of an era that would soon test the limits of the communist ideology both in China and what was then the USSR.

Her eyes unexpectedly clouded. She cleared her throat. Why revisit a painful past that she felt she had come to terms with? She pushed it away as she always did with a resolute nudge.

Nancy shuffled the papers she had bought before joining Edwina for lunch. She intended to look once more for news of Gary's death. Pole had promised to call her with the preliminary toxicology results as soon as they came through.. She certainly wanted to see Pole again but there was no need to invent some strange twist to an already complicated crime to spend an evening with her favourite inspector.

They were going to see a show together – God, it was another date. Nancy almost blushed. She had not felt this flustered for a very long time. Hesitation, her worst adversary when it came to love.

She opened the *FT* and started reading her newspaper, more about the financial crisis of course, but nothing on Gary. The odd-looking man she had noticed earlier on had settled at the far end of the pound. His back was turned to her but there was something familiar about the way he hunched forward to make what she presumed was a call.

* * *

A couple stood up, took their tray and moved away. Brett frowned; the table was perfectly positioned but dirty. He signalled to one of the waitresses and demanded the mess be cleared. The young Asian woman smiled and apologised. Brett hardly acknowledged her. He was about to sit down when he noticed a few crumbs left on the table. He called the Asian woman back impatiently. The girl came back flustered, apologising profusely.

"Anything else, sir?" she asked nervously.

"It will do. Actually, a pot of tea would be good to make up for the inconvenience," Brett said with a dismissive gesture.

He sat down, pulled a notebook from his inner pocket, a well-used fountain pen from another and got out one of the burner phones purchased earlier on. He composed himself for a few moments before placing the call. The people he was dealing with exasperated him, but he could not show his contempt or get angry.

His open disdain for Henry Crowne had brought him very close to being investigated. MI6-Steve, had not been amused and yet Steve had been curious about Crowne. Even after Crowne had been thrown in jail, his minder's interest had persisted.

Brett shook his head. He needed to make his call and a public place was the perfect environment to ring his Italian contact. He would have to show restraint.

"*Ciao Antonio, come va*?" said Brett in perfect Italian, the privilege of an upper-class upbringing. He opened his paper and looked for the crosswords. Brett would wait a little before interrupting Antonio's rant: the state of the trafficking business was deteriorating by the minute – much easier and more lucrative to traffic people than works of art: just put them on the boat and off they go.

Brett read the first of his crossword clues – Pilfer, 7 letters. Brett smiled. How apt – Purloin. He kept moving swiftly along the other clues until almost half of the grid was full. Brett looked at his watch and interrupted Antonio.

"Back to our business if you don't mind old chap" There was no way he was volunteering an increase in the already extortionate price he was paying to smuggle the artefacts out of Iraq.

"I am about to speak to the purchaser who I believe is ready to buy."

"What will I be shipping out-ah then?" Antonio's accent had become much stronger now that he was miffed at the interruption.

"The gold jar… And possibly the bust of Ishtar from Babylon."

"These are big-ah pieces. They'll need-ah moving separately. Two-ah weeks for the first one and two-ah weeks later if I'm moving the second piece."

Brett scribbled on his paper. "I see… Can't we do it sooner?"

"Not-ah sure. The Libyan route has become-ah tricky?"

"Really? I would have thought the mess in which Libya is at the moment makes it easier… Gaddafi is gone, and Libya is an almighty mess. I would have thought it a good thing for smugglers."

Brett looked around. He had raised his voice a little too much for his liking, but the place was by now nearly empty.

"And much more-ah dangerous… these people, they are-ah loose cannons." Antonio complained.

"Look, I need the consignment delivered in the next two weeks. The deal is worth £50,000 to you. It's a year's salary for some people in the UK and as ever I have been overgenerous."

Brett sat back in his chair and let Antonio rant again. He knew his contact would eventually come down and agree to his price. Brett could not help but smile. Antonio did justice to the popular conception of Italians: talking, complaining and eventually agreeing to something illegal.

Brett dropped his weak chin and returned to his crossword puzzle, solving a couple of more clues before interrupting Antonio again.

"Antonio, I have a meeting in five minutes," Brett snapped.

"Okay-ah… but I'm underselling myself. One-ah week from now."

"Good man. I know you will deliver, as you always do in the most difficult of circumstances." Brett carried on showering compliments on his contact; a proud Italian man would always succumb to flattery.

Brett terminated the call, relieved Antonio had once more caved in. Brett had tried other routes – Greece and Turkey – but his Italian counterparts delivered not only on time, much to Brett's amazement, but also understood how to handle high value artefacts and the pieces arrived in pristine condition.

Brett folded his paper but didn't move, still pondering whether the Libya route was as Antonio said – too dangerous and perhaps too expensive. People trafficking was a lucrative business with which he was competing. It was perhaps one piece of information that MI6 Steve might like to know, It might get his minder of his back for a short while. Brett's mind returned to the issue at end… his share of the spoil.

The Iraqi rebels took a 30% fee and so did Brett. The rest of the money raised by the sale of the looted pieces went to the various intermediaries. And so what if he was helping a bunch of terrorists? I t was all a matter of perspective.

The word terrorist made Brett smile. It reminded him of one of his most high-profile clients – Henry Crowne himself. The Northern Irish peasant had ended up in prison, a delightful thought. But who could have predicted the link between Henry and the IRA? When Henry had been accused of the murder of one of his banking rivals, Anthony Albert, Brett had not believed his luck. He had been grooming Albert's wife for a while, and here was Adeila, available and ready to be plucked. But it had all come to nothing, and Brett had felt bitter disappointment when it turned out that Adeila had been made destitute by her husband.

Still, seeing Crowne sent down for thirty years had been music to his ears. Brett had a score to settle with Henry. He had hooked him on the sale of (legitimate!) art from Asia and had wondered whether Crowne would buy some of the Middle Eastern pieces he was smuggling in early 2004. Henry had been mesmerised by the quality of the artefacts Brett was showing him, going firm on a series of superb cuneiform tablets. The price was agreed, a hefty £450,000. And then – Henry recanted.

MI6 had picked Brett up just has he was convinced he was about to meet a sorry end and a bullet put through his head. Brett inhaled and refused to let the memory blur his focus. Crowne was in prison. He had lost most of his wealth in fines and lawyers' fees. It could not have happened to a better man.

Brett's newspaper was still open in front of him. He checked he had recorded the relevant information. He would soon destroy the paper and leave no trace of the details scribbled on it. Brett stretched his gangly body, looked around and started walking towards Barbican station.

***

Nancy had finished reading her newspapers; her second cup of cappuccino was empty. The pond was now deserted apart from the scruffy man she had noticed a while ago. He got up, stretched and leisurely made his way towards the steps that rose to his left. He briefly turned his head towards her. She knew him.

Nancy dropped the wad of papers on the table and scrambled in her bag for her glasses. She found them just in time to look at the man who was nearly out of sight – Brett Allner-Smith? Could it really be him? She stood, uncertain at first as to what to do. But as he was pulling away, she started climbing the stairs too.

She slowed down, surprised by the outfit: old slacks and a tired blue jacket. Gone was the immaculate three-piece suit and the subtle tie she had seen him wear at his visits to Scotland Yard. Brett's pompous personality did not fit the current attire.

She slowed down further… Yet the walk, the fair hair with a nascent balding patch on top, looked just like him. Nancy decided to keep following the man. She was after all going in the same direction, towards Barbican station where she could catch a bus. The man was about to disappear down a flight of stairs. His mobile rang. Nancy stopped. The man answered.

"Antonio, what now? I told you before, I am the one making contact."

Nancy was all ears. It *was* Brett. She recognised his voice, the contrived way of pronouncing certain common words. Irritating.

"The consignment must arrive on time. My client will not wait and more importantly my Iraqi contact will find another buyer."

Nancy froze. She was about to emerge into the open if she kept walking. She came as close as possible to the corner of the wall and waited. Brett had slowed down and was hovering at the top of the stairs. "How much more?" Brett said, sounding exasperated.

"No chance… I will think about it… I said I will think about it… *Ciao.*" Brett switched off the phone. "Bloody Italian Mafioso." Brett was on the move again.

Nancy could hear his footsteps disappear down the stairs. If she followed, he may recognise her, no – he would recognise her. How could he forget? He had been involved in Henry's case and he would recognise her as part of Henry's legal team.

All was silent now. Nancy reached the top of the stairwell. She could see Brett disappearing into the street. She followed quickly, feigning to search for some lost item in her large bag. She stood at the crossroads.

Brett had walked into the tube station. She briskly crossed the road as the light was turning red. An impatient driver used his horn and gestured. Nancy did not bother to apologise. She entered the station and reached the platform on time to see Brett boarding a train towards King's Cross. She jumped into the nearest carriage just as the doors closed.

What was she doing? It was none of her business. If Allner-Smith was involved in some dodgy deal, did she really want to know? But her heart was racing, and her curiosity aroused.

"Curiosity killed the cat," she whispered. Then again, cats had nine lives and she had a few of those left in store. She stood near the doors and watched people coming in and out of the carriages. They reached King's Cross and when the doors were about to close Brett squeezed out quickly. Nancy just managed to follow. He was moving towards one of the exits. She kept shadowing him. Outside he turned in the direction of St Pancras and took the escalators. The Belle Epoque brasserie was packed, Eurostar travellers enjoying a quick meal before departure: a couple celebrating something important with champagne and caviar, a family of five struggling to keep the children in check. Brett hesitated. He stopped at a quiet terrace table, looked around, and sat down nonchalantly.

Nancy dived into the restaurant, flashing a broad smile at a young waiter. He accompanied her towards the ideal table, providing the perfect shield. The doors were open: Nancy inside, Brett on the outside, a 50–50 chance she would hear his conversation.

"I presume you don't serve Earl Grey?" Brett asked a waitress that had come to take his order.

Nancy could hear Brett clearly. She smiled, the same arrogant arse. "You do? How amazing – a pot of Earl Grey, lemon, no sugar, and can I expect proper China?"

Nancy sat back. She had indeed the perfect seat. The waiter went out with Brett's order. She could not bend forward to see what was going on and was starting to wonder whether anything would actually happen when she heard Brett's voice again, a voice discreet but audible.

"*Bonjour Mohammed, votre contact anglais à l'appareil.*"

Nancy was surprised. Brett's French was excellent, a soft English accent but perfect grammar. He must be speaking to someone with North African origins. Brett asked to speak to *Le Capitaine* and *Le Capitaine* came online.

"Good afternoon, Captain. Are you ready to ship the consignment?"

Nancy was intrigued by the switch to English. Maybe the captain was Middle Eastern? Brett had mentioned Iraq.

"Yes, my contact can do the transfer within the deadline we have fixed… The price stays at $1.2 million… My client is ready to proceed."

Nancy stopped her hand in mid-air, her cup not quite reaching her lips. $1.2 million was a pretty hefty sum in the world of art. Or was Brett dealing in some other products – illegal substances perhaps?

"We are using the normal route for payment… I agree we need to stay alert… The Swiss are far more cautious than they once were… I see, I will find a way."

There was a long pause. Nancy was tempted to move but what if Brett saw her? The smuggling business was a dangerous one and he would not take any risks. She knew what these people could do to an unwelcome witness.

"Very good, I believe we are done." Brett's voice had lowered. "I will get rid of this phone so any further calls from this number will not be from me." Brett hung up. His tea had arrived.

Brett asked for the bill, poured a cup and drank quickly. As soon as the waitress returned, he paid cash and left. His chair made of faint screeching noise as he rose. Nancy froze. If Brett looked back, he would inevitably see her. He stopped for an instant, checked his pockets and carried on walking. She waved at the waiter to settle her own bill and noticed her hand was shaking. "Serves me right. I'm not a trained spook."

When she stepped onto the terrace of the Belle Epoque Brett was nowhere in sight. She moved slowly towards the top of the escalator looking at the sea of people below. A Eurostar train had arrived. She gladly joined the crowd, safe in its midst.

* * *

Belmarsh prison had only been a name linked to one of Henry's favourite films *V for Vendetta* until he set foot in it. Aa a Category A closed prison, it had a reputation for housing lifers as well as those convicted for crimes carrying long sentences and within Belmarsh itself, the High Security Unit.

HSU Belmarsh was a prison within a prison, a concrete block, grey and windowless. Little known to the public or even to the other eight hundred and forty-three prisoners, it had been the "home" of Abu Hamza until his extradition to the US. Getting into Belmarsh itself involved crossing fifteen gates and having fingerprints scanned but when you reached HSU the scans would start all over again.

Henry's former limo driver, Charlie had warned him it would be no picnic. Although he had done time himself, Charlie had never been a Cat A con. He had nevertheless been an inexhaustible source of information and comfort. Charlie would not have wanted to be thanked for it. An armed robbery that had turned bloody had cost him ten years of his life; he was only eighteen at the time. He had decided on the day he had been sent down that he would walk out a free man and never return – classes, education, psychological support, he had done the lot and finally been given his chance to turn the page when he was freed on parole. Now on licence, Charlie had become a reliable limo driver, a jazz fan who had managed to land a position at his favourite club.

Henry had used Charlie as his regular driver. He had guessed his heavy past, yet always treated him with respect.

"Funny how things can turn out," Henry had said when Charlie came to visit him the first time. "Here I am banged up and here you are free as a bird."

"I know. I would never have imagined—" Charlie looked shy and tense. "I hope you don't mind if I don't stay for the full duration. It got to me to walk back in here, even after all these years."

"Charlie, mate, I am simply glad you came to see me." Henry had managed to smile.

"Listen, I have brought you something, only a few pages. A sort of guide to prison life." Charlie unfolded a few crumpled sheets of paper. "It's good you know, although the bloke who wrote it was not a Cat A con."

Henry nodded and looked at the pages. Charlie had put one hand in front of his mouth as he spoke and lifted an eyebrow towards one of the guards.

"Yeah, be careful. They sometimes employ screws that can lip-read, so watch it."

Henry had looked at him in disbelief, but Charlie had done time and he, Henry Crowne, was about to find out what Her Majesty's Pleasure had in store for him.

Henry had stuck to his routine, gone to the gym in the morning and yet again worked doubly hard. He had joined the few courses allowed within the HSU, an essential lifeline to the outside world, a sanity check to ensure he was still part of the human race. He had been assiduous, even though they sometimes depressed him.

He had, naïvely, seen prison as a way of redeeming himself, a way to atone but he had started to doubt that the release he was so craving would ever be granted to him between the four walls of a cell.

He had faced reality. The murder accusation that had turned to nothing and yet had unveiled part of an unsuspected iceberg, his deep involvement with the IRA. The entrapment, mercilessly organised by his rival Anthony Albert, had nearly destroyed his sanity, a revenge delivered by a dying man and never seen before even by City standards. He had in a moment of absurdity and utter despair believed he was guilty. He would still believe it and would have been condemned for it had Nancy and Pole not persisted in their belief Henry was no murderer.

Henry still had Albert's letter in his file. It was there in his prison cell, a few steps away from him, a few steps away from the bed on which he was sitting. He had read it only once on the dreadful and yet liberating day it had been delivered to him.

Henry stretched. He laced his long fingers together and reached over his head. The crack of his bones gave him some small relief. But the terrible question was still haunting him. How much involvement had he truly had in Anthony Albert's demise? He had not executed the plan but he had hatched that plan. Still a very young man in search of belonging, he had elaborated the means by which a bomb could be delivered onto a plane and shared his idea with Liam and Bobby O'Connor. He had so wanted to be part of that tightly-knit family and yet he had escaped to London.

The City, the money and the power had made no difference. He could not let go of the violence that a Belfast upbringing had driven into him. He had done all he could to support Liam, his only friend and a known IRA operative. And he needed to belong, if only to find out one day why his father had been murdered and by whom.

Albert had been a devious bastard but also a true genius. Aware of his impending death he had trapped Henry in the most methodically planned revenge. He had seen an opportunity at a Dublin high-profile closing dinner and dared to think the unthinkable, his own assassination.

It had worked perfectly, with implacable precision. His only mistake had been the letter. His need to triumph absolutely over Henry, to make certain he would topple him over the edge, had saved Henry. The letter that explained every single detail, the letter that exonerated Henry, had been found on time.

And today Henry was paying for what he had done: the support of a terrorist organisation. But the more he thought about his need for redemption, the more he felt he needed to use his ability, his powerful intellect and his capacity at taking risks, to earn that absolution.

What could he do in prison? He was educated, a maths degree, a solicitor's qualification. He had built one of the most innovative teams in the world of structured products. He still read several books a week and had managed to become one of the librarians of HSU Belmarsh's small library.

The anger that had always fuelled him had perhaps abated a little. He felt much more in control. He knew he could not let it rise in a Cat A prison, let alone within the confines of HSU Belmarsh. Henry did not fancy spending time in the segregation unit where prisoners had to spend twenty-three hours a day in their cells.

Henry was surrounded by terrorists, murderers; not fancy bankers who talked tough but had no idea what it would mean to deliver. IRA dissidents had done time there before him, now replaced by al-Qaeda terrorists. The hardcore criminal Ronnie Biggs had done time in HSU together with the unexpected Lord and liar, Baron Archer of Weston-super-Mare, simply known as Jeffrey Archer to HMP.

Henry had deliberately avoided the former and certainly had no desire to be further embroiled with the latter. There was no way he was giving free investment advice to a bunch of maniacs. He would probably end up with a knife sticking between his shoulder blades despite the somewhat reassuring track record of HSU – no one had ever been murdered there but there was always a first.

The greatest punishment Henry had to endure was a lack of freedom to do something, to contribute in some way, any way. Although the concept of reparation was bandied about a lot around the prison system, Henry took it to mean shut up and don't make a fuss.

But Henry no longer wanted to shut up. After the shock of incarceration, the months it had taken to absorb Liam's betrayal, and the annihilation of his career, he needed to exercise this brilliant mind of his. He needed a plan and the forbidden word had started creeping into his brain more and more often: escape.

Chapter Five

The preliminary toxicology report on the jumper, as on Pole's desk. Gary Cook was a user, nothing hardcore, more recreational, a little skunk for good measure, amphetamines – a lot of amphetamines – and then something new, something Pole was unfamiliar with, nootropics.

The coroner's opinion was clear. Cook used the amphetamines for sporting competition; boxing was his thing: broken nose and displaced jaw, broken fingers on both hands. Cook had been a keen boxer in his youth and still belonged to a boxing ring in the City. He must have enjoyed giving the bankers-would-be- boxers a punch for their money. An East-End upbringing was an absolute that he would have been trained in bare knuckle fighting.

Pole had visited Cook's home in South Kensington on the day after Cook's murder. The range of bodybuilding equipment was impressive and even more so was the private boxing ring built in the basement, so he agreed about the amphetamines.

Pole had sent his Detective Inspector Nurani Shah back to Cook's place after the tox report had landed. If there was anything to find, she would. Maybe that would shed some light on the rest of the report.

He headed towards the coffee machine.

"Talk of the Devil," Pole said as he spotted the DI in front of him.

Nurani smiled. She was rattling a bag full of plastic jars of various pills. Gary Cook was indeed a naughty boy.

"What have we got here?"

"I have to say, it's pretty impressive. A great collection. And I can tell you that a lot of them are not legal. All purchased through the dark web from a specific American website."

"Let's go into my office."

Pole gentlemanly gave way to Nurani and closed the door.

"How much of that stuff is used for bodybuilding and how much sends you on a high?" Pole asked.

"A lot of that stuff, as you put it, has to do with energy and resilience. These little red ones are amphetamines, and these little yellow ones are steroids. I have not yet found the one that really sends you on a high. I am forwarding all these to the lab but I'm pretty sure that the Yankee ones will be strong."

"OK Nu, deal with the tox guys. I want to know whether any of these combined with booze would have sent Gary as high as a kite."

"You mean a kind of acid trip? Pushing him to jump?"

Pole looked at the bag. He recognised some of the names, but nothing sprang to mind.

"What I can see here tells me more about pushing the body to its limits, aggression in sport, but not enough to kill the bloke. Although it might explain the arguments with people at the conference."

"Agreed, the competitive edge is more his style – the winner's drug." Nurani nodded. "And if you take enough steroids it can make you suicidal."

"It depends how much of it he was taking. The tox report doesn't indicate he was taking too much, but I'll check with forensic." Pole said. "Is there any cocaine?"

"Zip, not a trace. And we went through the entire house, top to bottom with a fine-toothed comb, floorboards up, emptied book-shelves – you name it."

Pole smiled at Nurani. She too was pumped up. Nothing better to draw out her skills than an investigation into the banking world. She had excelled and earned her stripes on the Crowne case. Pole didn't even want to imagine the state of the house she had just searched. She would have shown little sympathy for the grieving widow and children. Nurani was on a mission to prove how excellent she was I what could be yet again a high-profile case.

"What did Mrs Cook have to say for herself ?" Pole asked.

"She admitted to smoking a bit of weed but she had no idea how much Gary was consuming. I gather that he was not the sort of guy who was going to share his innermost thoughts with his wife."

"Was he depressed after GL had sacked him?"

"More pissed off apparently than depressed. He was talking to his lawyers and simply volunteered that he was onto a good deal – and he was networking a lot."

"Networking – more specific."

"She did not come forward with much. Again, not a great deal of confidences when it came to work but she said that he was going to a lot of conferences and networking evenings at his City club."

"Old school," Pole nodded. " earn the crust whilst the Missus stays at home to look after the kids and cooks for the hunter who brings back his leg of mammoth."

"I thought I was the one who did not like the bankers."

"It's not the bankers I don't like. It's the sort of guy who still thinks women are second-class citizens."

"Hear, hear, my honourable friend" said Nurani knocking on his desk repeatedly.

Pole waved a reproaching finger at her.

"Now, now, missus. I mean it and you know it."

"I know Jon, I could not have had a better mentor," Nurani replied in earnest. And she meant it too.

"I don't really want to say this," Pole changed the subject to avoid more unwanted compliments. "But I am going to say it anyway. This suicide does not feel quite right."

Nurani moved a pile of documents that lay on Pole's single spare armchair and sat down. She was also gathering her thoughts.

"Despite what his wife says he might have felt bad about losing his job. It is not uncommon for macho guys to lose their rag. In particular, if his job was given to some young buck or, worse, a woman."

"I might agree with you if he was left with nothing. But he was about to settle for a lot of money, possibly enough to start his own consultancy or hedge fund."

Nurani looked unconvinced.

"We are not in the north of England, Nu. He is not a miner or a factory worker with no hope. That sort of guy will always find something new to do. Actually, do we know how much he was earning from GL?"

"Not yet, I have spoken to HR at GL–HXBK. I should have the final number tomorrow. The HR woman simply said it was a generous offer."

"OK, we're talking millions. Do we know why they wanted to keep him quiet?"

"A long-serving employee?" ventured Nurani. "Remember, GL were up to their eyeballs in subprime debt. I bet you they don't want another scandal."

"What do you mean another scandal?" asked Pole, sitting up in his chair.

"I don't pretend I have new evidence but depending on the size of the deal between Cook and the bank, perhaps we are looking at another HR scandal."

"That's a very good point, Ms Shah. Maybe there is something else too that will come out. My sources tell me the disclosure of the crappy deals the City has been involved in is far from over."

"I see," said Nurani pursing her lips. Pole knew the expression well. She was frustrated she had not followed through on a potential lead.

"I'll go back and ask."

"Do. And you may want to emphasise we are not the FSA. I don't care what they have been cooking – I'm looking for a motive."

Nurani shook her head and was about to leave, eager to repair her mistake.

"Not so fast young lady. We did not speak about the new drug that was found in Cook's bloodstream."

"Nootropics – There was nothing at his home, and we still don't have the full picture on these," replied Nurani a little too sharply.

"Really. These are meant to enhance a person's mental performance, so why are you ruling them out completely? Surely it is not enough that you have not found any nootropics at Cook's house in Belgravia? Do you have a theory?"

"Well according to wife and kids, they don't use that stuff – at all. And again, we have looked—"

"I know, absolutely everywhere. Don't you think it is strange?"

"Well, I spoke to the kids straight after their return from Uni. I don't think they had time to rehearse the story."

Pole stroked his goatee. "In these days of mobile phones, I doubt they would not have spoken already."

Nurani shrugged. "Maybe. But what he was taking was not illegal, so I guess he was free to stash it at the office."

Pole sat back and remembered what Nancy had told him. Gary was a party animal in the naughty nineties.

"Do we know whether these networking events involve a bit of partying afterwards? I am not necessarily talking strip joints but some private club, preferably gentlemen only and the company involves a bunch of escort girls." Pole asked.

"He certainly would not have bragged about it to his wife either." Nurani stood up. "Good point, I am on it."

She left Pole's office unhappy. His DI was brooding a lot lately, Pole had noticed. And he knew why. A trip to the office coffee machine a few days ago had illuminated Pole perhaps more than he had wished.

"She seemed to be a good adviser on the Crowne case... and very pleasant," their colleague Andy Todd had said whilst stirring more sugar into his coffee. Nurani was leaning against the coffee machine, back towards the small corridor that led to it. Pole had slowed down as soon as he'd heard the word adviser.

"True enough, but she is not a trained officer. And she defended some pretty slimy people in her time as a QC." Nurani spoke as someone who had done a deep dive into the past of the adviser and Pole knew they were talking about Nancy.

"Perhaps, but why do you care anyway? You're up for promotion, aren't you?"

"But if there is a procedural cock-up because we have used the said consultant, I can kiss goodbye to that and it's not strictly by the book anyway."

Andy had not replied, and Pole had not believed his ears either. Was this the same Nurani, now all concerned about doing it *by the book*, who had proven a mercenary when it came to negotiating with the IRA for Henry's head? The same woman who had help convince Henry's best friend, Liam, to betray Henry.

Pole had retreated to his desk without a coffee to ponder on what he had heard.

Nancy was an excellent consultant and Ms Shah would have to get used to working with her if she wanted to continue working with Pole.

Pole pressed 1 on his phone's speed dial. And the phone chimed away. He grabbed the receiver and waited for Nancy to answer.

* * *

Nancy cursed as she entered the ground floor hallway of her luxurious apartment block. She had just missed Pole's call. She shouldn't have lost time following Brett. It was just silly. She had enough on her plate and so had Pole. She would call back as soon as she reached her place.

She pushed the door open and picked up the mail that the concierge had slid through the letterbox. A large envelope attracted her attention. The paper had a different texture, unmistakably foreign, Asian she thought. She hesitated. It had been posted in Hong Kong. No, she would open it later, one thing at a time.

"Jonathan, I am so sorry I missed you. The wretched phone's ring is too low against the noise of traffic on Angel's Corner."

"Not to worry… A few things have emerged that I needed to discuss with you."

She listened to Pole's description of his findings without interr-upting. "I'm starting to come to a different conclusion when it comes to Cook's death." Pole concluded.

"So, in a nutshell, you are now also in doubt about Cook's suicide but have no concrete evidence. I'm sorry to be a spoilsport but I can't imagine GL volunteering information about any financial problems they may have."

"I'm sure you're right but then again it is a criminal investigation, and we might now be talking murder."

"Still, until you can prove to them it is murder and not mere suicide, the bank's litigators are not going to budge, and neither will HR of course."

"And very annoying it is as I need to understand the deal the bank had agreed with Cook, to decide whether he was under threat."

"Well, there is one person who might be able to help," Nancy said, waiting to see whether Pole would take the bait.

"I see where you are heading *ma chére...*" a phone ringing interrupted him.

"You mean... Ah, sorry, a call for you on the other line. Not to worry. We have our Sadler's Wells' evening tonight so we can discuss without interruption. Looking forward."

Nancy smiled. Pole had been a solid friend for the past four years, a man whose company she enjoyed but, as ever, she could not quite make up her mind whether to go a little further. She pushed the idea aside, got up and went to the kitchen.

She boiled the kettle and was about to make her much loved Sichuan tea. Nancy went through her tea ritual to settle herself, warming the teapot, measuring the amount with precision. She chose her favourite mug and went back to the lounge.

The large envelope from Hong Kong was still unopened on her coffee table, but she decided it could wait a little longer. She poured some tea and moved to the sound system in the lounge. Nancy selected some easy listening music, *The Best of Julie London* and sank into a soulful tune.

The smoky voice of Julie London transported Nancy to another time and place. She had not been born in the fifties, but Nancy sometimes wished she had known America then, before so much happened in the world over the next forty years. Her mind was slowly drifting back to China, and she was about to push it away again when her favourite song came on.

The languid vocals of 'Cry Me a River' moved Nancy in a very different direction – a jazz club, the cosy atmosphere made for intimacy and the man she was meeting that night. Pole had stood up and offered a dance with such effortless charm that she had found herself on the dance floor before she had said yes. The 606 Jazz Club was full, as you would expect a good jazz club to be, yet not so packed that there was no room to move. Pole turned out to be a surprisingly good dancer.

Nancy stretched on her sofa; eyes closed. She could still feel Pole's touch; his hand on her back, fingers slightly stretched. She had tensed and then relaxed. Pole moved slowly, giving her time to adjust to a feeling she had not had for a long time, and she suspected neither had Pole.

She opened her eyes; the memory was both delicious and annoying. Yet, she was not ready to fall in love.

It was time to change subject and she turned her attention to the envelope that she had so far managed to ignore. She slowly lifted the flap and looked inside. She took out the letter and recognised Philippe Garry's signature. She had met him a few years ago. He had sold Henry his first important piece of contemporary art, *The Raft of the Medusa*. She had followed the evolution of Philippe's gallery with interest. He too had gone to Hong Kong, for the now much sought after HKG Art Fair. Whereas his London gallery had a clear contemporary art focus, Philippe's new venture in Hong Kong had a more open brief: contemporary, modern and some high-quality artefacts that provided unique selling opportunities.

His letter was written on an attractive sheet of rice paper.

Dear Nancy,
Join the "River Crab Feast!" On November 7, 2010 one of China's most prominent artists, Ai Weiwei, was placed under house arrest in Beijing. Since then over 1,000 people have attended the River Crab Feast at his Shanghai Studios. On January 11, 2011 the Shanghai city government, having declared the studios an illegal construction, proceeded with their demolition without ap- peal or prior notice.

The letter went on to talk about abuse of power *and human rights violations* and gave a link to a video of the demolition inviting Nancy to watch it, share it on social media and comment on it.

In solidarity with a friend and colleague whose freedom is under threat. They silence him, yet his voice grows louder and louder.

Nancy froze, a shiver rippled through her body. A sense of fear she had thought no longer existed within her shook her. She slumped back on her sofa and dropped the letter on the coffee table

She wanted to tear the letter to shreds and yet the more reasonable part of her was protesting.

She had lectured Henry so much about coming to terms with his own past and the past had decided to catch up with her too. Henry had been honest about the loss of his father at the hand of a masked gunman who'd never been identified, let alone convicted and yet she couldn't bring herself to speak of her own loss to anyone. Perhaps it was time she started to trust a friend.

* * *

The clock had moved very little since he had last checked it – 5:35 pm. Pole stretched and ran his long hands through his salt-and-pepper hair; he fingered the tickets in his jacket pocket and smiled. Meeting Nancy for something other than discussing the latest crime he was investigating made his pulse quicken. He enjoyed the keen feeling of expectation, but he was also a patient man. There was no rush. Nancy was an emotional enigma that he wanted to solve slowly. He would soon get ready, change his shirt and tie for the inevitable black turtleneck sweater. The Kodo performance started at 7.30 pm; they had planned to meet an hour before for a pre-concert drink.

Nurani knocked at the door and stepped in. Pole cast an eye at the clock again, 5:41 pm.

"What can I do for you?"

"Just had a real interesting call with HR," Nurani said, excited.

Pole raised a quizzical eyebrow. "Thinking of moving to Traffic, are you?"

Nurani shrugged her shoulders. She didn't seem amused. "Nah. They won't have me. I'm too tall – I mean with GL HR."

"That's more interesting."

"Sure is. First, the woman said the redundancy package for Cook was standard. Then she said she could not comment in detail, so I asked to speak to her boss. Anyway, to cut a long story short, the Head of HR came on the line. I have a feeling that Cook was helping 'the FSA with their enquiries'," Nurani said, air quoting. "GL does not want to be seen to have an axe to grind against Cook."

Pole sat up. Nurani had his full attention. "Is he a whistle-blower?"

"I don't think so, not exactly. At least not according to HR."

"They would have said so if it had been the case. Interesting, Did they volunteer any details, or do they want to speak to the Compliance department first?"

Nurani nodded with an approving smile. Pole was always one beat ahead when things mattered.

"HR are checking."

"They know. They just don't want to make a big boo-boo. And I presume they also will have to speak to their gators."

"What, alligators? I know it's banking but still!"

"You are not far wrong. I mean their litigators and other fancy lawyers. If it is what I think it is. e could have our motive here."

"Goody, a bit of banker bashing. Just the way I like it. And more information has come in, take two of the prelim tox report."

"You mean more details have emerged??" Pole asked.

"Yup, and now we not only know he was taking nootropics, but he was loaded with them."

"You mean he might have OD'd anyway? And how many prelim tox reports are we going to get before we get THE FINAL report? Who's the pathologist on this?"

"Someone new. Don't recognise the name but I think she is delivering in stages to help us."

"Ask our Head Pathologist to cast an eye over this newbie's shoulder, will you?" Pole pulled the file towards him.

"Sure, will do. But back to that nootropic stuff. Apparently, it expands your brain capacity. I am checking what else it can do. And don't be impatient… the guys are giving us the info as soon as they have it so that we don't lose time."

"OK, fine but get hold of the Drug Squad team; find out if there are any reported incidents in the past month or so involving the same type of nootropics around London. And I also want to know who sells the stuff, where and how to get hold of it."

Nurani crossed her arms over her chest in mock anger. "Already on it, sir."

"You're the best. And I am just an old fart trying to make sure he's keeping up with the younger generation," Pole said amused. He eyed the clock again – 5:55 PM. Time to get changed. Pole closed the file he had finished reading with a thud and moved it onto the to- be-continued pile.

Nurani did not take the hint and sat herself down in the armchair facing Pole's desk.

"Actually Jon, I was wondering whether I could have a chat with you about something else?"

Pole had another five minutes and nodded. He had intended to leave early but if his DI needed him, he would be there for her. Nurani's eyes fell on the tickets that Pole had mechanically taken out of his pocket. Pole noticed her stubborn look over the tickets.

"I know you'll put me forward for promotion, Jon, and I am really grateful. But do you think they'll take it seriously? I am a bit anxious." Pole sat back and looked at Nurani closely. She was not the anxious type so why pretend? She had been equally vocal about her ambitions, so why hide it behind fake humility?

"I can't guarantee anything, but you know I gathered very good reports from senior members of the force. I got Pat Murphy in Northern Ireland to support you after your excellent performance in the Crowne case. Liam gave us the evidence against Henry, his friend, after Pat and you cut a deal with him. It all looks pretty solid, believe you me."

"That's reassuring, still I'm not exactly the typical DCI, am I?" Nurani's voice trailed. She was now comfortably sitting in the chair with apparently little intention of moving. Pole looked at his watch – 5:59.

"You mean your Asian background. With the service record you have it won't be a problem and it shouldn't be anyway. You know I would not tolerate any setback in that respect. If it doesn't go through when I make my recommendation, I will be asking questions."

"I know you will, Jon."

The clock struck 6pm. Pole stood up. He was leaving right now whether she liked it or not.

Nurani looked frustrated. Pole's constant open-door policy irritated some of his superiors but enthused his colleagues and juniors. Today however he was leaving on time and would resume his conversation tomorrow.

Nurani simply wanted to hear how good she had been, was and would be, perhaps she needed encouragement after all. Had she guessed he was meeting Nancy tonight? DI Shah soon to become DCI Shah might well have done. She was after all a very good cop.

"I have to go…" Pole said clapping his hands together.

He grabbed his bag and gave Nurani a broad but uncompromising smile. She returned a dark look and stood up without a word.

Pole followed Nurani through the door of his office, locked it and moved swiftly towards the corridor. He was off on a date."Glass of champagne or beer?" Nancy had texted. Stuck in traffic, Pole felt a little irritated. She had just beaten him to the theatre. He deliberated over which was the most appropriate. Beer was a bit too copper-like. Champagne, he did not like the thought of Nancy having to buy her own glass. Champagne should be bought by the gentleman. Oh God, what to do?

"Shit, I'll go for what I like," he muttered and went for Champagne.

The traffic Pole was stuck in eased of and he was parking his car near Saddlers Wells theatre 15 minutes later. He entered the building and spotted Nancy perched on a high stool at one of the tables set up in the small theatre wine bar. There was always a relaxed elegance about her no matter what she wore. Her black- and-white trouser outfit, vintage haute couture perhaps, was a perfect smart-casual choice that enhanced her tanned skin and jet-black hair. Nancy waved and gave Pole a broad smile.

"Don't worry. Perfect timing. It would have been pitiful if I had not beaten you to it since I live three minutes' walk from here," she said anticipating Pole's objection.

"You're too kind. I'll order for the interval. You look well," Pole said bending forward to kiss her cheek.

"Thank you, Jonathan," Nancy replied whilst returning his kiss. "I just came back last week from a few days in France."

They briefly caught up on the latest developments in the Cook affair but there was little Nancy did not know already. Their conversation drifted into a more enjoyable chat until it was time to take their seats.

* * *

The Kodo drums were in full swing, the rhythm and intensity rising and ebbing to reach unimaginable crescendos. Pole was on the edge of his seat and Nancy was transfixed. He had cast an eye towards his companion at the beginning of the performance.

Nancy had been hooked from the first beat the players had struck. Each number they played was a complete success and the crowd erupted in applause every time. The final number was about to start when Pole heard the low vibration of his phone. Someone wanted to talk but he was damned if he would even consider taking a discreet look. *They'll leave a message if it is that urgent.* Sure enough the phone interrupted again. Pole discreetly looked at his watch – only ten minutes to go till the end of the first half.

"This is extraordinary," Nancy said with complete enthusiasm as they made their way out of the auditorium. "I never would have gone on my own. Kodo didn't sound that appealing to me. Thank you."

Pole grinned. He was glad he could introduce the much-cultured Ms Wu to some new music. Next step was jazz fusion but all in good time. They reached the small table they had left an hour ago. The two glasses Pole had ordered were waiting for them. Pole dragged his phone out of his pocket with an apologetic smile.

"Jonathan – remember, I used to be a QC. I am impressed you have waited till the end of the last piece. I would have been out of the performance like a shot."

Pole had put the phone to his ear in a distracted fashion to listen to his messages. He was about to reply to Nancy when his focus became absolute. Nancy read his face and forgot about her drink altogether. Pole inhaled deeply and was about to apologise once more.

"Do tell Jonathan – someone else jumped?"

"No but was found in his garage – dead in his car."

"You're going?" Nancy asked more as an observation than a question.

Pole nodded. "Want to join me?"

Nancy grabbed her bag and coat. "Who is he, if I may ask?"

"Tom Hardy, Chief Executive of the British Bankers' Association."

Nancy frowned but did not look surprised. Something was bothering her and with this new death Pole wanted to know why.

Chapter Six

The recognisable white-and-blue barricade tape had already been placed around the scene. Pole had parked his car in the middle of Holland Park. Forensics was following him on foot. They waved as they recognised him. Nancy had got out too, standing outside the restricted zone and simply observed: Pole absorbing the information, the details of what the first PC on the scene had gathered, the opinion of the paramedics. Nancy admired his effortless mastery of the situation, focused, controlled and yet inclusive. He waved her into the controlled perimeter.

"She is with me, consulting for the Met," Pole said to the other PC manning the surveillance of the enclosure. He handed a pair of gloves to Nancy, and they entered the garage in which the body of Tom Hardy lay.

The odour of petrol fumes was still overwhelming. Nancy gagged but she stilled herself. She would not let Pole down. The driver's door was open, and Tom had slumped in his seat. Nancy could not see his face, but she noticed his hand stretched towards the passenger seat. He was still wearing a seat belt. Nancy noticed that the passenger door had been taped.

"Who found him?" Pole asked.

"His wife. DI Shah is with her at the moment," replied PC Thomas who was briefing Pole.

"You need to go in on your own," Nancy said. "I will take a look and see what I can make of it. I'll see you back at the car."

"I might be a while. But you're welcome to join me." Pole looked concerned.

"Don't worry. It's probably just as well if you start on your own." Nancy replied. Nurani was on the crime scene and Nancy had learned to be guarded in her presence

"Are you sure?"

"I'll make my own way if it takes you too long. I don't have another date to go to," Nancy replied with a teasing smile.

Pole nodded, smiling back, and disappeared.

Nancy did not trust Nurani and Nurani had made it clear she did not trust Nancy either. There was something oddly competitive about her that Nancy could not quite make herself comfortable with. Too bad though; Nancy would keep consulting with the Met whether the young DI liked it or not.

The SOCO team was setting up a tent outside the garage and a small pudgy woman arrived on the scene. She extended her hand to Nancy after removing her gloves.

"Are you *the* consultant?" she said with a twinkle in her eye.

"I did not think my reputation was that good. Or perhaps that bad," Nancy replied with equal amusement.

"Well, we all like a good gossip. And the boys are the worst." She gently moved Nancy out of the way. "So, what have we got?"

"Do you mind if I join you?"

"Not at all. And I'm pretty sure you know the drill." She was already palpating the man's body, looking for initial clues. "My name is Yvonne Butler by the way. The Yard's Head Pathologist."

"Mine is Nancy Wu. But I guess you know that. I would say very nice to meet you but it may be inappropriate."

Yvonne shrugged. "OK, no sign of struggle, position of body and face consistent with asphyxiation."

Yvonne took a small torch out of one of the pockets of her protective white overalls. "Mmmm, might have taken drugs – not uncommon in this sort of suicide," she said whilst checking one of the pupils of the dead man.

"You mean he was asleep before asphyxiation?"

"Very likely, I need to carry out a full autopsy to be sure, of course." She stood up to face Nancy. "Who is he anyway?"

"Tom Hardy, chief exec of the BBA."

"BBA?" Yvonne said moving away from the car to get her camera.

"British Bankers' Association," Nancy replied.

"Another banker! Gee, I have not even finished processing the last one."

"You mean Gary Cook?"

"The very same. Are you also closely *consulting* with Pole on that one?" Yvonne asked mischievously whilst pulling out her camera.

"I'm afraid I am. And since we are talking about it, I presume you were there to photograph the body?"

Yvonne looked at Nancy with a hint of surprise. "Why do you ask?"

"Did you think it was consistent with suicide to have the body land on its back?"

"A very good observation," Yvonne said, clearly convinced of the sharpness of Nancy's mind.

"And—"

"Unusual but not impossible. He was drunk and drugged. He may have lost his footing before he actually jumped," Yvonne replied as she started taking pictures. Nancy moved away slowly, turned around and said, "And Tom is still wearing his seat belt."

"Odd indeed," Yvonne acknowledged.

* * *

Nancy would have stayed longer were it not for Nurani. Pole had a long night in front of him and did not need a jealous spat between two strong- minded women. She smiled at the warm feeling Pole elicited in her but the proximity of the SOCO team sobered her up rapidly.

She texted Pole and called a cab.

The taxi drove past Sadler's Wells on the way back. The theatre was emptying slowly. An excited bunch of people were talking about the show with evident appreciation. She and Pole should have been part of the crowd and yet she enjoyed being part of his other life too. She could never be cross with a man who had a tough job to do.

Nancy entered the magnificent hallway of her block of apartments and took the lift to reach her landing. Until Henry was out of jail, she would be the only one living on Floor 5. She was glad he had been able to keep the apartment opposite hers despite a crushing fine and lack of income. The tabloids had made a meal of it. How could a man involved in supporting terrorists still be able to afford such an expensive property?

But Nancy knew the intimate side of the story: the childhood terror, the mixed-marriage nightmare in seventies' Belfast where Catholic and Protestant did not cohabit, let alone marry. She knew of the desperation to belong, the blind faithfulness to friendship that ultimately had brought Henry down. As ever, the barrister she was passionately believed that everyone should be allowed to find redemption and one day be absolved.

Nancy was surprised to find herself standing in the middle of her landing and opened the apartment door briskly. It was good to be home. She moved to the kitchen, made herself a pot of tea and a sandwich and removed her Louboutin Hot Jeanbi 100 with great relief. "Really Nancy, walking a crime scene in five-inch heels," she said almost amused.

She collapsed into her favourite armchair and picked up the yellow pad she now had a habit of leaving on the coffee table. She methodically reported all she had seen, smelt, heard, even touched and drew up a list of questions.

1. Suicide?
Nancy did not know Tom Hardy very well but he did not seem a candidate for such an act of desperation. Edwina had spoken about his appointment as an excellent move for the financial institution he represented.

The BBA was becoming old-fashioned, a lobby group for the various banking organisations and bodies that populated the City. More importantly, it was the institution that fixed LIBOR, the primary benchmark for interest rates, not only Sterling but also an impressive range of other currencies including Dollar LIBOR.

She jotted down UNLIKELY after her first bullet point.

2. Financial crisis put pressure on him?
Nancy poured a cup of tea. She inhaled its fragrance before taking a

sip. How wonderful – tea, the cure for all ailments. She picked up the pad again and jotted ASK HENRY next to the question.

3. Tom Hardy's enemies?
This would be a question for Edwina. Nancy was not entirely certain whether he had worked with her directly. It did not matter that much; in the rarefied sphere of the City's trading floors she would have had contact with him anyway. Henry might have a view as well.

ASK EDDIE AND HENRY.

4. Seat belt?
This was the most puzzling part. That question would go to Pole. Or perhaps she could make friends with Yvonne. Nancy's excellent intuition was telling her it was a material element.

She looked at her watch, gone 1am. She was due to meet Henry the following day for her regular visit. Should she speak to Pole and get Henry involved? He knew the people who worked in the City better than anyone and he had worked with Cook. She would be surprised if he had not known Tom Hardy as well. More importantly he would almost certainly have a view about what unsavoury deals these people might have got involved in

But she shook her head – too early in the case. She sat back in her chair, put her legs underneath her and poured a second cup of tea, savouring the peace and security of her surroundings. Her eyes came to rest on the rice-paper letter she had received that morning.

"Not now," she said, annoyed at having left the Hong Kong letter on the table. "Too much death for one night." She stood up and climbed the flight of stairs to the shelter of her bedroom. She had an early morning meeting at Belmarsh prison.

* * *

The early visiting slot opened at 9:15am. Belmarsh had strict rules for visitors requiring them to present themselves an hour in advance and be processed through the various gates and security checkpoints.

However, Nancy was still using her Prerogative as counsel. The advantage was that she could hold and transfer documents that would never be checked by the guards. The contents of the folder she brought with her would never be examined.

She went through the gates with a crowd of people, mainly women some of whom she recognised and greeted. The early morning visits always drew the same kind of people. She acknowledged a short black woman and nodded. There was no fraternity but a certain amount of unexpected amiability. The processing started and the usual checks were performed. Legal counsels and solicitors were given their fair share of questions but nothing like the circus of what other visitors had to endure.

Nancy knew the drill too well to accept any nonsense from the prison officers and they knew it too.

"Anything else you need, officer?"

The man took his time to pat her down and go through her handbag. "Nope, all in order."

"As ever," Nancy said with the most courteous of smiles.

She was accompanied out of the main prison block to start the checks needed to enter the HSU. The small reception was carpeted, yet the comfort stopped there. The rest of the unit was bare.

Nancy removed her shoes, and her belongings were scanned. She walked through the metal detector unperturbed and let the guards check the lining of her suit and even the inside of her mouth. HSU guards themselves were subjected to the same strenuous checks. Nancy thanked the prison officer and moved to the meeting room. There were only three tables in the parloir, unlike in the main prison. HSU did not engage in a mass visiting program, but rather a tightly controlled one.

She and Henry would have an hour and a half which sounded too little but sometimes was oddly too much. It was important to feel comfortable she had learned. She certainly had news to share but was equally keen to carry on the conversation they had started on her previous visit. Something was bothering Henry over and above his incarceration and she needed to know what She had sensed it in his last letter.

* * *

The door clanged open. Nancy turned her head as Henry entered. The prison officer removed the handcuffs. Henry rubbed his wrists, a mechanical gesture to check that his hands were indeed free rather than do away with the pain. Nancy stood up and took his hand with the usual kindness. He smiled, squeezing Nancy's hand in turn.

"Morning Nancy."

"Morning my dear."

Getting the conversation going was always a slow process. Nancy had come up with a routine that Henry liked. They would speak about his flat, the latest art exhibition; Nancy would feed him bits of gossip from the art world that made him feel he still belonged to the community of Collectors. The serious stuff would trickle through gradually.

Nancy put the copy of *Tate Etc.* on the table between them. "Actually Nancy, I caught the news this morning. What is the story around Tom Hardy?"

"Officially, suicide – unofficially, I am not sure."

"So incredibly odd. First Gary, now Tom."

Nancy smiled. Henry was always on the ball. She told him all she knew.

"Still working with Pole as a consultant I s'pose?" Henry teased. "I told you I wanted to reconnect somehow with my old profession. But no funny business, I promise."

"Good girl." Henry teased. "Although I remember a particular letter that indicated otherwise."

"Argh. I should know better than to commit compromising information to paper." Nancy laughed. "Swiftly diverging our conversation, back to Tom and Gary. Do you see a connection?"

Henry pushed his chair back and lifted his face towards the ceiling. His short hair made the features of his face stand out even more. No doubt an attractive one to some, a resolute jaw, deep furrows slicing his cheeks and a slightly hooked nose gave it an intensity that could attract or disturb.

"A connection? That's an interesting thought."

Nancy looked at him incredulously. "You do have an idea."

"Well – I see one connection but I'm not sure whether it would matter."

"Pray tell."

"LIBOR, the interbank interest rate."

"Why? Gary was on the trading floor at GL and Tom was chief executive at the BBA. I can't see it and, yes, I know how LIBOR is being used."

Henry smiled. "I am not talking about LIBOR trading. Although it might also be a link come to think of it. I am talking about LIBOR fixing. To be more precise the process through which the banks decide where LIBOR sits daily, weekly, etc."

"I am sorry. I feel particularly dense this morning but what's the connection between Gary and Tom?"

"You're not being thick Nancy; you just don't know these people as well as I do. Gary Cook was the guy who gave his estimate of where the bank, I mean GL, estimated LIBOR to be at. In other words, he estimated at what level GL could borrow in the interbank market and he was the official submitter of GL as far as LIBOR was concerned."

"And Tom?"

"Tom would preside over the fixing process. Not directly of course – but, still, remember BBA publishes LIBOR on Reuters."

Nancy remained silent, taking the information in.

"And how big is or rather was GL's Sterling rates book?"

Henry clapped his hands and gave Nancy the thumbs up.

"One of the largest on the market, a game changer in times of market turbulence."

Nancy's face grew serious.

"You must speak to Pole." Her dark eyebrows had come together so close they nearly formed a line. She meant business and Henry smiled. He liked it.

"Do I want to speak to the guy who put me in this place for starters?" Henry replied dryly.

"You are being unfair. He brokered a deal to get you out of the mess in which you had put yourself."

Henry stood up, turning his back to Nancy. The prison officer reappeared.

"Please sit down, Henry."

Henry's fists were clenched but he obeyed. "Does that mean I get to come out?"

"Is there any reason why you should?" Nancy frowned.

"Pole may want me to look at evidence on-screen, consult records and carry out a data search on Bloomberg."

"What are you expecting to find?"

"Nancy, if there is something to find that is market related, I will need to track it by myself and I don't want that to be done on Belmarsh's computer."

"You are not serious? You mean another banking scandal," Nancy said incredulous.

"I won't know for sure until I see the data." Henry was sticking to his guns. .

"OK, I'll speak to him."

"If this is LIBOR manipulation in size, it goes right to the top of the tree. You understand that?"

"You mean CEO level?"

"I mean government, Whitehall and the Bank of England." Nancy looked Henry in the eyes. He was not joking.

She thought of Edwina. Henry was perhaps overdoing it. He had been an equity boy all his working life. Was the manipulation of LIBOR a real prospect?

"I'll bear that in mind," Nancy replied. She was now keen to change the subject but did not need to find an excuse. Henry had noticed something or someone and his attention had shifted away from her entirely. She waited. Maybe this shift had something to do with what had been bothering Henry of late.

"Sorry, Nancy." A deep line was digging into his forehead; his blue eyes had grown a shade darker.

"Something's wrong?" Nancy asked resisting the urge to turn round. "Not something – someone," Henry said slowly. "I usually don't worry about the many nutters that live round the corner from me but this one is bloody odd."

"In what way?"

"He has just arrived, thankfully not on the same landing though.

His name is Ronnie Kray." Henry's attention was still on the space behind Nancy. He did not see her face drop in disbelief.

"You mean like the Kray brothers – but Ronnie died in the mid-nineties."

"I know." Henry's focus came back to Nancy. "This guy has changed his name by deed poll apparently. The Kray twins are his favourite gangsters. He has carried out the inspiration a tad far for my liking – he is in here for murder and trafficking."

"Has he spoken to you?" The tone of her voice had taken on the professional edge he knew meant business.

"Not yet but he is looking, picking the moment of his choice. Charlie warned me about his type. They have a grudge and if you are on the wrong side of that grudge, beware."

"Do you need me to do anything? I can ask for a transfer at least out of the spur and—"

"I should not have worried you with this Nancy, it's the HSU after all," Henry said now more relaxed. Speaking up had had a comforting effect Nancy gathered and Henry moved the conversation back to the topic of art. Nancy knew better than to prod for more information, but she needed to stay alert. It was her turn to feel a little defocused on what Henry was saying. But Henry uttered the word netsuke and Nancy's face broke into a smile. It was naughty of him to mention the small piece of art he held secretly in his cell.

"I re-reread *The Hare with Amber Eyes*. I so wish I had started collecting these much earlier on." Henry had positioned his hand strategically around his face. No one would be lip-reading his words as he spoke about his new-found passion.

Nancy frowned half seriously. "And you're going to get me disbarred if you keep wanting to build this collection of yours. Without mentioning the fact that netsuke are Japanese, and I have Chinese ancestry – very bad form."

Henry winked but his attention shifted again

Nancy followed his gaze and the violence of Kray's glare hit her in the chest as powerfully as a well-aimed punch. Henry did not lower his eyes and kept the contact going for a few more seconds, enough to tilt the balance in what was a challenge, a test of Henry's mettle.

"Henry…" Nancy's voice made him break off his stare. "Not a good idea."

"You're right." Henry nodded. His face regained his composure.

Nancy glanced at the clock on the wall It was almost time to go. She knew better than to discuss Kray again with only a few minutes left, and yet couldn't shake the feeling that Henry might have made his first life-threatening mistake.

Chapter Seven

TOP BANKER TOPS HIMSELF screamed the all-caps headline. Edwina had bought the tabloid on her way into work. She had read the article twice. She felt nauseous. Tom Hardy had been a close ally of hers for years. They had worked together, planned part of their career together. They had pushed the envelope as far as it could go... possibly even further. And there was something that Edwina was absolutely convinced of, Tom would never commit suicide.

She emerged from Bank tube station and turned left into one of the little alleyways that so characterised the City. She had come to know the Square Mile by heart and the little passage was exactly what she needed. A secluded place to make a call.

"Gabs, it's me. Are you in already?"

"Of course...already slaving away at my desk."

"Good man, I am at Bernie's. We need to talk."

"I'll meet you there."

She dropped her phone nervously into her bag. Gary first, now Tom – it could not be a coincidence. Edwina made her way to their meeting place, weaving her way through the narrow alleyways of the City.

Edwina entered the small café and sat at a corner table.

Bernie waved at her and Edwina ordered two lattes, with an extra shot for Gabriel, and two croissants. She sat in the window and took a sip of coffee. As she raised her cup, she noticed her hand was shaking. Why was Gabriel taking so long? She was about to call again when he appeared through the door, his presence already reassuring her. She was almost certainly overreacting.

"Hello Eddie. What terrible problem will I have to sort out today then?" Gabriel said smiling.

"Hello Gabs." Edwina smiled tentatively. She waited until her number two had sat down. "Have you read the news?"

"Always. Are we talking Tom Hardy?" Edwina nodded.

"Very sad," Gabriel said. "I can imagine it is a shock. You guys were close."

"Yes, we were, and I am very sad but..." Edwina hesitated.

Gabriel lifted his hand to silence her. "Are you about to refer to the conversation you and Tom had in 2009?"

Edwina nodded.

"No one could have known. Right?"

"I'm not so sure."

"Why? Tom was the most discreet man I have ever met."

"Yes, but he had to act and get someone on the market to move the benchmark," Edwina said lowering her voice.

"And?"

"He would have contacted someone like Gary."

"Did he tell you that?"

"He said he had a contact at GL."

"Mmmm, I see," Gabriel replied. He took a sip of coffee. Edwina could see he was measuring the importance of the information.

"I thought I'd told you."

"Nope." Gabriel gave a negative nod. "You only mentioned Tom."

"Sorry, I thought I had. In any case, it was GL, and if it was GL—"

"It was Gary Cook, I get it." Gabriel took another mouthful of coffee. He bit into his croissant and started chewing thoughtfully.

Edwina's throat tightened and her eyes tingled. She pictured Tom's serious face breaking into a smile as he spoke about his daughters.

"Eddie, what are you exactly worried about?"

"I don't know. It is – odd. Two suicides, one after the other," her voice trailed. She avoided Gabriel's eyes and toyed with her croissant. "And these two guys were not the suicidal types."

"Do we really know that? I'm not sure."

"Come on Gabs, Gary Cook would have slaughtered half of the City before he incurred so much as a paper cut. He was a fucking bastard and fucking bastards like him don't commit suicide."

"Well, maybe he no longer could slaughter half of the City as you put it since his early retirement," Gabriel said stressing the word early. "And that got to him."

"I don't buy that, but if, and that is a big if, it explains Gary, no way does it apply to Tom. No way."

Gabriel shrugged. "I heard his marriage had some issues."

"What? Rubbish. He and Jane were a tight couple."

"That has not always been the case," Gabriel replied aggressively.

"That is very old history. They had forgiven each other."

"OK, let's assume you are right. Who would want to bump off these two guys? And why?"

"How about the very 'call' we talked about earlier?"

Gabriel looked at Edwina in a way he never had before. The scar on his cheek looked even paler than usual as his face had coloured in anger. He brought his hand to it and traced its outline mechanically.

Edwina froze. There was something ferocious and determined in the movement that shocked her. But just as quickly as it had gone, his amiable face returned. He moved towards her reassuringly. "The LIBOR fixing will never come out. Trust me."

Edwina nodded. Gabriel's look had sobered her thoughts The LIBOR matter should never be discussed – she got it now. And yet she could have sworn that she remembered Gabriel in conversation with Tom and come to think of it, Gary at the Whitehall summer party a few months ago. Would they not have been discussing the forbidden subject?

* * *

The art consignment was on its way to Macau. Brett did not want to know through which route. The less he knew about the traffickers' business the better. Half of the cash had been deposited into his Swiss account. The other half would be paid when the artefacts had been received and checked for damage. Brett hated this moment of uncertainty.

His Chinese client was a reliable collector. But he would also be ruthless if the quality of the pieces did not live up to expectation. In a couple of weeks Brett would be on his way to Hong Kong. He would then make the trip to Macau on his client's private jet.

A phone was ringing. He did not recognise the ringtone at first but realised, with annoyance that it was his burner mobile.

Unexpected.

"Hello?" Brett answered, cursing himself. Why had he not got rid of his phone more promptly?

"This is *Le Capitaine*. The consignment has reached its destination."

"Excellent… I will see the client in a couple of weeks and as agreed payment will be made then…"

Le Capitaine interrupted Brett. "I have a deal for you… something a little different but lucrative."

"More artefacts moving to Europe? What's the commission?"

"£300,000. As I said something different. I'll call back with the details in the next 24 hours, perhaps sooner."

Le Capitaine hung up. Brett should be pleased. £300,000 would be a welcome addition to his meagre income. But the assumption that Brett would be interested come what may, rubbed against the grain.

"Who the hell do they think they are?" Brett muttered.

Brett took his pack of cigarettes out but decided against having one. This was not the way it was supposed to be. He was the one giving directions. He walked to the elegant desk he had managed to salvage from yet another disastrous divorce. He took an antique decanter that had belonged to one of his most illustrious ancestors, sat down and poured a large helping of whisky. Neat. Just as his father had taught him, and his father before him.

Brett closed his eyes and let the amber liquid do the trick. By the third glass he felt bolder. What if he said no? This Middle Eastern riff-raff knew little about him: no name, no address. His only contact in London he had known for years, and Brett had accumulated enough on him to condemn him for several lifetimes.

But then there was his business with MI6, that which gave him ultimate protection should any of his shabby dealings be discovered. He had told Steve he would call with fresh information no matter how small, but Brett felt he needed a little context to decide on the timing of that call. Being an informant for MI6 had to be played skilfully. Brett finished his glass and stood up with a slight stagger.

"Steady old boy, or you won't enjoy your hard-earned money."

Brett sighed. He stilled himself and pulled back the silk Hereke rug that spread underneath his coffee table. His index finger pressed one of the wooden slats of his immaculate French parquet, a small part of it pivoted to reveal a hole large enough to contain a laptop and some documents.

Brett placed the laptop on the table, logged in – time for an update on the latest developments in Iraq and Syria. Perhaps he could anticipate what *Le Capitaine* had in mind. Brett received first-hand information that would never reach the public. He retrieved a small token from the safe and started stage two of his high-security log in. The remote access process lasted for a few minutes, testing his patience. When the website came live, he chose the sequence of options he knew by heart and started reading.

No new post since he last accessed the site, no military and financial developments – frustrating. The rise of a new terrorist faction had been reported. It was now a matter of weeks before the time bomb that had started ticking in Iraq after the US-led invasion failed, exploded.

More turbulence and the need for more money coming from art smuggling was all good news for Brett's business. This steady source of income was unlikely to disappear soon and yet the information coming from the Middle East was alarming even for the rogue dealer that Brett was.

The new type of fanaticism that secret intelligence was talking about seemed worse than Al-Qaeda: even more ruthless, better organised both militarily and financially. Art, oil and people's donations straight from the heart of Wahhabism in Saudi Arabia. Although Bin Laden had come from Saudi too, the family was well known, and it was possible for governments that were so inclined to trace Bin Laden's business.

But tracing this new group's dealings was proving more complicated. The new group also had the advantage of starting to control a region that spread over a number of countries struggling with religious conflicts – a perfect recipe. The movement had been founded in 1999 but it had failed to attract the attention of the intelligence community until recently. The word ISIS or DAESH had started circulating; no one had yet leaked the information to the press.

"Very unwise," Brett muttered.

He closed the laptop with disappointment. Tomorrow he would have received details of the deal *Le Capitaine* was proposing, and he would discuss it with his MI6 minder.

* * *

The mortuary still made Pole queasy. It was not the sight of the flesh but the despicable smell. Pole would have felt less human if the stench of death had become habitual and he had become immune to it. He was listening to Yvonne's initial findings with an uncomfortable sense of déjà vu.

"Alcohol and drugs is my best guess at present. We need to wait for the toxicology report to confirm. Then asphyxiation by inhalation of CO – took less than half an hour."

"I gathered as much," Pole said. "But a couple of things disturb me."

"Such as not finding any booze laced with drugs in the car?"

"Right, there was nothing in the house indicating he had drunk anything or taken any pills of any kind. Odd don't you think?"

"Until we know what he took exactly, I would not draw any conclusions. He might have organised it so that he did all his preparatory business somewhere else."

"Why? And it means a lot of planning – taking booze and drugs then giving yourself enough time to get home, arrange the car..."

"He might not have wanted to leave evidence at his home address."

"Perhaps, but his suicide is going to distress his family no matter what," Pole said raising a hand to stop Yvonne disagreeing. "And you are going to say that he had passed the point of no return where death seems the only option. But that would mean serious mental health issues and his wife was adamant all was well. He was worried about the financial crisis, obviously – but as she put it so is the whole bloody City."

"I presume you have not spoken to his BBA colleagues yet?"

"Not yet, Nurani is on the case. It's only 9am."

"I'm not criticising, just asking."

"Sorry, something escapes me and I don't like it."

"By the way, I met your *consultant*, Nancy. Very clued-up and as sharp as my granddad's razor."

Pole blushed slightly and he smiled at Yvonne. "Your granddad's razor must have been a lethal weapon."

"Yep, the old-fashioned throat slitting type."

"That's my girl. She would be mighty annoyed if she heard me call her girl by the way."

"Don't be fooled Jon; all women still have a part of them that is young and cute."

"Is that so?"

"Uh-huh. And it's a bloody good tip by the way, if you're trying to woo a lovely woman like Nancy." Yvonne said, whilst removing her gloves with a precise gesture, inside out, one into the other, and immediately throwing them into the hazardous material bin.

Pole's mobile was ringing. He reached below the protective apron he had donned.

"Speak of the Devil. Nancy, how are you?" Pole's face turned unexpectedly serious. She wanted a word urgently, but he would have to call back.

"There is nothing more for the time being. Take your call," Yvonne said waving Pole out. He mouthed "thank you" and stepped out of the mortuary into the corridor.

"Nancy, I'm still here. What about Henry?" Pole listened and broke into a slow jog towards the exit. "OK, let's meet outside the office at our regular place. I will be there in fifteen."

* * *

Nancy had broken with their usual ritual – she had arrived first and was waiting for Pole outside their favourite cafe. She waved and started coming towards him.

"I am sorry, Jonathan. It looks a little full. Let's try to find somewhere more discreet."

"Let's go round the corner. There is a small square and we can sit on a bench," Pole said, gently offering his arm to her to guide her to their destination. Nancy fought the immediate desire to break free and relaxed into Pole's warm guidance. He let go of her only when they arrived at the wrought-iron gate into the square and made way for her to enter first.

"So, what's Henry's opinion?" Pole said as they sat down.

"First of all, Jonathan, do you know how LIBOR works?"

"Not in detail. I know what it does broadly but do tell."

"Let me cut a long story short. The part that is relevant for us is the fixing of LIBOR. And before you even comment on the word *fixing,* it is the correct terminology. But let's call it *setting,* for our purpose."

Pole nodded. "Go for *setting.*"

"LIBOR is set every day by a number of selected banks that submit the rate at which they can borrow on the market from one another for various maturities, intraday, weekly, monthly etc—"

"Are those banks all British?"

"Good question, no. The current panel comprises a number of foreign institutions too."

"Would I be right in guessing that both GL and HXBK are members of that panel?"

Nancy gave him an appreciative look. "Spot on *mon che*r."

"And who fixes, sorry, sets, the rate for each bank?"

"Not so fast. I know you need a name, but you must first know that LIBOR is set by the BBA, which receives from each bank the information it needs. The BBA discards the highest four and lowest four responses. It then averages the remaining numbers. The average is reported at 11.30am daily for all maturities."

"The BBA is involved? You mean the same BBA Tom Hardy was the CEO of?"

"The very same and, to answer your previous question, banks will select traders that trade Sterling – I mean Pound Sterling – and one of them will establish the house view."

"Don't tell me. That person at GL was Gary Cook."

"*Voilà. Vous avez tout compris, mon cher.*"

"*Incroyable.*"

"I think you may have to dig around a lot more but if, and I still say if, there is some fixing then—"

Pole finished her sentence. "We have the beginning of a motive."

"We have indeed."

"So, Henry put two and two together to give us our *motive*?" Pole said, both amusement and irritation flashing in his eyes.

"He has but I don't think he is going to volunteer anything else unless—"

"What? First of all, I am not sure I need more information from him yet. The banks might speak up if I wave the spectre of a full-blown investigation in their faces."

"That may not be very effective, Jonathan. And I can tell you straight away that the banks would rather have a murder investigation on their hands than admit to LIBOR manipulation."

"I don't owe Henry anything," Pole grumbled. "And why do you think the banks won't talk?"

"Because the size of the financial market that will be affected if there is manipulation is unimaginably large. I don't even know how to quantify it."

Pole jerked in astonishment.

"I know. But consider this. LIBOR does not only cover mortgages in the UK, it also covers mortgages pegged to Dollar LIBOR and other currencies. That is a hell of a lot, Jonathan. Whether you like it or not, you need Henry."

Pole stood up and leaned against the backrest of the bench. His forehead had added a few lines in a characteristic frown.

"Why do I think I am not going to like his terms?"

"Because you know him so well by now. He wants to work on this outside Belmarsh." Nancy had just laid it out straight. There was no point in working on Pole to get the desired result. Raw truth was sometimes what it took. Pole moved away from the bench as if it had become electrified and a flash of anger showed in his eyes.

"Does Henry remember why he is a Cat A con?"

"He does. More than you can imagine, Jonathan. I understand your anger at the request, but frankly do you want him to work on a subject as sensitive as that from the confines of the HSU Belmarsh library?"

"I'll think about it."

"*Bien sûr*. He is not going anywhere."

"I bloody well hope he is not," Pole replied vehemently.

Nancy smiled. "HSU Belmarsh is the most secure prison in the UK and possibly in Europe."

Chapter Eight

The laptop was booting up in the library where Henry had booked some IT time. The device was painfully slow, but Henry had by now acknowledged that his days of impatience at the speed of his trading floor computer or his Tech Team were over. The screen finally came live with two icons appearing, a dog and a cat. The inmates were allowed access to computers to prepare formal documents, but the functionality amounted to little more than that of a word processor.

Predictably, inmates would have clicked on the cat. The little animal, silent and lithe seemed to fit the con population perfectly. The prison officers had access to the system too and would have, equally predictably, clicked on the dog. The dog had, of course, much increased capability, in particular, access to the Internet.

The password changed very regularly for increased security, but Henry had been able to keep track because he helped out in the library. He knew how to wipe his Internet history or access the net in incognito mode. Any sign the computer was abused, and the privilege would be withdrawn.

Henry smiled and confidently clicked on the dog, entering the latest password he had managed to crack. Henry moved swiftly to Google and searched under LIBOR. He remembered reading an article published by *The Wall Street Journal* in 2008 which had attracted his attention. In April of that year the *Journal* had published a controversial article on how LIBOR had been deliberately low-bowled by banks for years.

Henry urgently needed to refresh his memory of what the journalist had claimed, if he was going to convince Pole he needed Henry to crack the case.

Could he risk printing the document? Not worth it: he would commit what he was reading to memory and jot down the information back in his cell. The small library was quiet, not always an advantage. He may attract attention.

Henry started a new draft of a document he was writing for Nancy. She was part of his legal team, an excellent cover if asked. He switched back to the article. *The Wall Street Journal* had written their well-informed piece about the possible manipulation of LIBOR based on credible interviews. He might have paid more attention to it at the time of its publication, had the takeover between his bank GL and HXBK not been at the forefront of his mind.

The threat to his position, culminating in the titanic battle with his arch- rival Anthony Albert, had pushed this significant piece of information to the back of his mind. But his well-organised brain had stored pieces of crucial information as efficiently as ever, ready to recall these as soon as they might be of use. And here they were. The assertion that LIBOR had been understated was credible, even obvious.

It was in the interest of banks at the time the credit crunch was biting in 2008 to understate the level at which they estimated they could borrow money from one another. The first reason was to lower the level of interest they were currently paying on their own borrowings; the second to detract from their current financial difficulties or impending bankruptcy. High-borrowing costs indicated lack of confidence from other market participants. A state of play that no bank was willing to accept.

A lack of confidence amongst banks would have meant one thing: the collapse of the financial system, just the way it had during the '30s Great Depression era.

Henry's pulse quickened. He had not been this excited by a piece of news for months. His mind raced to calculate the impact on the market. He knew the size of the GL derivatives book was around $49 trillion. He quickly extrapolated. Other banks he knew had lower exposure than GL but still their exposures were in the trillions. He sat back in his chair; the number he was coming up with made him, Henry Crowne of all people, gasp.

"Wow, over US$300 trillion," Henry murmured. He was about to return to *The Wall Street Journal* article when a movement at the periphery of his eye stopped him. He called his cover-up document to the screen and tried to look focused.

"You allowed a laptop?" Someone had moved next to Henry.

"Yeah, got some legal work I'm working on," Henry said without looking up. He recognised the North London accent of a new inmate.

"You're the IRA banker, aren't you?"

Henry looked up slowly. This guy wanted his attention badly. Even his short time in prison had taught Henry he needed swiftly to ascertain why. The intensity of the dark eyes startled him. This young chap was a believer, and no prison sentence would extinguish his fervour. He had seen the same look on Bobby's face many years ago.

"Not my favourite nickname but, yes, I was a banker who was close to the IRA. Why do you ask?"

The eager face broke into an attractive smile that made the inmate's dark beard look less severe.

"My brother worked at GL."

Henry closed his documents as casually as he could. His computer session was over, much to his annoyance.

"GL is a pretty big place."

"You mean was a pretty big place. The takeover has been a bloody affair."

"So I hear but frankly not my problem anymore."

"Not my brother's either; he is back in Saudi."

"Good for him, now if you don't mind. I have a class to go to."

"Certainly, good speaking to you. My name is Kamal."

Henry nodded and moved away, taking his time. The dark eyes followed him right through the doors of the library.

The chain of gates and prison officers he had to cross before he reached his cell still daunted Henry. He knew most of the guards by now: their habits, what may set them off or appease them. Charlie had warned him, never trust but be trusted.

And golden rule number one: never think you are going to make friends. There is always an agenda. Henry had quickly realised that the concentration of psychopaths to the square inch rivalled that of the City.

He had been naturally guarded in his City life and he remained even more so as an inmate, with a few exceptions. It was impossible to serve thirty years without any decent human contact. Big K had become a mate and could be relied on for info on the latest gossip. He would know who Kamal was. But what mattered now more than anything else to Henry was to get involved in Pole's new investigation. It was nearly lunchtime, and he could bring his food tray to his cell to save time. Henry left his cell and made his way to the canteen.

A short queue had just started forming, the soft shuffle of feet rhythmically following the stop-and-go along the self-service line. Henry looked around. He recognised some faces but no one he knew well, a relief.

Henry put the most appetising looking lunch option on his tray. The queue stopped; one of the inmates had dropped his spoon. The only cutlery cons were allowed in prison. Henry had been shocked at first. He was not a five-year-old. But after four years in HSU, he was now grateful. He had seen what damage could be done with the handle of a spoon – eyes nearly gouged out in the latest fight he had witnessed. What would some of these nutters do with a fork? And a knife, even plastic and blunt was out of the question.

The queue was moving again. Henry was about to push his tray when a clunk startled him. Someone further down the line had just joined and he wanted everyone to notice. Ronnie Kray was two inmates away.

Henry was nearly done, just needed to grab a chunk of bread. Kray had started whistling a tune low and the two inmates between them responded to it – they moved out of the way fast. Despite Henry's best efforts Kray had seen him and kept his eyes focused on Henry's neck, a sharp sensation at the bottom of his skull convinced Henry of it.

As he was retracing his steps to move out of the canteen, the whistle intensified to a high pitch. Henry forced himself to slow down, his eyes brushing over Kray, distant. The shuffle of feet had nearly stopped. Everyone was waiting to see who of Kray and Henry might cave first. But Henry kept moving, deliberately taking his time – and he was saying to Kray:

You don't scare me.

Henry returned to his cell. The hour's bang-up time would start soon, allowing the prison officers to have their lunch. He had left Kray behind and refused to think about what the encounter meant. Henry focused instead on the all-important matter of improving his lunch. The pasta looked predictably overcooked, but Henry took an assortment of dried herbs from a corner of his bookshelf and sprinkled it over his food. A luxury he had negotiated hard to obtain with the help of his former driver Charlie. There was no time for self-pity over the dismal quality of the food though.

Henry had work to do.

He sat down at his desk and started writing all he could remember of the article he had just read. He then proceeded to write all he knew about Gary Cook, Tom Hardy and all the people he knew whose work involved or who had an interest in LIBOR.

Within half an hour he had an impressive list of names and institutions that would be involved if manipulation had taken place. Henry had spent enough time in the City, nearly twenty years, to see the signs and believe that *The Wall Street Journal* was onto something substantial.

He had to make Pole listen and he would make this happen through Nancy. His intuition, a quality that had served him so well as a star banker, was again making him restless: the slight tightening of the chest, the hair rising on the back of his neck. Or was it simply the need to be doing something meaningful? Henry moved to his bed and sat down. In this diminutive space, he had found a way of distancing himself from prison life. The papers spread on his desk were alive with what had been his past.

Was reconnecting a way of finding a solution to the conundrum that had been haunting him since his conviction? Was life in prison the path to redemption he so craved? Henry lay on his bed, eyes closed. The dark bubble of anger swelled again in his chest. He knew it would pass. He was learning the power of letting go. Of letting the past rise again without answering to its call. But Henry was also under no illusion. His redemption, if it ever came, would be brought about by an action perilous enough that his life might hang in the balance. He was now certain he would never find atonement within the confines of HSU Belmarsh.

The bell rang again, indicating that bang-up time was over. It was time for him to resume his work at the library. No funny business and no risk taking until he had spoken to Nancy though.

* * *

His meeting with Nancy had left Pole uneasy. She was close to Henry as a friend would be. Pole had never questioned how close that relationship was. But for the first time since he'd known her, the seed of doubt had been sown. Would Nancy see through Henry if he ever tried to manipulate her? Yesterday, Pole would have unequivocally answered yes but today was another day. He would have been comfortable having these doubts about anyone else but having to step away from the woman who had so captured his imagination was much harder.

Pole returned to the double suicide of Gary and Tom. He needed Nurani to deliver so that she could unequivocally secure her promotion. Her task was to force GL to talk about Cook's settlement. He had tried her mobile without success. He dialled Forensics, a little nudge on the prelim tox report's next version might yield something.

"Pole here."

"It's on its way." Yvonne replied.

"You read my mind..."

"No, I read your number... Call me if you have questions."

"Will check my inbox straightaway."

The reward of not being a constant pain in the butt was that a request for high priority was always well received.

The latest tox report was extensive but simply confirmed the pathologist's initial findings. Gary Cook's blood contained a cocktail of drugs including the latest kid on the block – nootropics. And, no, the nootropics Cook had taken had not been tampered with.

Pole frowned. It seemed this new drug had become a real craze. Cook had not been a long-time user. Yet, Cook did not seem the type to mess with his health. The new question was why purchase nootropic drugs at all? Pole had a vague memory that they were used by Silicon Valley developers once upon a time – might still be?

The latest tox report was clear on another key point: the drug would have caused enhanced perception, greater brain activity. Cook was after a bit of brain enhancement. Nothing very wrong with that or indeed very lethal.

Nurani was coming back with what the Drug Squad had on the ir tablets. She'd sent a text to Pole giving him a summary of her findings so far. Nootropics were illegally import through the Internet, not exactly a Class A drug scandal.

What puzzled Pole the most was the absence of nootropics in Cook's home in London. Nurani had carried out an exhaustive search that had yielded nothing. Why hide these so well?

There were some steroids as well. Yet another illegal drug if not prescribed by a physician. Another Internet purchase? Or perhaps a UK dealer that could deliver quality?

Pole paused for a moment. There was another place they had not searched yet. He dialled Nurani's mobile.

"You on your way back?"

"I am because goddamn GL HR is not budging… "

"OK, we'll speak about that when you're in the office. In the meantime, are you going to search Cook's office?"

"Already done, of course and with a proper warrant."

Pole grinned at Nurani's frosty reply.

"You need to loosen up your sense of humour, dear lady," he said, hanging up.

The combination of drugs and alcohol might have pushed Gary Cook over the edge – literally, thought Pole whilst flicking through the report. But Pole found himself drifting again towards Nancy's theory. It was out of character. Cook was taking drugs to enhance his performance, not to get on a high.

So, an accident? Again, Gary Cook was not the absent-minded type. Nevertheless, without further evidence there was little Pole could do. And the idea that yet another banking catastrophe was looming sounded far-fetched.

He picked up the phone and dialled Yvonne's number. Tom Hardy was still on the slab, but Yvonne would not mind Pole calling.

"Afternoon, anything for your old pal Pole?"

"If you keep interrupting me like this, there won't be... What do you think I can achieve in two hours?"

"But you are my best forensic," Pole exclaimed.

"Flattery will get you nowhere, still this is what I've got so far

No sign of struggle. He'd ingested a cocktail of drugs before he turned the ignition key and said goodbye to the world."

Pole had started jotting down notes. "What sort of drugs are we talking about?"

"I need more time..."

"Are you planning to spring a surprise on me?"

"Not sure but the one odd thing was that he was still strapped in his seat when we found him."

"I had noticed. He had not unbuckled his seat belt."

Pole thanked Yvonne. He roughened up his goatee. Another unlikely suicide. He stood up, moved a couple of piles of documents around, irritated. He would wait for the new tox report on Tom hoping for a plausible explanation. In the meantime, Henry Crowne may have to wait a little longer before he was allowed to play his get-out-of-jail card if it was what he was looking for.

The voice reached Pole's ear before the man walked through the door of his office. Superintendent Marsh was visiting Pole's neck of the woods and he liked to advertise his presence way in advance. An advantage for those wary of Marsh's reputation as a man who liked to hog the limelight.

The smell of a profile case always attracted the politically savvy. Pole was simply surprised it had taken the superintendent this long to turn up on his doorstep.

"Inspector Pole, I hear you are on a large City case again." Marsh walked to Pole's desk and looked around hoping to find space to sit for a chat. He prided himself on walking to meet his officers, never overdoing the prerogative of summoning his people to his office.

"Perhaps, sir. But we are very much at the beginning of this double suicide and—" Pole looked at the state of his office and wished he had had time for a little tidying up. He would be reminded in a memo, yet again, of the clean-desk policy the Yard was keen to promote.

"I hear you. Although you seem to believe there is more to it than simple suicide, don't you?" Marsh was still looking around, for a seat. He awkwardly picked up the file that was laid on the only chair in front of Pole's desk. Pole grabbed it and put it on top of a dangerously high pile.

"Is that safe?" Marsh asked looking at the perilously high stack of papers.

"I do lock my door when I leave for the evening," Pole replied. "Right, right. There seem to be a lot of stuff around that's all."

"Good point. I'll see what I can do." Pole removed the file from the pile and moved it to another marginally more secure stack.

Marsh sat down, smoothing the panels of his uniform as he did so. He said nothing, the slight tap of his fingers on the armchair a cue for Pole to give a full account of the situation. Pole was considering a reply, letting the silence drag a little too long for Marsh's liking.

"Why don't you speak to me about this consultant of yours?"

Pole had not expected that question. He looked at Marsh blankly and felt his face turn a shade of pink.

"You mean—"

"Well, yes, the consultant you are using on some of your profile cases. Nancy Who."

"Wu – You mean Nancy Wu," Pole said irritated.

"That's right, as I said Nancy Wu."

Pole was about to launch into a description of Nancy's many attributes, but Marsh did not seem interested. A question had been planted in his mind and it came out well-rehearsed.

"Why would she think it is not suicide?" Marsh asked.

Pole's face froze. *Nurani, you little...*

He sat back in his chair, about to defend a theory he had not endorsed fully yet. Marsh listened now to every detail. Pole decided to underplay Henry's role in expanding on the LIBOR theory.

"In a nutshell we could be on the brink of yet another financial scandal?" Marsh summarised.

Pole nodded; much to his annoyance Marsh seemed to relish the idea.

"You realise this will need to be well substantiated. We have not even started recovering from the financial crisis," Marsh said, his lips pursed. And yet Pole knew he would revel in the thought – his team uncovering, yet again and before the regulatory authorities, another financial scandal, another feather in Marsh's cap.

"Which is why I have been particularly cautious and not wanted to inform you before I have good evidence..."

"But now that I know, I would like a daily update."

As Pole was about to protest Marsh raised an appeasing hand.

"I know you are busy, Jonathan, but I am sure that your young DI, Ms Shah, will be a very good liaison – if you don't have the time of course. She should be put on the next promotion roster in any case."

Ms Shah must have decided that a conversation with The Super was a way to speed up her elevation. Perhaps the first mistake she'd made for a long time.

Pole knew exactly what Marsh meant: say no and you will imply that she can't do the job of reporting to me and if she can't why are you seeking to promote her? Marsh stood up and was moving towards the door. He half-turned back to ask his final question.

"And why don't you organise a meeting between Ms Wu and me?"

* * *

The meeting with Pole had left her with a bitter taste in her mouth. Nancy suspected that the same was the case for Pole.

I should have thought it through a little more. She had never felt torn between Pole and Henry until now. Pole had given Henry plenty of rope to change his destiny when he first arrested him after Henry had managed to breach security at GL and assault its CEO, Douglas McCarthy.

Nancy had admired Pole's sense of fairness, his ability to see through the pretence. True, Henry was a Cat A convict and Pole would have to have an unassailable reason to involve him in his high-profile case. But Nancy's intuition was pushing her, as it had always done, to tread in uncharted territory. There was possibly one person who may have a view Pole could not ignore, her senior contact and friend at Whitehall.

His insight had been invaluable when she first took Henry's case on. She had thankfully seen William a few times after they had reconnected. Nancy felt less embarrassed to call upon him for yet another tip on the investigation's ramifications. She picked up her mobile, hesitated only for an instant, and dialled her friend's number.

He picked up the phone almost immediately.

"William, what a surprise. I was expecting your PA," Nancy teased as he answered his phone. "This is very last minute but—"

Nancy did not have time to finish her sentence.

"Then great minds think alike, let's do coffee at the usual place, say 4pm." William suggested.

"Unless you're too busy and we could do a drink this evening."

William's voice rose a little. "Nonsense. It will be good to get out of the office for a while."

William would meet her that afternoon at Tate Britain – the William Blake Room. But for the first time since she'd known William, and she had known him a very long time, Nancy had the feeling he was agitated and was the one who wanted to talk.

Chapter Nine

Tate Britain was buzzing with the anticipated effervescence the Turner Prize created. One of the most prestigious contemporary art prizes was on and it drew the crowds.

Nancy paused before entering Tate Britain. She had called on William four years ago when she had decided to help Henry with his case. Nancy had been open with William. She had not considered deceiving him for one moment no matter how desperate the situation was – and Henry had been in dire straits. The accusation of murder that hung over him was rooted in a mounting level of evidence that had been hard to dismiss. And yet Nancy had had doubts.

William had been happy to rely on her judgement. She knew he had always been intrigued by her personality. Her ascent to the Bar, her taking Silk at such an impossibly young age, her fascinating mixed cultural background – everything felt like a challenge and an interrogation for William. He, by contrast, felt the product of an antiquated aristocracy: Eton, Oxford, the Civil Service and yet his open-mindedness often contrasted with the stale idea people had of him. William did not make friends easily; he fussed, picked and chose. Nancy felt privileged to be one of them. Not because he was fastidious but because friendship was precious, always to be honoured.

Since Nancy had become a consultant to the Met, he had been generous with his time to discuss any matter that troubled her. He had a dispassionate way of tackling a problem that helped her see more clearly. Today however William had sounded different: a slight change in the rhythm of his speech, a slight hesitation where there should be none told her he needed to talk.

Nancy walked around the rooms she knew so well to finally reach the room that displayed their favourite pieces, the William Blake prints. She glanced at her watch; she was dead on time. She turned around but William was nowhere to be seen. He was late. So uncharacteristic, she felt alarmed.

She sat down again and would give it another five minutes before she rang his mobile. She stilled herself, helped by the exquisite lines of Blake's drawings. A slender but firm hand pressed her shoulder and she found herself face to face with her friend.

"Thank God William. I was getting worried," Nancy said before noticing his ashen-white face, his eyes still wide open with shock.

"Not here, let's go to the Members' Room." They chose a quiet corner. The small coffee table and two armchairs was what they needed for their chat.

"So sorry Nancy. Good afternoon," William said regaining some of his composure.

"Do settle down. I will get the tea. No apologies required among friends."

William nodded and settled down into a comfortable armchair, wincing as he did so. He seemed in pain, and Nancy moved forward to help, but he waved her off.

Nancy returned promptly with their favourite drink, an excellent choice of Darjeeling, and a couple of small pastries. William needed a pick-me-up.

"Shall we dive straight in with the reasons for our meeting? I feel we have a lot of ground to cover." Nancy said as she was pouring.

"I would rather you start with your news, Nancy. I am still deciding how to present what I have to say to you."

"Always happy to go first," teased Nancy. William managed the beginning of a smile.

"I am sure you have heard about the death of both Gary Cook and Tom Hardy. I am working on the case with Inspector Pole and the working assumption is that it is suicide," Nancy said after taking a sip of tea.

"You don't buy it?" concluded William. It was not a question but rather a forceful statement William sat back, closed his eyes bringing his hands together, fingertips touching at the level of his mouth. Nancy did not interrupt his thinking. The process that was going through William's mind was about to deliver a verdict, a statement based on facts and experience, an immensely powerful combination.

"I think you are right," added William finally. He was leaning towards his cup wincing again in pain. He took a sip without looking at Nancy. He had not looked at her once and when he returned his cup to its saucer his hand was shaking.

Nancy sat opposite William, the position she preferred when talking about a subject that felt like business rather than an intimate conversation. She stood up and moved next to her friend. She sat close to him and took his hand.

"I have never, in the twenty-five years I have known you, seen you so distraught. Please talk to me."

William inhaled deeply.

"I will. I just need to gather my thoughts. Something has happened and I don't think it is a coincidence."

"Do you know about LIBOR?" Nancy said. She was not fishing for information about what could be a thorny topic, and William knew it.

"Your greatest strength as ever, my dear. To the point and no shying away from it."

"I gather the answer is yes. What happened this morning that has so thrown you?"

William took another sip of tea. He was enjoying a moment of slight reprieve.

"For a few days now, I have had the impression that I was being followed. I dismissed it to start with. There is always a temptation in a senior position like mine at Whitehall to think we carry secrets about the workings of government that makes us a target; that we are at risk."

"And do you carry that sort of secret, William?" Nancy asked. "We had a conversation during the Henry Crowne investigation which I remember vividly."

"Ah yes, I said I was trying to salvage the UK financial system." William replied with amusement in his eyes. "Rather pompous I know."

Nancy's formidable memory was at work again.

"And now I ask, have you? It seems to me we are not yet out of the woods."

William hesitated.

"Why don't you finish first telling me what happened this morning?" Nancy suggested, trying to keep the momentum going.

"You're right, I felt his presence, saw someone hurrying up behind me as I crossed the road, turned a corner. And I could have sworn it was to keep track of me."

"I see. Is the same person following you?"

"No. Which is why I thought I might be overdoing it. As I said, I thought I was getting a touch paranoid. But then—" William stopped and swallowed hard. He finished his tea. Nancy picked up the teapot and poured a fresh cup, an indication to carry on and seek comfort in his favourite drink.

"I was about to cross the road. You know me, I am a creature of habit. I leave my flat in Pimlico at the same time. I always walk to work whatever the weather. The crossing is on a timer. I am an obedient citizen, I wait. It turns green. I start crossing. A white van comes out of nowhere and accelerates. He can't *not* have seen me. I drop everything and I run. I squeeze between the SUVs parked at the end of the crossing. I can hear the scrape of metal against metal. Those two cars saved me Nancy, otherwise..." William's voice trails. He couldn't bring himself to say the word and for the second time today Nancy squeezed her friend's hand. William's face was ashen white again, and again his hands trembled as he reached for his cup.

"You are certain the van was going straight for you?"

William shook his head. "He swerved across the road to get to me. I am sure."

"Did anybody else see this?"

"The street was pretty empty at 6am."

"And you did not get the registration number?" William shook his head again.

"Of course, you must have been so shocked."

"I fell to the ground on the pavement, by the time I got up..."

"Have you been to the police?" Nancy asked, her stomach lurching once more. But her friend needed her to be composed. She had kept her hand on William's.

He squeezed back in return. "Thank you, Nancy. You are here and I wanted to speak to you before doing anything else."

"Because I asked to speak to you about Gary and Tom?"

"Exactly right," William replied, colour coming back into his face. "But you can't fully comment because it is one of the 'secrets', involving the government."

William simply smiled.

"Why don't I tell you about the information I have gathered, and you can confirm?" Nancy suggested. William retreated into his armchair. "Perhaps, you can redirect me if I go wrong in my assumptions?"

"Much better idea," William said relaxing considerably.

"Gary Cook, Head Trader at GL, runs the Rates book. Every day he submits the LIBOR rates to the BBA. He is the voice of GL as far as LIBOR is concerned."

William drank some tea and Nancy carried on.

"Gary is leaving GL, but he seems fired up about something. Knowledge that can get him back in the race after his sacking from GL."

It was Nancy's turn to drink some tea. She was on a roll and engaged with what she did best, relentless deductions.

"Tom Hardy, Chief Executive of the BBA. The British Bankers' Association has had the huge responsibility of delivering LIBOR to the market, in all its maturities and currencies, since its creation in 1984. It has a process that it follows but it relies on the banks delivering an honest figure about what they estimate their own borrowing costs are. The BBA could ask questions of the banks I presume but I have never heard it reported that it had."

William finished his cup of tea.

"LIBOR, an essential benchmark in the financial system, from mortgages for Mr Nobody to derivatives for large multinationals. And not only in the UK. I have looked it up on Bloomberg; the size of the LIBOR market is around $350 billion – I mean trillion!" Nancy continued.

"A sensitive matter as you said, Nancy."

"Now that I have the facts, let me tell you what my assumptions are. I should have probably mentioned that I have had some crucial help from a friend," Nancy said frankly.

"You mean Henry is bored in Her Majesty's Prison?" William said.

"He is still a banker who knows how the City works," Nancy replied, a little too much on the defensive.

"He is a clever man, and I can only imagine that given enough information he will understand pretty fast what is really going on."

"His take on Gary and Tom is that LIBOR has been manipulated, probably a low-bowling by the banks to cover their true financial position in 2008–2009, possibly before, and that it may have an impact on their deaths."

William's composure evaporated again.

"If we remain hypothetical and there has been a manipulation of LIBOR then people at the highest level must have known. Bank of England. Government."

William moved his hand absent-mindedly towards his empty cup. Whilst Nancy had been speaking, he had averted his gaze; now he was looking into her eyes.

"Low-bowling LIBOR as you call it may be an unorthodox way of controlling the crisis, within reason." William's voice no longer hesitated. Nancy sensed his confidence returning.

"You mean that the government may have initiated this idea?" Nancy asked incredulous.

William nodded. "I told you Nancy. We need – no, I need to salvage the financial system in this country. I did think long and hard. I have discussed the impact of the crisis with numerous people. I had to act, even if it meant using methods which…" his voice trailed off, as he searched for the right word, "are questionable."

Nancy was speechless. She looked at William as if she had met a totally new person. He sensed it and blushed slightly.

"Desperate times, desperate measures. Although it is really not a satisfactory excuse, I know."

"Sorry William. I can't pretend I am not amazed but I suppose…" Nancy couldn't really yet believe that her friend, a man she had seen as most honest and dedicated, had just admitted the unthinkable – the manipulation of financial system on a large scale. The next question she uttered in a low voice, because it could topple yet another of her greatest hopes.

"Who did you speak to – the Bank of England, the BBA, any particular bank?"

"No Nancy, that business has to be done so carefully, as you can imagine. I can suggest, in hypothetical fashion. I don't need to directly instruct."

"Who William? Please."

"I can't say, not yet," William exhaled. His hands must have become moist with perspiration. He rubbed them mechanically on his paper napkin.

"Please, don't ask me to disclose a name yet. The only thing you need to know is that the impact of LIBOR was discussed and a preference for a lower number was expressed with the relevant people."

"In other words, Whitehall. You asked for LIBOR to be low-bowled so that the impact of the 2008 crisis be smoothed. And it actually happened." Nancy said.

"Correct."

Nancy exchanged a quick look with her friend and shook her head.

"I am sorry I ended up disappointing you Nancy," William said gently.

"No please don't apologise. I don't envy your position. I can understand it. I can't condone it though." Nancy frowned. "But William, coming back to you and what happened this morning – your near-miss accident. Are you telling me these two events are linked?"

"Possibly, I don't know. I have felt exposed recently in a way I have never done before, and I have seen a lot in my twenty-five years as a civil servant."

"I know how senior you are now. Or should I say Sir William?" Nancy managed to tease.

"A little humour at this dire point is welcome, my dear. Going back to your question. I fear I will be next; Gary, Tom then..." William said, failing to complete the sentence.

"If you are concerned you must speak to the police," Nancy said in a pressing voice. "Speak to Pole; you know he can be trusted with delicate matters." A piece of jet-black hair had escaped from her hair pin. She brushed it back slowly. "Oh God, I have been so stupid. You want me to speak to Inspector Pole for you. Is that it?"

"I understand it is a big ask but I don't want to go to the police, not just yet. I might be overreacting anyway, although I don't think so. If I come forward the police will have to investigate not only Whitehall but also the Bank of England. We, I mean the country, does not need that at the moment. The longer I delay the better."

"William, you are willing to...," Nancy looked for the word but could only be blunt, "risk your life? What happens if you are right, and you are a target?"

"So be it," William said closing his eyes.

"But you are my friend. I am not sure I can let you take that sort of risk," Nancy said anxiously.

"Then I will have to find someone else," William replied determined. No one would make him change his mind. He would see it through whatever the cost, Nancy gathered.

"You know this is the right thing to do. You know," William said looking at Nancy with intensity.

"You are expecting me to speak to Pole and hope he can find the person targeting you before he strikes again?"

William nodded.

"Fine," Nancy said finally. She took her yellow pad out of her bag and started taking notes. William raised an eyebrow. "Don't worry, I write in cryptic words. Let's recap on some information. The race is on."

* * *

The phone call was short but amicable. Chancellor George Osborne had not trusted his aides and wanted to hear the news directly from the Bank of England. Edwina had assured him that Mervyn King would agree to the next round of quantitative easing.

"What does George want from his blue-eyed girl?" Gabriel asked amused.

"He wants to make sure that I will slap back the old dinosaurs who think QE is only for the rich," Edwina replied flatly. She would have normally engaged with Gabriel in a banter about Osborne-chancellor-of-the-exchequer-blue-eyed-girl but today she didn't. What she had seen in Gabriel's eyes this morning had startled her.

"You know what that means, right?" Gabriel asked, crossing his hands behind his head and stretching.

"I am sure you will soon enlighten me."

"You're in pole position to succeed Mervyn-The-Oracle-King."

"The Oracle refers to Greenspan not King," replied Edwina tersely, no longer amused by the displaced nickname.

"Don't be a bore. You know I am right," Gabriel said unfazed by Edwina's tone. "Don't you want it?"

"I don't want to speculate."

"You mean so close to your goal. You're not superstitious, not you Eddie."

Edwina ignored him and resumed typing the email she had been writing when Chancellor Osborne called her.

"Are you still worried about Tom and Gary?" Gabriel asked.

"No, it was just a silly idea. Forget I ever mentioned it."

"Good, I am glad you've given up on that," Gabriel said with a forcefulness that surprised Edwina again. He did not simply seem happy she had given up on the idea. He was positively pleased – as if the idea could be dangerous in itself.

Edwina stopped typing the email and looked at him. For a few seconds she saw again the cold harshness in his eyes, replaced promptly by a smile that no longer convinced her. The scar on his intelligent face looked angrier than ever. She must seek advice from someone else. She must speak to Nancy as soon as she can.

The phone rang again, and Edwina gave it an irritated look. *What now?* The prefix told her it was the US. She hardly looked at Gabriel.

"I need to take this call on my own."

Gabriel stood up without a word and closed the door behind him.
"Tim, good morning. How good of you to call back."

"Don't mention it," replied Tim Geithner, the Secretary of State of the US Treasury. "We are on a secure line by the way."

"Excellent, I just wanted to conclude our conversation on US LIBOR."

"Absolutely," Edwina replied, but she was damned if she caved in to any of Geithner's requests.

The governor of the Bank of England, Mervyn King, had received a memo from Geithner in 2008 alerting him to the issue that LIBOR was facing. King had delegated the sensitive project of investigating the allegations to Edwina, a mark of trust she had been proud of. Today, however she called this thorny project a typical hospital by-path if there was one.

Secretary of the US Treasury, Tim Geithner, and his team were fully aware of the potential and even probable manipulation of LIBOR, but the financial crisis had tied their hands. Now was not the time to challenge the way this well-used benchmark was calculated. Geithner had been more forceful of late, calling her regularly himself.

But Edwina knew better than to be impressed by this show of strength. US LIBOR represented around forty-five per cent of all adjustable mortgages and eighty per cent of subprime mortgages. She had held firm since 2009 when the memo had landed on her desk. No, now was not the time for yet another full-blown crisis.

If she could hold back until King retired and she was in place as governor of the Bank of England, she would have free rein to carry out the much-needed reforms. In her view, an up-tick adjustment to the benchmark would have an immediate repercussion on the mortgages it underpinned and therefore calculated by reference to it – meaning more foreclosures, more crisis... more people losing their home or livelihood.

As she listened to Geithner's proposition about how the LIBOR calculation could be improved, she remembered another conversation she had had with Tom Hardy when he took over as CEO of the BBA.

Geithner's irritated voice brought Edwina back to the present. Did she have a plan? Of course, she did but not just yet. Geithner was a decent guy and a very smart one too. She knew he would not want just to rock the boat. They both needed more time to handle the worst of the crisis. And Edwina needed to wait for her elevation. The call ended as all the previous calls had – "let's keep in touch."

Edwina sat back in her chair, letting her mind return to Tom Hardy.

She had called Tom one late evening as the crisis was taking hold and had asked him for a much-needed *little* chat. She had recognised right from the beginning that this crisis would not be like any other. It was deeper because it did not affect only a segment of the economy; it affected a vast number of people whose mortgages were about to foreclose – in the US, in the UK – and take with them all the institutions that had speculated around those mortgages.

Tom had dealt with mortgages. He would understand and, more importantly, trust her judgement.

It was so late when she reached his office that only a security guard was manning reception at the BBA offices on Old Broad Street. Tom came down to collect her. His equine face, normally so detached, showed strain. They hardly greeted one another and did not speak until they reached his office.

"More bad news," Edwina had said, a statement of fact.

"The worst," Tom had replied. "I am not going to dance around the issue Eddie. It's about LIBOR. I fear it's about to implode; there's no trust left in the market and the levels are being scrutinised more closely."

"Shit!" Edwina blurted.

"You are aware?" Tom asked taken aback. "Can't tell you who my source is but I have just had a memo sent to me to discuss this."

"Who knows about it?"

"You mean who suspects?"

Tom waved his hand in the air, a detail but was the implosion of LIBOR in the open?

"OK, just because it is you and I trust you." Edwina hesitated for a second. "The Yanks, but don't ask for more."

"No need."

They both fell silent, hardly looking at one another and waiting to see who first voice would a view that both shared.

"How many banks at the moment?"

"One I know of, for sure."

Again, they fell silent. As they were both moving closer to what seemed an inevitable conclusion, Edwina stood up and moved towards the window. The City had fallen quiet. Even as disaster was striking, the City trading floors had closed. The trail of disaster had passed to New

York, then Asia, to come back fiercer than ever at the opening of the next trading session in London. She kept her back to Tom as she spoke.

"But it means the market is panicking less..."

Tom did not respond immediately, and Edwina waited for him to say the word.

"True," Tom replied eventually. She turned towards him but remained silent. They knew what had to be done next.

"Do we need to lowball LIBOR more in the UK?" Tom asked

"Who will ask?" Edwina said without anxiety. It was now a matter of planning, no longer debating.

Tom sat down, heavy in his chair. "I will."

Edwina opened her eyes and shuddered.

The memory of her conversation with Tom and call she'd just had sobered her up. If she spoke to anyone, even Nancy, she was putting her career at risk. Years of hard work, planning, enduring. She was convinced that once she got the top job, she would make the changes that needed to be made. She couldn't go back, not now, not when she was so close.

Her phone rang and she saw Mervyn's personal assistant was calling. Another round of emergency talks was about to start in five minutes and more than ever she was ready for them.

Chapter Ten

The pudgy little doorman had seen him turn the corner. Brett would soon enter the Club. The cul-de-sac in St James was suitably discreet. The Club's door, a small unassuming affair, opened onto one of the most powerful gentlemen's clubs still standing. Brett's father and his father before him had belonged. Men in his family had joined from the day when the Club had become an establishment for the nobility to meet in the eighteenth century. Brett had sent an emergency message to his handler. He could not wait for the planned meeting date. Brett hardly acknowledged the doorman who kept his distance. He handed over his trilby and rain mac to the white-gloved butler.

"My Lord, your guest has arrived."

"Very well, do we have a quiet corner?"

"Indeed, the library as requested."

Brett nodded, satisfied with the unctuous tone the butler was using, and headed for the library.

Steve didn't t bother to stand up. "You got something for me awfully fast…" Steve frowned. "How come?."

"Give me some credit. I know what I'm doing when it comes to Jihadists." Brett said as he sat down. "My Iraqi contact is trying to introduce me to someone new. I think this is big. I don't have all the details yet, but they want me to meet him in the UK… and that is unusual – in fact unheard of."

"OK, I'm listening."

"I have had two calls from them already. It's all about a one-off deal and a large, very large, sum of money. But no details yet."

"And you think it has nothing to do with art trafficking?"

"Nothing. They are talking about a consignment, but I can tell they are testing whether I am interested and more importantly whether I can deliver. It's armaments or possibly people."

Brett's guest studied him for a moment. He was about to speak when drinks came through.

"Macallan?"

"Of course," Brett replied. "What else?"

Brett noticed a faint smile on the other man's lips. "So, you think they have taken the bait?"

"Almost certainly," Brett replied as he started savouring his whisky. "Why are you so sure?"

"Because for the past five years I have solidly delivered on my promises. Steady flow of clients, at the high end of the art market, cash payments without delays. They have also done quite a bit of digging."

"You mean about your previous trafficking?"

The remark unsettled Brett. Such harsh words should not be spoken in such an august establishment. He preferred the word facilitation.

"Well, let's say that my facilitation in the Far East has come under scrutiny."

"Who told you?"

"I still have good, in fact very good, contacts in China. They do not like people asking questions and they wanted to know who was asking."

"Is it going to become an issue?"

"No, I told them it was a particular client I knew well doing some research because of the size of the deal involved. It seems to have pacified them."

"Seems?"

"Well, I have done a lot of business with that particular Chinese client, but would I trust him with my life? No."

Brett's handler did not respond. Brett had no secrets from Steve, much to his annoyance and regret. Steve knew all about his art trafficking, his divorces, his financial machinations and the disastrous Crowne deal. The agency had stripped him bare. They knew details of his life he had wanted to forget about but they had handed him a deal he could never refuse once they knew they had him.

"You will soon need backup, but you need to ride this alone for a little longer I'm afraid."

"I thought you might say that."

"And you were right," Steve replied whilst putting his empty glass on the small table next to his armchair. Brett looked at the glass. What an exceptional drink to waste on such a thug.

"But I will make sure we are ready. I'll also see what we have picked up that might give us a better picture. We are monitoring a lot more dark-web info traffic these days."

"I will probably have to travel there – wherever 'there' is. They will want to see me before they finalise. They won't trust me otherwise."

"As soon as you know, you apply for a visa for 'there.' We will pick it up. I will then be in contact with you."

Brett nodded. Working for MI6 was not a ball.

* * *

Henry's regular routine was nearly at an end. Big K had finished his round of press-ups too and was nonchalantly moving towards the showers with the easy swagger of a Jamaican rapper. Henry had told Big K he needed information on Kamal. It may come at a cost but Henry had asked very few favours so far. It was time for him to spend some of the brownie points he had accumulated against his name. He followed Big K into the showers. At six foot three Henry was not used to having many man look him in the eyes but Big K was one of them. He relaxed; posturing would have irritated Henry in a previous life, but he liked to have this slumbering giant in the next door cell, a man whose intelligence was not in question.

"What do you have for me?" Henry asked as soon as they had turned on the showers.

"Your guy Kamal is the latest bloke charged with terrorism. Comes from a rich Saudi family," Big K said as he lathered his armpits furiously. "Got caught 'cause someone grassed him up. Well-connected guy in high places."

Henry anchored his arms against the wall and let the water run over his body. He needed its warmth to stop the shaking that had started as soon as Big K uttered the word terrorism. He closed his eyes and clenched his fists. Big K's voice had become distant and vague. Henry inhaled deeply and forced himself to move.

"Such as?" Henry asked, slowly running his long hands over his greying hair to lather in shampoo.

"Government, oil industry, high finance. No drugs though," Big K replied regretfully.

"Not a user then?"

"No man, prays five times a day; no booze either."

"Did he actually do something or was he the brains?"

"You mean did he plant the bomb in Paddington?"

Henry froze. In an instant, the shower room vanished.

He is back in the police van that is taking him to the Counter-terrorist Squad's HQ for questioning. The police know his involvement with the dissident IRA and Henry is bracing himself for his first encounter with the CT Squad.

And then there is the bomb... the deafening noise, the short silence after he has been thrown around the van, the empty eyes of the dead policeman who sat in the van with him.

Henry wills himself back from the abyss with an unbearable effort of strength.

Big K was clicking his fingers in front of his face. Henry had turned white, and his body was ice cold despite the scorching water. He moved away swiftly, embarrassed by the show of weakness.

"You were there?" Big K asked.

Henry nodded. "That's where they were taking me for interrogation."

"Shit, man."

"So, this fucker was involved," Henry managed to ask through gritted teeth. "That's why he is in here."

Henry grabbed his towel and wrapped it around his waist. He could feel Big K's eyes following him. He had just broken one of the golden rules that Charlie had given him. Do not expose your feelings; do not get involved in any controversy.

"What do you wanna do, Bro?"

Henry turned back to face the other man. He had shown fear, but he would not show anger. His blue eyes had turned a shade of steel.

"I need to think about that. What do you want for the info?"

Big K nodded. "I'll let you know."

Henry moved to the drab changing rooms and got dressed slowly, a man in control. He could not run away this time. He maintained composure enough he hoped to deceive Big K as well as the guards he was about to meet along the corridors.

Back into his cell, Henry slammed his hand against the far side of the wall, the one facing the outside. The shock reverberated through his entire body, setting his shoulder on fire.

"What have these mother-fucking idiots in the prison service done?" Henry said barely controlling his voice. A thousand questions assailed him. Did the prison governor not realise? Was it a way to get to him? Yet another devious plot as insane as that elaborated by Anthony Albert? Henry did not believe in coincidences. An entire career on the trading floor had taught him to trust his intuition.

"Did the little fucker of a governor not know who Kamal was?"

Anger had crept into his belly again the way it had done so many times since his Belfast days but today he had no one to savage but himself. Henry was trembling. Out of nowhere the images that had punched him in the face in the showers resurfaced, more vivid than ever.

He could smell petrol, the spilt guts. He could feel two hands grabbing him, dragging him out of the burning vehicle. He remembered the plea of one of the guards to help him with the trapped driver, his lethargy, his fear. He had been a coward on that day.

Henry was shaking so badly that he had to sit on the floor and lean against his bed. He had not felt so lost since his final arrest in the quietness of London Fields. On that day Nancy had been at his side. He so wished she was here today. But prison meant solitude.

Henry finally managed to stand up and go to his small desk. Henry reached for the pile of correspondence that sat on it permanently. He would read Nancy's last letter, his greatest source of comfort. His little radio babbled away on his desk. In a few minutes time, he would make his way to the library to start his job.

The noise of hurried footsteps hardly registered. But the thick clang of his prison cell being shut automatically punched him in the stomach. Henry rushed to the door and shook it hard without creating so much as a ripple in the heavy steal. He stuck his ear to the latch and listened hard. It had not been closed properly and Henry could just about make out a few words from the guards outside: him down... medics... breathing. Henry pressed his body against the door so hard he could feel the cold metal seeping into him. More hurried footsteps and now shouting voices... not breathing... medics. Henry dropped slowly to the floor. He no longer wanted to hear. Just a few cells away, an inmate he hardly knew had decided to set himself free in the only way he could.

Henry had been asked as soon as he entered the prison system whether he felt suicidal. He had made a flippant response.

"Me, never."

But today he understood why people would regularly take their own lives. The world he had started to construct around him, the routine put in place to survive the next thirty years – God, he would be an old man by then – was crumbling around him.

He must find a way out of this hell.

* * *

Tom Hardy's latest tox report was in. Nurani had laid a copy on Pole's desk, and she was already ensconced in the only spare chair he had in his office, reading her copy when he arrived. Pole still could not shake the irritation that had overcome him at his disappointing meeting with Nancy and he certainly could hardly contain his anger at Nurani's conversation with Marsh. Her intrusion into his space was only a cause for further aggravation.

Pole managed a suitably friendly "What's up?" The time to speak about her conversation with Marsh had not come yet.

"Hardy's tox report just arrived," Nurani said. "Hot off the press. I have not finished reading it yet."

"And – what do we have so far?"

"Well, a cocktail of painkillers. Strong. Prescription drugs only. Something to check of course and then—" Nurani frowned, having turned the page to read the last paragraph of her copy. Her face turned dark. Pole knew the look. There was something she had not anticipated or worse she did not want to read.

Pole removed his jacket, rolled up his sleeves, stroked his well-groomed goatee and sat down. He did not bother to read the whole of the report and jumped straight to the last page.

"Nootropics!" Pole exclaimed. "This cannot be a coincidence." He pushed a pile of documents that was dangerously high, managed to extract Cook's file without dropping so much as a paper clip and went straight to the page on which he knew he would find the information he was looking for.

"Same nootropics," Pole pondered.

Nurani was about to speak but Pole interrupted her, unusually. "OK, so they almost certainly have the same provider. Nurani, where else can these guys stock their meds without them being uncovered by a nosy wife, housekeeper, kid or colleague?"

From the look on her face, Nurani was not expecting Pole to take this tack. She had expected him to follow the lead she advocated. Pole tapped his fingers in succession on his desk. He was irritated at himself. He could not let his nascent feelings for Nancy cloud his judgment, but Nurani had overstepped the mark with Marsh. Nurani looked confused for a few seconds, then her face brightened suddenly.

"The gym," she said clicking her fingers.

"Well done. The gym it is. Did you fancy a little tour of one of those posh City gyms where bankers sweat out their boozy lunches while wearing Lycra?"

"Gross. I don't even want to picture it."

"Very well, I will—" Pole did not have time to finish his offer to 'do' the gym.

"But I am a devoted team player. I'll go," Nurani said all eager after all to check on the Lycra brigade.

"I knew I could count on you. Be gentle, will you? No savaging of those bankers yet. The time will come."

Nurani gave Pole a blazing smile. He nodded.

"Which will give me time to *brief* Superintendent Marsh," Pole added. "He was in fact so well *briefed* about this new *High-Profile Case* that he wants to meet my consultant."

Nurani's smile evaporated, but she kept her cool.

"Whoever spoke to him about Nancy must have created an impression. He is very keen for the meeting to be ASAP," Pole carried on, his fingers still drumming on the desk.

"Well, I suppose it is important that Superintendent Marsh meet with Nancy," Nurani said, voice in control.

"Is that so?" Pole shot her a look. "Let's hope he does not question any of my other choices." A mean reference to his support for Nurani's future elevation but warranted he thought.

"I'm sure he won't," Nurani mumbled as she left Pole's office.

Pole waited for a few seconds, troubled by what might lie ahead and started dialling a number on his phone.

"Some actions have unforeseen consequences," Pole said too late for her to hear. He closed the door after her. As the loudspeaker on his phone was telling him Nancy was out, he hung up.

No one would dare enter his office until he had reopened a door that so seldom remained shut. Pole moved the precarious pile of documents to the chair on which Nurani had just sat. He selected four files in addition to the one already on his desk, logged onto his computer and searched for the word that had started intriguing him more: LIBOR.

A flurry of webpages appeared: definitions, fixing rather than setting, the involvement of the BBA. He sat back in his chair: nothing there that would validate Henry and Nancy's concern. Then again, it was unlikely he would easily find the information he was looking for. Pole reluctantly admitted that the use of the same batch of drugs by both Tom Hardy and Gary Cook was not taking the case in the direction he had hoped.

The idea that both men used the same provider merited attention.

Nurani was now on the case of determining who that person was. This line of inquiry also focused her away from a confrontation Pole knew was coming. He no longer cared about sparing Nurani's latest desire to adhere perhaps a little too strictly to the *Rules*. If the case had to move in the direction painted by Henry and Nancy, so it would.

Nurani had proven a ruthless operator in the Henry Crowne case, extracting information from Henry's best friend Liam in the most unforgiving manner. She was right of course. Henry's secret involvement with the fundraising operations of a dissident IRA group was an unexpected bargaining chip against Liam's brother's life. But the way in which she had relished getting the deal done had surprised Pole. No, what he feared was not Nurani's wrath but rather his own antipathy for Henry.

As ever Pole had been fair. He had kept going with the case when everyone had thought it was sealed. Even after Henry's dubious confession he had persisted in getting to the truth. And Pole recognised that Henry was smart, in fact extremely smart. If he had seen something in this LIBOR story, Pole would reluctantly have to take note.

The phone rang and Nancy's name appeared on the screen. Pole hesitated. His hand hovered, moving involuntarily towards the handset. He stopped himself. Pole would come to a better formulated view before he took the call, and he was in no hurry to arrange the meeting with Marsh.

He came back to Henry. How could he have known? Or taken an interest?

"Option One, he is trying to get out." Pole considered the idea aloud. Very possible: a man like Henry, accustomed to making decisions and free to roam the globe would suffer in prison, more than most.

"Option Two, he had prior knowledge." The idea sounded interesting. Henry had the most phenomenal memory Pole had ever encountered. He had witnessed it first-hand during interrogation. Henry would use the same words, recount the same facts, no deviation or omission. This had made Pole suspicious to start with, only for him to realise that this unusual behaviour for a man telling the truth emanated from a highly trained and controlled mind.

Only Nancy had proven a match for Henry. The thought made Pole uncomfortable. But he was not a jealous man and his excellent ability to read characters had told him there was deep friendship between the two but nothing else. A warm feeling and small leap of his heart made Pole grin. Nancy would be his, no matter how long it would take.

The light on his phone was flashing, no doubt a message from Nancy that was urging him on.

If Henry knew anything it would have to be from his GL days but Henry was not an interest-rate specialist. Nevertheless, Henry had been top management. He had used his knowledge of GL's undisclosed dealings in subprime to topple his former boss and compromise the crucial merger between GL and HXBK. Henry had revealed in a damning fax the eye-watering large loss position that GL held in subprime to the CEO of HXBK. Why would he not disclose more of what he knew now? Henry had no reason to hold back.

Pole considered the idea. Would something else have triggered Henry's interest? He was an avid reader of news, as every trading floor MD would be. Pole extended his original Google search. He combined LIBOR and news articles. The *FT*, *The Guardian*, *The Times*: a flurry of new webpages appeared. But all seemed to concentrate on LIBOR as a benchmark.

He was about to give up when he spotted an article from *The Wall Street Journal*: BANKERS CAST DOUBT ON KEY RATES AMID CRISIS, (16 April 2008). Pole could not help but smile. Henry Crowne was indeed a smart-arse. Pole's phone rang once more. He picked up still thinking about Henry and cursed his decision.

"Hello Jonathan, this is Denise, Superintendent Marsh's PA."

"Hello Denise. Is he about to pay me a visit again?"

"Nope but he wants to meet Ms Wu – *urgently.*" Denise imitated Marsh superbly.

Pole sighed. "And you want her phone number, mobile number, fax number, email address so that you can invite her *urgently.*"

“Spot on.”

Pole waited a few seconds, feigning to be looking for the details he, of course, knew by heart.

Chapter Eleven

The bus lumbered away from its stop outside Tate Britain. Nancy broke into a sprint to try and catch it but the driver ignored her waving arm. She cursed. Perhaps she needed a brisk walk. She left Victoria station and turned towards Grosvenor Place. Thoughts buzzed around her head like threatening insects, preventing her from creating a coherent picture of the situation.

William had asked her, no, begged her, not to reveal his identity. It was so unlike him to lose his cool, to be rattled by what could have simply been a clumsy driver talking on his mobile phone whilst driving. And yet, William was convinced he had been targeted. Could she truly leave his name out of a conversation with Pole? And, more importantly, let her friend take risks that could cost him his life?

The last question made her stomach churn. She stopped to recover her breath. Nancy had defended some unholy characters in her time. She had come to consider the implications of what some of them had done in retrospect. She had managed to look at her role for the defence as an essential service justice must provide in a democracy worthy of the name. The job of the police and prosecution was to build the case following due process and according to what the law of the land permitted. Her job was to make sure that it stacked together.

The promise of success, her much wanted elevation, had gradually made her lose track of what she thought of her clients. She had become supremely adept at extracting the information she needed, not to assess the value of the case she was accepting, but in order to win the battle. She recalled the moment when, at the height of her career, she had received a call from one of France's most notorious and controversial barristers, Maitre Jacques Vergès. She knew full well why Vergés' story had re-surfaced. It was reminding her of the success that warranted his contact. She had defended Vladislas Karsik successfully against war crimes. This obscure figure had never been directly involved in the Kosovo genocide, but he had been instrumental in supplying armaments and logistics to the armies of Slobodan Milosevic.

The prosecution had been mounted expertly by barristers she knew well, and the evidence gathered was credible. Karsik had managed to keep a low profile, covering his tracks, always ensuring that evidence would be destroyed along with the people who knew too much with it. The most frustrating moment for the Prosecution had not only been to lose but also to know that Karsik was still supporting other wars from his prison cell – and yet the evidence they had gathered was far from watertight.

Nancy had reached Piccadilly. She was walking alongside Green Park and in a couple of minutes would be in front of the Royal Academy. She entered the courtyard and briskly walked into the members' room.

She looked at her watch, only 3pm. Was it too late or early for a small pick-me-up? She shrugged, so what? She ordered a large glass of Merlot, chose a bowl of sad-looking olives and sat herself at the window. The meeting with William had moved her in ways she had not felt for a long time. She no longer wished to be associated with the dark shadows that power and politics cast over people. Most of all, she did not want to be responsible for someone's death.

She took a large gulp of wine, passably good but it did not do the trick. The thought of William coming to any harm because she had not divulged his identity became unbearable. Nancy closed her eyes and breathed deeply. William may never forgive her. He was doing what he believed was right for his country. But he had put her in an impossible situation. She should be angry with him for presenting her with this awful choice. She picked up an olive mechanically from the bowl and chewed on it. She would call Pole, speak to him and go with the flow – when she spoke to the man, she trusted more than anyone else perhaps a decision would emerge. Yes, Jonathan Pole was indeed her most trusted friend.

Her mobile rang. She fumbled in her bag, cursing, and answered with a curt "hello". A charming voice was asking her for her availability to meet with Superintendent Marsh. She felt herself relax. Pole must have made the right decision – he was involving Henry. If she went to the Yard now, she could meet with Pole and speak about William too.

"Of course, I would be delighted to meet Superintendent Marsh... Today, 5pm. Perfect... It will be my pleasure." Nancy took another sip of wine. Put her glass down and pushed it away. Being tipsy now would not do. Marsh was Pole's superior after all. Meeting William meant she could indulge in dressing couture. Was she too overdressed? She considered her immaculate Louis Féraud suit, black-and-grey herringbone pattern, yellow shirt that suited her tan so well, black pearl jewellery.

"No," she whispered. "A good bit of power dressing always impresses the likes of Marsh."

* * *

The call startled Brett. He was not expecting his contact to demand a meeting so quickly. Brett was still feeling the effects of his favourite whisky. He needed to sober up significantly before making his way to Finsbury in North London. Steve's instructions were clear: go with the flow and get as much intel as possible. Each piece of information was worth harvesting for an information thirsty MI6 that needed to infiltrate the Salafi network which was fast expanding in Europe.

Their Jihadi strategy was to introduce people into a country early, let them become part of the community – years, perhaps decades – before they would be asked to act. Brett's MI6 minder had been surprised that they should trust him. But the Salafi network needed access to places and people they could not yet reach.

Brett had told him that this was a very specific piece of work, a narrow target, not in his view a bomb or mass shooting. Decades in Art's black market, navigating the trafficking world and doing business with the most dangerous of collectors, had brought him knowledge and instinct. He was on the ground. And he, Brett, was still alive.

He made himself a cup of strong coffee, Middle Eastern style letting the grounds sink to the bottom of the small glass. The powerful aroma filled the room. Brett poured the liquid into a small ornate glass, took a lump of brown sugar and plunged it into the coffee only releasing it when it was about to disintegrate.

The bittersweet taste sent a shiver through his body, a reminder of how his life had unfolded since his last divorce, the cruellest of them all. Brett checked his watch and released the strap. He was not taking his beloved Patek Philippe to a meeting in North London. He finished his coffee and moved to his bedroom to get ready. The shabby blue jacket and faded slacks were waiting for him still carelessly thrown onto the back of a chair. Brett changed, casting a quick eye outside his flat.

The weather was turning cold, and it would soon be dark. He sat on the side of his bed, checked his new burner mobile. A text had come through confirming his meeting – Finsbury Park station, N4. Mohammed would be waiting for him there. Nothing else. Should he alert his minder?

"Not yet," Brett murmured. "If they are going to kill me it won't be today. Today they want to talk."

As he walked out of the Finsbury Park station, Brett was hit by an unexpectedly harsh wind, a sharp contrast with the snugness of the Tube. His hands were moist with sweat. He adjusted the cotton scarf around his neck and scanned the faces in the crowd: men in long white robes, white crocheted hats, and well-trimmed beards; women in scarves, many of them wearing the full-face mask.

Brett felt out of place despite his low key, well-worn jacket. A hand grabbed his arm and before he could say anything Mohammed was pushing him towards the exit, down the street. A car was waiting, the door opened, and he was pushed inside. Brett had expected it would not be a cosy ride. He protested. They could not think he was eager or even prepared. Mohammed tried to sound reassuring, but Brett could tell that he was more scared than he was. The man sitting next to him in the back of the car was wearing the requisite dark glasses, his leather jacket contrasted with the outfits more common on the streets of Finsbury. He handed Brett an eye mask.

"Put it on," he said. His voice had a slight Middle Eastern accent that Brett could not place. Brett looked at Mohammed with an offended look.

"Come on – just to be on the safe side."

Brett protested again and hoped his mixture of disquiet and offence was doing the trick. He donned the mask and sat back. Now the real work had begun.

The car was moving along Blackstock Road towards the north. He was counting the minutes, memorising the turns. They stayed in the car for just under half an hour, but Brett was almost certain they had gone in a circle at least once. He felt strangely relaxed. It was not the first time he had been hoodwinked and led to some unknown destination. At least he was in the UK; he was in London – not in a foreign country run by war lords who may decide to sever any part of his anatomy including his head.

The car stopped and a large hand grabbed his arm, making him disembark clumsily. He was led through a door and the blindfold removed. He winced at the bright light coming from a single bulb dangling from the ceiling. Mohammed was with him, and Brett realised that he too had been blindfolded.

"You're going on your own." Mohammed exhaled anxiously. "I don't need to be with you."

Brett nodded, avoiding eye contact. He could only have contempt for this coward, but he was of good use. No need to do damage to their relationship.

Brett progressed down a shabby corridor, paint peeling from the wall. The place was unusually warm, almost suffocating. The smell of spices and coffee told him it was lived in. The door on his left opened abruptly. The thick-necked man who was walking behind him gestured for Brett to walk in. The room was softly lit, in contrast with the corridor, a number of rugs and a couple of thick mattresses spread over the floor.

A small bony man was sitting on one of them. Despite the lack of furniture, the room felt cosy. Brett quickly assessed the quality of the rugs and the throws, once a dealer always a dealer – these were not a poor man's possessions. The man did not stand up but gestured for Brett to sit down. He crouched and sat easily on the mattress to the right of his interlocutor. A faint smile brushed over the man's face. Brett had done business with the likes of him before. Brett registered. He was doing good – so far.

"We have a business deal to put to you," said the man with no further introduction. His English was fluent, educated in the US.

"I am listening," Brett replied with the coldness of a man prepared to do anything as long as it made money.

The man eyed Brett for a few seconds. Tea carried by a woman in full niqab appeared. She left the platter in front of the man and the scent of mint filled the air. He took his glass, again gestured to Brett to help himself, and started sipping at the burning liquid.

"We need to bring someone into the UK along a new route."

Brett also took a sip of tea and slowly placed the glass down on the floor in front of him.

"I don't do people," he said calmly.

"Yet," replied the man, "the price will be right." Brett finished his tea.

"Why me?"

"You have a good track record. You smuggle unique pieces almost everywhere in the world but in particular into the UK and – you do not do people," said the man with a hint of irony. Brett paid more attention to him for the first time. His face was young enough, with the expected untrimmed black beard. His hat came down low on his forehead unexpectedly emphasising his eyes. There was a level of determination, cold and unyielding, that Brett had seen only a few times before. A pang of anxiety surprised him.

"It will be a one-off," he said

The man nodded and finished his tea. "How much?"

"Only one man, no – equipment?"

The man nodded again and clapped his hands. The woman reappeared, poured some fresh tea and disappeared without a sound.

"How quickly do you want this done?"

"Next week, possibly sooner."

Brett's hand stopped in mid-air as he was reaching for his tea.

"I need a little more time if it is to be successful."

"You don't have it."

Brett drained his glass. "£1 million," he said without flinching. The man's eyes bore into Brett. "We will contact you."

Brett stood up. The door opened and the same thick-necked man moved him towards the door. The meeting was over, and Brett knew he had won the deal.

* * *

The cell door had opened an hour ago. Most inmates had gone to the canteen to collect their dinner. Henry always made his trip downstairs at 7pm. He did not like to mix with the lot that needed to seek comfort in food. This was not food in any case. This was fuel that kept the body going. Even canteen at college had been better than that. Still, it was part of the deal. It was part of the atonement process.

Today, however, Kamal's presence had made his environment taste even more bitter. He was still reeling from the discovery. Henry stood up. He had to make a move, or he would miss a meal. He slowly walked along the corridor, down a couple of stairwells. Big K was not in his cell. He too liked to get his food late – "Caribbean style, man." He always smiled as he mentioned Jamaica, uncovering a set of perfect white teeth.

Henry walked past an empty cell. He shivered. The sounds of the failed attempt to save the life of the inmate who had lived only two doors away came back with a disquieting clarity. Someone would be moved in as early as tomorrow Big K had told him. Henry straightened up and focused on the way ahead, slowing down his pace…

He was looking down the staircase when he saw Kamal at the bottom of it. He slowed down further almost to a stop. He had not yet decided what he should do. He could turn around but the urge to face up to the little shit grabbed him. No more excuses. Henry knew his anger, the deep marks left by a Belfast upbringing. But the rage that had seized him in the gym was still fresh and potent.

"I've got to find out," he said through gritted teeth. "No matter."

Henry started moving again. He forced his pace to remain measured. Every move on a Cat A wing had to be thought through. He could not afford to be misread by the other cons, so Henry willed himself to maintain the calm appearance he liked to adopt. The queue was short. Kamal seemed to have slowed his pace too. He was only a couple of people away.

He cast an eye towards Henry and for an imperceptible moment made eye contact with him. He turned back to pick up a tray and started slopping food on his plate. A politically correct prison service was offering a halal option and he took it. Henry moving along the queue hardly noticed what he was putting on his tray. Today he would eat at one of the tables. Big K had just finished and was putting his tray away when he nodded. He moved towards Henry with the nonchalant swagger of a man strolling along the white beaches of his native island.

"See who's here?" he murmured as he passed Henry.

"Yep, can't miss the beard," Henry replied. He could feel Big K's smile but did not lose his focus. Kamal had chosen a solitary table. Henry chose the corner of the room from which he could observe him discreetly. He started assessing the small built man.

Kamal looked boyish, a quiet young man who no one might notice. Henry had remarked how delicate his hands were, almost feminine. His voice was soft and yet the unmistakable echoes of fierce single-mindedness could be heard by a trained ear. It was not the type of fanaticism he had been used to with Bobby, although he had thought so to start with, or the fiery determination of Liam. It was deeper, methodical. Kamal would not, would never be turned from his path.

Again, Henry wondered why Kamal had been moved to Belmarsh. He would check the information he had gathered from Big K with Charlie. Too much was riding on this for him to rely on only one source. He could speak to Nancy too, but he discarded the thought immediately. He needed her for some more pressing issue – getting involved with Pole's new investigation. Kamal wanted to establish contact, so be it. "One terrorist to another," thought Henry bitterly.

He would play the game for a while. The explosion at Paddington came back in a quick flash of disjointed images. The look of his half-eaten plate of beans disgusted him. He pushed it away and sat back in his chair. Would Henry ever be a killer? He doubted. Yet, he needed the proof, irrefutable, that he could, one day, re-join the human race. Maybe that proof, that opportunity had presented itself and he was ready to grab it, run with it even if it laid him in the depths of hell.

Another inmate joined Kamal's table. They did not speak but when Kamal stood up the other man quickly placed a small piece of paper in Kamal's hand as he walked past. Henry slowly averted his gaze. Kamal walked past Henry's table to reach the tray conveyor belt. "Let's talk," he said.

Henry did not respond. Kamal walked past him again not expecting an answer. The game was on, and Henry had an inkling as to where it was leading.

* * *

Marsh was standing at the window, in full uniform, when Nancy entered. He was poised to impress. Nancy gave him her best smile. She too was on a charm offensive. It was a formal "How do you do?" all around, followed by the softer "A pleasure to meet you – likewise." Marsh locked his eyes into Nancy's as they were shaking hands and she knew she had made a greater impact than she had anticipated.

"I have read your CV, Ms Wu. Very impressive. I can see why Pole needs someone like you for the more complex City cases."

"Inspector Pole is a very capable man. I input solely on the more technical issues," Nancy replied.

"Pole is perhaps a little unconventional," Marsh added with a hint of sarcasm.

Marsh called for tea. He enquired whether Darjeeling would do and whether she'd prefer milk or lemon, and they settled down in the more comfortable corner of his office harbouring armchairs and a sofa.

Marsh sounded genuinely curious about her background. Nancy gave him a well-rehearsed story. He kept interrupting, not in a way that was irritating but with the questions that a good listener might ask. Marsh was sitting comfortably, relaxed, one arm over the back of the sofa – encouraging her to feel the same, comfortable and ready for a revelatory chat. If Marsh was testing her to validate her credentials, she would play the game. Even more important was to validate Pole's decision to involve Henry.

Nancy volunteered a few titbits of information.

Marsh courteously poured more tea. His right arm was once more spread over the back of the sofa, his hand moving mechanically in slow motion patting the leather affectionately. His eyes had not for one instant left Nancy; to someone less accustomed to scrutiny it would have been intimidating.

"And your experience of the City tells you it is not suicide?" Marsh asked out of the blue. Nancy smiled, drank a little more tea. She would not be drawn out that easily. he game of influencing and toying around with arguments was on.

"I am sure Inspector Pole has told you but I was unfortunately, or perhaps fortunately, present when Gary Cook died. I saw the body."

"Your conclusion?" Marsh asked, also taking a sip of his tea, all nonchalance and yet observant.

"He certainly was drunk when he spoke to me but not that drunk. The body fell at some awkward angle."

"And Tom Hardy?"

"No sign of alcohol or pills in the car, still strapped in his seat – unexpected."

"Still a little slim, in terms of evidence." Marsh smiled. His eyes widened a little and his eyebrows moved up. He wanted to be convinced otherwise.

"But so far no personal crisis that warrants such a dramatic move has been uncovered for both – no motive. And these two men were certainly not the type to commit suicide."

"Cook had lost his job." Marsh had done his homework, read the file or spoken to someone who knew it well.

"Cook had been in the City for a very long time. He almost certainly would have seen his dismissal as a means to getting a large sum from his former employer."

Marsh bent forward suddenly; his knees made contact with the small coffee table that separated them. His elbows rested on his thighs.

"How do you propose we move the inquiry forward? Pole is expecting the final toxicology report on Cook imminently. Hardy's final report will follow shortly thereafter. I have made it clear it is priority." Marsh was flexing his seniority muscle to impress. Nancy gave him a "you're-so-clever" sort of smile.

"And Inspector Pole can certainly speak to Henry Crowne as soon as he has received the OK." Nancy nodded.

Marsh's head moved sideways, his eyes questioning. "Crowne?"

Nancy stilled herself. "If he is so minded of course." Had she just gone over Pole's head? Bad, very bad idea.

"Henry Crowne; you mean the IRA banker?" Marsh said slowly. "Because of his understanding of the City?"

"It's a possibility," Nancy replied. Her mind was screaming danger. She could try to force the issue with Marsh now that she had presented the idea but Pole might never forgive her. It would certainly dent the trust they had for one another. And yet, Henry needed to be heard.

"What does Pole say?"

"I have hardly broached the subject with him."

"Why not? You should." Marsh settled again into the sofa. His eyes had finally left Nancy. He could see it all: another high-profile banking case triggering much media attention. He loved it. "In fact, why don't I give Pole a ring. I am due an update in any case."

"I am due to see Henry Crowne tomorrow. Why don't I gather more information and let you know whether this is worth it? You would not want to make a premature assumption that he has much to offer." It was the best Nancy could think of to soften her blunder and delay until she could speak to Pole.

Marsh pursed his lips. She had a point.

"Very well, I shall await your call. What time are you meeting him?" Nancy gave Marsh the details and extricated herself from the meeting. Marsh insisted in accompanying her to the lifts where she was finally allowed to go. Nancy took her mobile out of her bag and dialled Pole's line. No connection.

"Bloody lift, come on," she blurted. The door opened and a couple of people walked in. She terminated the call, pressed the close- door button. The lift stopped again. She grumbled and pushed her way through. She would call from whatever floor she was on. Pole's landline went to answer phone, so did his mobile. Nancy left a text message marked *genuinely urgent...*

Chapter Twelve

Nancy restlessly pushed away the book she was attempting to read. But even an Iris Murdoch novel, her favourite writer, could not do the trick. She had tried to reach Pole a few times since their last meeting, but he hadn't returned any of her calls or messages.

She stood up and went to her large window. The light was fading away fast, and it would soon be dark. She had cornered herself into the tightest of spots; a classic mistake of assuming the case was going in her direction - an assumption she should not have made. She had to reach Pole before Marsh did.

Marsh had been impatient at the thought of this new high-profile case and he might give Pole a nudge before tomorrow. She would go back to the Yard today if necessary or even cross the river and see Pole at home. She took a deep breath to release the tension in her shoulders and rolled her head slowly. The disquiet she had felt in Marsh's office at the thought of losing Pole's trust had risen a notch. The word Love floated across her mind, and she pushed it away. She could never get close to anyone – lovers perhaps, but love.

She moved away from the window, back to the coffee table on which the letter from Hong Kong was still laying. She focused on it with intensity, eager to remind herself why she did not want to, could not, let any man into her life. She had taken many risks in her life but that of abandonment she couldn't face, even after all these years.

"Why did you have to go back?" Nancy murmured, torn between anger and sadness. The memory of that moment savaged her once again.

She is running alongside the train that is taking him away, her father. The man who has enthralled her with his immense knowledge of art and philosophy. He dares everything when it comes to art, new ideas, new media; there is no limit to his skills and his inventiveness. She's barely seven when they leave China but already seventeen when he decides to go back. Deng Xiaoping has been put in charge and her father considers him a bringer of progress. The Cultural Revolution is soon at an end. Mao is now dead. He must return to China to fight.

"With what, Your paint and brushes?" Nancy said through gritted teeth. But she knew she was was wrong. Art has always been a powerful tool and it can make a difference.

Her mobile was ringing. She snatched it from the coffee table and was about to answer when she noticed the number. It was marked withheld. She threw the phone onto the large sofa. It bounced once and nearly fell off. Nancy caught it just in time.

"Bloody hell. What's the matter with me?" she said impatiently. The ringtone was telling her the caller had left a voicemail. She picked up the phone and listened to the message.

"Ms Wu, I hope you won't mind me calling you at this late hour, but have you given any more thought to Henry Crowne's involvement?" Marsh said as eloquently as he could. Nancy listened to the convoluted message. She sat back on her sofa and managed a half smile. Marsh was asking for another meeting, or rather for the pleasure of her expert opinion as he put it.

"Well, Jonathan Pole you've just found yourself some serious competition," she mused; Marsh was perhaps a little too keen.

* * *

Pole was in a meeting with his team, recapping on the various interviews they had carried out when Nancy called. He had noticed Nancy's calls. With a hint of hesitation, he turned the phone face down. Andy was recapping on their findings so far, nothing: family, friends, colleagues – not one single noticeable connection. And yet within the rarefied world of high management in the City this was inconceivable. Seniority exacerbated visibility and tightened the circle in which bankers operated.

Pole was particularly keen to explore both men's work contacts, clubs and outside interests. Both Gary and Tom had worked at the same bank when juniors. They understood how to navigate the world of finance. They were experts on bonds and interest rates. Pole's research on LIBOR had been fruitful but irritating only proving to him that Henry had a very valid point.

The article published by the *WSJ* had been well researched and it had sown a seed of doubt in his mind that kept growing the more he read around the subject matter. But Pole was not ready to yield. Nancy was probably pressing for what she believed was right - Henry's involvement in the case. Pole needed more than a personal hunch; the evidence needed to stack up and so far it did not, or so he told himself. There was also Nancy's meeting with Marsh. His mind drifted a little. Nancy would know what to do, surely. Pole's slight discomfort in the pit of his stomach was not mere professional anxiety. Nancy was a strong judge of character and her help invaluable – nothing was more attractive to him than a strong intellect combined with charm and a compassionate nature.

Andy was wrapping up and the team dispersed.

Pole hung around.

"Good job, even if a bit frustrating."

"I know Guv." Andy hesitated.

"But you have an idea?"

"Not so much an idea but an... observation."

Pole raised an inquisitive eyebrow.

"It feels like something is missing. People are not talking. I am not saying they are doing it voluntarily, more like they're not wanting to remember."

"That's an interesting view," Pole said slowly. "Walk with me to my office."

Andy adjusted his thick glasses on his baby face, walking awkwardly alongside Pole.

"What makes you say that, apart from the lack of information?"

"I read the transcripts again," Andy said craning his neck toward his boss.

"All of them?" Pole said suppressing a smile.

"I'm not losing time by doing it again, just wanted to make sure..." Andy turned a deep shade of red.

"I'm not saying you are." Pole smiled encouragingly. "And..."

"It's all about work, the office. There is nothing private. I mean, l what it was like to know these guys on a personal level. But all the answers were very vague as though the people they worked with didn't care. ."

"Even with friends' interviews?"

"Specially with friends' interviews. They all talk about these guys and their work successes, but..."

Pole and Andy moved into Pole's office. Andy moved a pile of documents from the chair in front of Pole's desk. He took a roll of wine gums out of his pocket and offered Pole one. Much to Andy's surprise Pole took one and started sucking on it. Pole smiled at Andy's shocked face.

"I, too, was young... once"

Andy nodded,

"How do you want to take your hunch forward?" Pole asked.

"I thought I could go back into their diaries and look for lunches, dinners, parties."

"And you have already started it – so what do you have?" Pole asked. He knew a keen face when he saw one.

Andy wriggled a little on his seat. "Parties are really interesting. I mean, there is a bit more information like photos, snippets in newspapers or websites."

Pole nodded encouragingly.

"There are a couple of parties that did not quite turn out the way they should. At one of them there was a brawl, and the police were called – bit of a punch-up between some trading-floor guys, too much booze apparently."

Pole shook his head, and grimaced. "Not uncommon I would say. Most of the time the reason we don't know about it is because they don't call the cops. I mean us."

"But there is this other one where some young guy jumped from the top floor of the hotel where they were having a party."

Pole stood up. "Keep going." He took his phone out of his pocket and was playing around with it in a rhythmic gesture.

"A young grad, apparently he had been having a bad time and couldn't cope with the pressure."

"Who was at that party? Gary Cook and Tom Hardy?"

"Yes, Guv, and a lot more top people."

"You know what you've got to do? Get a full list of people there, and autopsy report on this poor bugger."

Pole dumped his mobile on his desk, showed Andy out and sat back down. It would not take long for Andy to find the information on the old case file. Another excuse to delay calling Nancy perhaps? Would Marsh have called her already though? 8pm. Marsh's PA would have gone home. He toyed with his phone for half a minute longer.

"Shit. I give in." Pole closed his door and was about to dial when the door opened again without a knock and Nurani entered. She was all smiles.

"You have the face of a cat that got the cream," Pole said with an amused smile. Nancy would have to wait a little longer.

"Oh yeah, the cream – or rather the little blue pills, the ones we were looking for."

"Pray tell." Pole sat up tall in his chair.

"The gym was a good lead. We searched the lockers and found a whole bag full of various naughties and I have taken the lot to the lab."

"Did you get a list of the gym members?"

Nurani crossed her arms over her chest and gave a smug look.

"OK, OK," Pole said putting his hands up. "I am just a DCI doing his job."

Nurani sat down.

"One of the guys is going through it as we speak. I bet you we will find Tom Hardy there."

"Couldn't agree more but I am looking for another connection," Pole mused. Nurani raised her eyebrows. "Weren't we keen to find the guy or gal that sold these chaps some dodgy drug?"

"Very true, and yet – and yet."

"You're not going to buy that conspiracy crap, are you?"

"Well, I have been doing a lot of reading of late," Pole said waving at a pile of printed articles. "And I am afraid the conspiracy theory is now sounding particularly attractive."

"This is bullshit, Jon. Really, all because *Nancy* is spinning it in order to help her mate, Henry."

Nurani's voice was trembling, her eyes filled with so much outrage that Pole was taken aback.

"Temper, temper Ms Shah," Pole said, trying but failing to find humour in the situation. His eyes met Nurani's, and he would not yield until she did.

Nurani stood up abruptly. She leaned forward towards Pole; her knuckles planted on his desk.

"This is not on, Jon. She is not a trained investigator. She has no terrain experience and OK, perhaps she is good when it comes to fake paintings, but this is an entirely different ball game."

"And I think your way of belittling her input is, in turn, not on, Nurani. She has a huge amount of experience in the field of criminality, and I am not asking Nancy to do your job or mine," Pole replied, more angered than he expected. "In any case, I do not have to justify my actions to you."

"Why not? It is also impacting the way I work on the case. And you certainly should have spoken to me about this LIBOR idea."

"What's the matter with you? You are senior enough and will almost certainly be promoted next year if not before. You are leading one of the main lines of enquiry in this case—"

"But," Nurani interrupted. "You are not involving me at the sharp end of the enquiry."

"Please shut the door," Pole's voice had taken on an uncharacteristically incisive edge. Nurani hesitated, yielding only to Pole's order when he went to stand to close the door himself. "I will not have you questioning how I run a case, not when it comes to my choice of experts. You know how I work. I don't only give orders. I do the work too including when it's hard graft. Some of my colleagues like to delegate or even over-delegate, not me. And I get results because of this – which, by the way has served you well so far." Pole paused. "I don't want to hear more of this garbage. Are we clear?" Pole was still seated, his tall body relaxed in his chair. Only his voice conveyed his anger and it worked. Nurani's face had turned red, her righteousness turned to concern. Pole had never spoken to her that way before. She uttered a barely inaudible "Fine" and disappeared, closing the door stiffly behind her.

Pole sighed. He hoped he wouldn't have to deal with more of Nurani's bad temper. This was not fitting for a soon to be DCI.

He snatched the mobile from where it had slid, under a pile of articles he had dumped on his desk, evidence of his hard graft as he had put it to Nurani. The word LIBOR figured prominently on most pages. He collected the papers together, tapped the bundle on his desk. He placed the wad of paper in front of him. Time to return Nancy's call.

Pole accessed he missed call list. He tapped his long fingers on his desk. He should not have dismissed Nancy's views so readily. Still, he had now gathered more evidence on the deaths of Gary Cook and Tom Hardy. The puzzle was falling into place just the way he liked it to. Pole reached Nancy's name in the list of missed calls – seven altogether.

He ran his fingers through his hair. "Shit."

* * *

Edwina looked at her watch, 9pm. She stretched, yawned and tried to focus on the email she was drafting. Yet another email to the Governor of the Bank of England justifying the need for a further round of Quantitative Easing. Her door had remained closed, and she had not checked on Gabriel.

He was no doubt still around. He would have otherwise stuck his head through the door to tell her he was leaving – made some silly joke, called to make sure she didn't need him. Gabriel was the most devoted deputy she had ever had. He could have easily been in her shoes had it not been for the horrendous accident that had cost him so dear.

She rubbed her hand over her face – *focus.* She read aloud the last sentence of her email. "The current level of QE in the UK has reached GBP 70bn." It did not have the punch and technical quality she was looking for. She stretched again and stood up. Her mind had not been on the job for a few hours. She went to her window overlooking Threadneedle. The flow of traffic had died down and only the odd cab rushed past, carrying another banker eager to get home.

The activity may pick up a bit, she thought. Most City firms no longer allowed their staff to use cabs before 9pm. The days of expense abuse were slowly disappearing. And yet so much work still needed doing to change mentalities

She rested her head against the cool glass. What was happening? She could not ignore the heavy feeling she had carried all day. Something about Gabriel had unsettled her and she could not shake it away. She moved to her closed door and eased it open slowly. Gabriel was still at his desk, working. She closed the door again. Her chest tightened, a moment of panic, then she was calm again.

The final round of meetings that would promote her to being the first female Governor of the Bank of England was playing on her mind, she decided.

I do not need this bloody stupid story: Gary, then Tom. How inconsiderate of them to drop dead. Humour may not be appropriate but who cared? She would work another hour and then call it quits. Her stomach grumbled; she needed food.

"Gabs," Edwina said sticking her head through the door again. "I am famished. Can we order something?"

Gabriel lifted his head, rubbing his eyes underneath his glasses. "Yep, great idea – pizza?"

"Deep, crisp and even." Edwina smiled.

"Gosh. It's not that time of the year yet."

"I know. A poor attempt at levity."

"Well, I know what Father Xmas is going to place in your stocking."

"You are convinced. Aren't you?"

"Absolutely Eddie. No one and nothing is getting in your way. Mark my words. You will be the next Governor." Gabriel winked whilst putting on his jacket. His smile was broad, perhaps too broad.

"Are you ordering?"

"Will do and just walk there when they call me to tell me the pizzas are ready to collect. I need some fresh air." He turned away and disappeared.

Edwina cursed herself. She should have gone home. The work she would do after eating a pizza with Gabriel would be rubbish and she would get home late, again. But old habits died hard, and it was difficult not to succumb to the investment banking macho pressure of working all hours. Whether quality work was produced, well that was another matter altogether.

Gabriel had disappeared on his pizza errand She walked to the window to see him cross the road. She swiftly moved to his desk.

He had locked his PC – something he should do of course but that he rarely did when they were working late together. She quickly went round his desk, lifted carefully the chipped Oxford mug that he used to hold his pens. She found a small post-it underneath, Metatron32.

How stupid.

She entered his password. The screen on which he was working materialised. Edwina's heart was pumping in her ears. Edwina checked his browser's history. Gabriel was checking flights. Edwina found a tab still open.

Gabriel was checking flights to Turkey. She did not recall him mentioning a holiday nor indeed any interest in a trip to the Middle East and certainly not, she had assumed, after the terrifying accident that had earned him a deformed face and cost his brother his life. The dates looked equally odd. End of the month, in exactly seven days' time.

She heard the doors of the lift chime, rapidly locked down the screen and disappeared into her office. She busied herself around her meeting table, making room for the warm pizzas she could smell already. Gabriel opened the boxes, tore out the tops, took out of his jacket pockets a couple of cans of lager and plunked himself in a chair. A well-rehearsed sequence meant to make them both feel at home, the way an old couple would, Edwina thought. She was still standing at her desk, away from the table when Gabriel opened the cans and gave her a surprised look – was she not hungry?

"La Reine pizza," he announced. "Thought it might be topical."

"What about yours? Sicilian pizza, extra pepperoni – that smells of La Mafia," Edwina managed to jest.

Gabriel's smile dropped for an imperceptible moment and was back again. "Anything to get the *Job* done, of course."

He grabbed a piece and took a bite. He gave an approving grunt, washed the first mouthful down with a drink from his can. "Won't you share my Sicilian Eddie? Just what you need at this moment in time..."

"As long as you share La Reine," Edwina replied short of finding something wittier to say.

"You bet I will," Gabriel smiled and helped himself. He started on his new piece and took another slug from his can. Edwina had stopped eating. The same feeling that had made her check his PC made her put her slice down. "What's keeping you so late today?" she asked forcing herself to resume her eating.

"There is always something to do. I need to finish the new report on the latest inflation figures. How about you? Still working on QE for Mervyn-The-Oracle-King?"

Why lie?

Edwina took her can of lager and drank from it in silence. Why lie about a holiday?

"I'm not finding the right words – frustrating," she heard herself say.

"Are you worried about anything in particular?" Gabriel asked whilst selecting another piece of pizza.

She gave him a surprised look, but Gabriel was talking quantitative easing – at least she hoped he was. "Of course, I'm worried. Worried that Merv is going to say no to the next instalment of QE."

"I meant beyond that?" Gabriel's effort at being casual filled her with anger. If he wanted to ask her whether she was still thinking about Gary and Tom's deaths he should, plain and simple.

His BlackBerry rang. He was about to ignore it when the caller's ID made him change his mind. His face showed concern for a moment and closed again to scrutiny as he put the phone down.

"I'd better try to finish this wretched email," she said.

"Yep. I might disappear soon since you don't seem to need me." Gabriel stood up. As he walked out of her office door, he looked at his BlackBerry again. She heard him put his coat on. A few seconds later the doors of the lift chimed open. Edwina moved to the window again.

Gabriel was on the pavement in front of the Bank. He was on his phone, holding what seemed to be an angry conversation. His right hand kept thumping the air. He stopped walking, looked around and finished his conversation abruptly. Whatever Gabriel was saying was not for anybody else's ears.

* * *

Nancy's mobile had barely rung when Marsh walked through Pole's office door. Pole killed the call. Marsh walked up to his desk and this time did not bother to find a space as more files were once again sitting on the office's spare chair.

"Pole, I'll be brief. I met with Ms Wu. Remarkable woman." Marsh marked a pause. Nancy had made an impression – oh, yes. He cleared his throat. "I think we should bring in Henry Crowne," Marsh paused again.

Pole had not moved a muscle. "And let me know when he is here." Marsh was halfway towards the door when he turned back. "Well done on your new high-profile case." His voice bounced off the room outside Pole's office as he walked past desks and made conversation with the few people still around.

Pole threw his mobile on his desk and stood up abruptly. He bent forward his arms outstretched, resting on the back of his chair.

"What the fuck is Nancy playing at?" Pole clenched the back of the chair and pushed it away. He closed the door of his office. A nasty word was creeping into his mind. Was it manipulation or betrayal – perhaps both? Pole snatched his mobile from where it had landed and dialled.

Nancy's mobile was ringing.

"Jonathan, where on earth have you been? I—"

Pole interrupted. "With Superintendent Marsh." Ominous silence on the other end of the phone. "Who has instructed me to involve Henry, which I will do in my own time whether you and Marsh like it or not," Pole's tone was ice cold.

"It's a stupid misunderstanding, an overreaction, but I have something more urgent—"

"The reason I work with you, Nancy, is because you do not overreact; not a woman of your experience and even if it involves Henry," Pole's tone had the bite of a wounded dog.

"This is ridiculous, Jonathan. If you had replied to my calls, you would have known about Marsh," Nancy's tone took a sharp edge Pole had seldom heard before.

"I am not at your beck and—" A knock at the door interrupted Pole. He would not have an argument with someone waiting outside his office. "I've got to go. I will call you later." Pole hung up. "Come in."

Andy opened the door gingerly.

"I have got the info you wanted, Guv, but I can come back."

"Nope. Come in," Pole said waving him in. He cleared his throat and sat down still clenching his mobile.

"I found the info about this grad, Felipe Martinez. Really bad stuff. He could not cope with the pressure apparently. That's the official version but the parents thought he was being bullied and he worked all hours – just like me really." Andy was waiting for Pole to indulge in a little banter, but he just grunted.

"How bad was it?"

"He was picked on by the traders – too slow at delivering the documents they were expecting, not quick enough at learning how to use the systems. There is a whole report by the guy who oversaw the team," Andy replied adjusting his thick glasses in an embarrassed gesture.

"Which bank was it?" Pole started leafing through the file in front of him.

"GL, a year before they went down."

Pole stopped in mid flick. "And are you next going to tell me that this young guy was on Gary Cook's desk?"

"Spot on Guv."

Pole grabbed his phone, balanced the handpiece on some files and started dialling DI Banks' number. Andy came closer and Pole indicated he should sit down. It may take some time.

DI Banks, the case officer was still at work.

"I can take you through the most interesting elements of the case." He offered.

"Please." Pole made room on his desk to accommodate Andy's writing pad.

"GL had opened an internal investigation into the behaviour of its staff, it gave very little... a bit of a whitewash but no one was willing to talk. The other grads seem to dislike Felipe, not an Oxbridge student and certainly not an MBA from Ivy league America or the LSE."

"Why was he recruited then?" Pole asked

"Part of a Diversity programme. GL used to offer a couple of spaces to underprivileged students every year," Bank said. "What was disturbing was that his parents and even his girlfriend had not realised how bad it was until towards the end – and no one knew he was on drugs either. You've got Martinez's tox report in the file I sent, right?"

Andy picked up the file and opened it at a page he had marked with a red tag.

"Not sure whether you heard about them, but he was on—"

"Nootropics," interrupted Pole without referring to the file. Banks whistled. "Don't tell me your two vics were on that too?"

"Yep, and some amphetamines too."

"You know nootropics are not illegal, right?"

"So, I gather but how these were purchased might be."

"Hmmm, maybe, but the bit that tipped the balance for the Martinez case and might be more interesting for you mate is LSD. Martinez had taken a large dose. In fact, he had finished the bottle of little pills he had on him, and you know what that does to anyone?"

Pole circled the word LSD in red in Martinez's tox report, thanked Banks and hung up. He was right; no one had been using LSD since the early seventies. Coke, Speed etc – these were the drugs of today's users. And why would Cook and Hardy's tox reports not show traces of the stuff? Pole looked at his watch, almost 10pm.

"I would like to speak to Martinez's parents and girlfriend asap. And tomorrow, we go through the list of guests once more."

"What are we looking for, Guv?"

"Not sure yet, possibly someone who is the supplier of all this stuff. Anyway, well done. Go home now and get some rest; tomorrow is going to be another long day."

Andy left Pole's office with a spring in his step. Pole looked at his watch again. "Too late and not in the mood," he murmured. He wanted to go home, play a little jazz on his old-fashioned LP player and drink a decent glass of wine. Then perhaps he would have mellowed enough to forgive the unforgivable.

* * *

The short man who had followed him stood up and leaned against the glass partitioning of the tube carriage that Brett had entered. He was moving his head in short rhythmic movements, listening to music through brand-new headphones. He looked too young to be any good. Was it a warning or did they assume he would not notice? The Jihadists were trying to find out where he lived.

He could try to lose this chappie. But those were not the instructions of MI6-Steve. *Not his neck on the bloody line though.* Brett composed himself, he would look cautious but could not let on he was trained. The skill was to spot the shadow, assess whether it was key to give it the slip or appear unaware. Brett disembarked at Piccadilly. The crowd was dense. He struggled towards the Regent Street exit.

His watch indicated 9.20pm. He disappeared into the buzz of Soho. One of the little bars he frequented there on occasion would not take any notice of his shabby attire. More importantly, that wine bar had a well-hidden side exit he may decide to use later on. Brett sat at the counter, ordered a whisky and took his phone out. The shadow had walked in. The headphones were still on. He was relaxed. So not a complete amateur. A table had become free. The young man sat down and ordered a Coke from the waitress.

Brett was taking his time. Scrolling down his email list, replying, deleting, ordering a second whisky. The bar had become crowded. A group of gay men were at Brett's elbow: loud voices, laughter, tight bums and rippling muscles in immaculate T-shirts. Brett glanced quickly towards the shadow. He was no longer looking in his direction. Choosing a bar with a gay clientele had been a stroke of genius, Brett thought. If he wanted to leave, now was the time.

The shadow would have to cross the room as soon as he had spotted Brett was no longer in his seat and wade through the group of gay men to reach the downstairs lavatory. It would take him a few minutes to spot the side door – by which time Brett would be in a cab.

This time though there was no other flat, no decoy address or hotel room that stood between him and those trying to track him down. Brett looked at his empty glass. The people who wanted to employ him wanted to study him. Let them, Steve had said. MI6 was expecting him to play the game. Brett put his faded blue jacket back on and left simply the way he had come.

* * *

In the cab home Edwina finalised her email. She rested her head against the headrest and slowly closed her eyes. They felt sore and she gently rubbed them. She looked out of the window. They were crawling through the West End. She had not bothered to instruct the driver about the route she wanted him to take. She still needed to think. The BlackBerry was resting loosely in her hand. She started composing a text to Nancy. It was well past 11pm but a text would not intrude.

Must catch up. Need to discuss a peculiar point urgently.

She erased the last sentence. Nancy was busy but not so these days that she would not make time for her. Better not show concern. *Let's do breakfast.*

Edwina dropped her BlackBerry into her bag, not yet ready to commit. A nugget of relief fluttered in her stomach. She had bottled up all her concerns after Tom Hardy's death. Nancy was her best ally. The need to speak to her was growing stronger and yet, once she had voiced her concerns, how could she stop there? Nancy would put two and two together.

She had been after all a most respected QC. Edwina's cab drove past the US embassy on her right. The compound's security had been reinforced. It looked more like a bunker than a Ferrero-Rocher fairy tale dwelling, a sign of the times. Life felt harsher and more unforgiving. Where had the crazy eighties gone or even the rich nineties? She picked up her phone again and looked at the unfinished text. She added a few words and pressed the send button.

Nancy would think it was about the appointment of the new Governor of the Bank of England. In some ways it was true. Edwina was ready. She was ready and had more than the required intellectual capacities, the technical capacity without a doubt, but more importantly she was willing to take the harsh decisions – for the greater good.

The greater good? Edwina wondered what would have happened if she had not made the call. A futile exercise in late examination of a momentous decision, she knew. The past could not be undone, only concealed. Then again, how could she not have agreed with Whitehall?

Tom Hardy had also been persuasive. He had first spoken to William Noble and eventually to her.

The taxi was driving along Holland Park Avenue. She would be home in less than ten minutes. Her husband John would still be awake, reading. She had not spoken to him either. She sagged into the seat and closed her eyes. She felt heavy, each muscle aching to release the strain and yet on constant alert. Her phone buzzed in her bag and she picked it up. Nancy had replied. She confirmed she was free the following morning and was awaiting a time. There was still time until their meeting. Edwina need not rush into a confession, at least not for now.

Chapter Thirteen

It was still dark when Nancy woke up to brew her first cup of tea. The leaves of the trees across the park below her looked shiny; a soft summer rain had cooled the temperature. A welcome relief after a stretch of hot weather that made London hardly bearable. She mechanically opened the cupboard, picked up the tin of Sichuan tea and boiled the kettle. Her eyes, still heavy with lack of sleep, could not quite focus. She consulted her BlackBerry – 4.45am. Pole had lost his cool and not called back. She had toyed for a moment with the idea of contacting Marsh, but it was stupidly vindictive. Still, William's life might be at stake.

She made tea, walked back into her lounge and stretched on her sofa. She could doze off perhaps. But her restless mind got the better of her. She moved to her sound system, selecting her favourite Philip Glass opera. The music was low, but the first bar propelled her into another world of minimalist melodies yet rich with subtle romantic undertones. She stretched again on the sofa. This time her body relaxed. She let herself be carried away by the sound she enjoyed so much and for the first time in a very long time she wished she had comforting arms around her to sooth her.

Her mobile rang. Nancy woke up in a jolt. She checked the time. It was not yet 7am. "Nancy?" asked a distraught voice.

"Speaking," Nancy mumbled with a pang of anxiety. She did not want to hear what that voice had to say.

"It's Paula, William's PA," the voice continued, barely holding back tears.

"My God. He has had an accident." Nancy collapsed back on the sofa.

"How did you know…but yes, he was hit by a car. He is in a bad way, in intensive care at St Thomas's."

"I'm on my way." Nancy did not wait for an answer before hanging up. A cry swelled in her throat and her eyes watered. She had not felt this helpless since she had arrived in Paris in the late sixties – a long, very long, time ago.

The furtive images and sounds of a bygone China materialised and dissolved almost instantly. The voice of her father telling her to hide, the arrival at Orly airport after weeks of travelling… She cast aside the blanket she had wrapped herself in and stood up almost in a panic.

She looked around, disorientated for a moment Nancy walked into the bathroom and splashed her face with cold water. Her hand searched for the towel. She brought it to her face. The soft smell of clean linen soothed her. She took a few minutes to collect her thoughts and get ready. William needed her.

Stepping into St Thomas's Accident and Emergency Department was like stepping into another world. The flow of people coming through was constant. The smell of disinfectant and human stench combined to give the waiting room its unmistakable odour. Nancy rushed to the information desk to be told that William was being operated on. Nancy held onto the edge of the receptionist's high desk and closed her eyes. Why had Pole not called back? A small hand pressed her arm. She turned back to face a pale Paula. She had been crying, her large blue eyes rimmed with red.

"They can't tell me anything until the operation is over."

Nancy inhaled deeply. She too felt like crying but she had no time now. As long as William was alive, she would fight for him, fight to find out what had happened. She swiftly brushed the corner of her eyes with delicate fingers.

"You'd better tell me all you know so far," Nancy said putting her arm around Paula's shoulders. They both walked towards the far end of the waiting room to what seemed a quieter corner.

Nancy fetched a couple of teas from the vending machine. They sat down and hugged their cups in silence for a moment. Paula breathed deeply and started.

"He came back from his meeting with you looking a little happier. William has not been his calm self of late. Not impatient but distracted."

Nancy nodded encouragingly. Paula hesitated. She had been William's faithful PA for over twenty years and speaking ill of him distressed her. Nancy gently took her hand and squeezed. "I need to know." Paula brought her crumpled handkerchief to her eyes and continued.

"He started working again on a file he had been putting together for a few years now. It must be ultra-confidential as even I have not been allowed access."

Nancy shot up an eyebrow. Paula agreed. "I know, virtually unheard of. And then he took a call on his mobile. His office door was open. He went to shut it and less than five minutes later he left with these specific instructions—" Paula drank some of her tea and cleared her throat. "I had to get in touch with you if anything happened." Nancy let out a small gulp of anguish. Why had he not called her then?

Paula continued. "I did not know what to make of it. But he looked dreadful again. I was about to ask him if he was unwell, and he must have read my mind. He said it would be fine in the end."

Nancy closed her eyes. She would not succumb to anger – would not. It would serve no purpose and yet. She forced her mind into composure to do what it did best: extract the right information, uncover the evidence.

"What happened next?" she asked, knowing the answer would involve a white van. "Was he hit by a car?"

"Actually, not a car – a van. That's what an eyewitness said."

"Have they found his mobile phone?" Nancy asked.

Paula opened her eyes wide. Nancy read the shock in her eyes. How could she suddenly ask questions only someone from the police would when William was fighting for his life?

"I know how it sounds but William asked you to call me for a reason."

"The police did not recover it."

Nancy fell silent. She was deliberating. She wanted to stay at St Thomas's, huddled with Paula, waiting for the outcome of William's operation, until she knew he had been saved. But she must leave now if she was to save him from the next attempt on his life. She also must speak to Pole before Marsh did. She looked at the large clock on the wall, almost 8am. Pole would be at work and if he was not she knew how to find him.

"Yes," she muttered, "I know where you live." Nancy was startled by her anger. Why had Pole not returned her calls? She was not a time-waster – he knew it. But Marsh had already spoken to him, and he was now justifiably angry. Nancy stood up slowly. Panic showed in Paula's eyes.

"Are you leaving?"

"There is nothing better I'd like to do than stay with you. But I must meet someone. Someone William wanted me to talk to. It pains me to leave you on your own. Just let me know as soon as you have any news."

Paula tried to look brave. She understood the urgency.

Last night Nancy had resisted the urge to go to Scotland Yard and savage Pole. He had a point, after all. She had made a mistake with Marsh. But as the cab whizzed past the Houses of Parliament towards the Yard, she pressed the send button on a text she had just finished. She hoped that Pole would see her when she arrived or else she would speak to Marsh.

My friend William Noble is in intensive care because you wouldn't listen. If he dies, I will never forgive you.

* * *

The yellow sticker that had been left on his chair told Pole that Martinez's girlfriend was on her way. Pole sat down slowly, considering the small piece of paper. He rubbed his eyes with his thumb and index finger. This new piece of evidence would matter.

"A drug deal gone wrong?" he said, transferring the post-it to the receiver of his phone.

"Morning, Guv, you saw my note?" Andy asked.

"Yep, and thank God I look before I sit otherwise I would be walking around with a post-it stuck to my backside," Pole replied straight-faced.

Andy swallowed a giggle and mumbled. "Sorry, Guv."

"Sorry in turn, today is a grumpy day," Pole said. "What else have you got for me?"

Andy moved swiftly towards the desk.

"Went through the guest list of the evening Martinez jumped and the day Gary Cook... well, also jumped." Andy produced a single piece of paper that he put in front of Pole. "I've got a few names..."

"And the name of *particular* interest is?" Pole said.

"Edwina James-Jones." Andy stabbed the paper where a name had been highlighted.

"The Bank of England woman? What sort of party was that then?"

"I don't think it was that sort of party," Andy said slowly, putting space after each word.

"I said party," Pole replied. "Not orgy."

"Well it's the City and—"

"In the eighties I would have said almost certainly; in the nineties quite possibly but 2011 – not in London, far too risky."

"It was a sort of networking event – sort of meet our senior management and senior alumni."

"So, Tom Hardy and Edwina James-Jones are both ex GL?" Pole's phone rang. Felipe Martinez's girlfriend had arrived. "Felipe's girlfriend responded fast. Any idea why?" Pole asked.

"I got the feeling she's hoping we might reopen the case. She said she never believed in his suicide."

* * *

The small radio had been on since he had woken up at 6am. Henry had brought his breakfast back to his cell. He'd hardly noticed what he had put in his bowl, porridge of some description or another. His mind had more important problems to chew on.

For the last couple of years, the prison routine that Henry had created in order to survive jail had slowed him down. He had followed Charlie's advice, kept a low profile. Nancy had been another precious source of advice.

Even Big K had been surprisingly generous with pieces of information that proved judicious. The length of his sentence had stunned him, thirty years: the maximum term applied for an act of terrorism. The message was clear: zero tolerance for the likes of him – a rich banker and an IRA operative. There would be no mitigating circumstances for Henry Crowne. True he had been deceived by his friends but above all he had deceived himself.

Like a man whose body had been crushed, Henry had taken the small steps to rebuild his identity. Since his downfall he had gathered more true friends around him than he had ever had in the City – Nancy, Charlie, perhaps even Big K. And as he gradually stumbled out of the daze of his conviction, the weight that had burdened him since his arrest on the bench in London Fields had lifted. The desire to make his life count had inexorably grown.

Henry switched channels – still nothing on the deaths of Tom Hardy and Gary Cook. Henry read the pages he had written since he'd started thinking about their deaths. He knew he was right.

He also knew that government and politics had to be connected to the manipulation of LIBOR. Tweaking LIBOR, as some of the traders would put it, had been common practice for some of the large banks; infinitely small adjustments of the basis point – perhaps 0.5bps or even 0.25bps – that made a large difference because of the size of the market, from mortgages to complex financial products. But this latest manipulation of the benchmark looked like it might go well beyond what had gone on in the past. Henry was not yet sure by how much.

The LIBOR market was probably one of the deepest in the world. Henry had created lists of instruments with best estimates, decision trees of who he knew would do what and for which institutions, network links to assess the ramifications of any scandal. And amongst all these names lay a killer.

The containment of the 2008 crisis was at the forefront of every single government agenda on the planet. This scandal would run deep, and the argument would be convincingly the same – needs must.

Henry's isolation hit him unexpectedly. He had felt alone in the City, never expecting to build ties of trust with any of his contacts. It was all show, networking, surface friendships to get results.

He had thought his true friends to be in Northern Ireland. He would never have spoken of his hopes or fears to anybody else. But even that small sanctuary had been destroyed by Liam's betrayal. Nancy's unexpected kindness had saved him from the abyss, even Pole's remarkable fairness had helped.

But this morning, as he was sitting on his small bed in his standard HMP Belmarsh brown tracksuit, he felt the stab of pain punch his stomach. He could not reach out. He had refused Big K's offer of a mobile. How he had managed to smuggle one into the HSU was nothing short of miraculous – no, it was miraculous. Henry had broken enough rules to last him a lifetime. He would abide by the rules imposed on him by HSU Belmarsh, the harshest of them all.

Yet, who was he kidding? He had bypassed the prison's computer system and accessed the Internet a number of times. He had an excuse – keeping tab on the markets, a ridiculous justification of course. And there was the netsuke: no excuse for that one. Henry stood up but there was nowhere to escape to. This was arrogant, stupid... unforgivable. The familiar feeling sent a shiver down his spine. His stomach tightened again, and a ball of fire burnt his throat.

Anger, no, fury.

He needed to lash out. His gym time was still hours away. His turn in the prison library was not until the afternoon. Henry removed his shirt and started rapid press-ups: fifty... a hundred. He collapsed on the floor in a pool of sweat. His arms and lungs were on fire, trembling. Henry rolled on his back. The coolness of the concrete floor calmed him a little. Images of Northern Ireland materialised. Restlessness crept back into him. He turned over for more press-ups. This time he collapsed face down. He groaned. He had once said it to Nancy and still believed it. He had left Belfast, but Belfast would never leave him.

The memory of that first supper at Nancy's brought a smile to his face. He was still free then. If Nancy had been a little younger, he might have fallen for her, a mistake of course. With time the friendship that had grown between them had become deep and true, its quality greater than he could have ever imagined.

Henry stood up slowly, ran cold water into the small washbasin nestled in the corner of his cell and splashed his face. He let the water trickle over his body, eyes closed. The burn of anger had subsided – for now.

"Thirty years," Henry whispered. He had taken advantage of all the facilities prison could offer to a Cat A HSU inmate. His psychologist was a decent person. He had expected to find do-gooders at his compulsory psychological assessment; instead, he had found patience and understanding, realistic, objective, yet considerate.

He had to reassess if he wanted to survive the ordeal. If he wanted to keep his sanity. He had come close to losing his mind once. Anthony Albert, his most prominent City rival, had made sure of that with the implacability of the dying man that he was. Henry's certainties had been shaken to the core. The tough lad from Belfast had a much softer centre than he'd like to admit.

Henry lay on his bed, the beads of water still rolling over his skin. Memories rushed into his mind once more, disorderly until the picture of a ten-year-old boy took hold. His mother had collected him from the police station once again. It would not be the last. Why did he have to stick around the O'Connor boys? On that day though his mother had had little energy left to scold wee Henry.

His father had not been seen for a few days and if he did not appear soon, he would lose his job again. Henry had never quite understood what his father's job was. He simply knew he was on the road a lot. Later on, he recalled the word salesman, selling pretty much anything and everything. He never kept a job long enough to be known as anything else but The Salesman.

But Henry could remember the joy he felt whenever his father crossed the threshold of their home. His little heart flipping in his chest at the sound of the heavy footsteps making the floorboards of the staircase creak. There was always something fun for him: a bright red toy car, some chocolate wrapped in the shape of a snowman. And of course, there would be the dancing. Henry on his father's shoulders, moving to a Rock 'n' Roll beat, his mother following the rhythm with delight. Then his father would once more disappear, having made a promise to stay that he would never keep.

The day his father disappeared down a dark alleyway at the back of their house and never came back alive would be marked in Henry's mind forever. The image of his father's lifeless body on the ground was still hard to keep at bay.

The sound of his tiny radio recaptured his attention. The beat of a Rock tune bounced off the wall of the small space. What a coincidence. Henry sunk back into the past. By his late teens Henry had convinced himself his father had been a partisan. Was it not much better than calling him a drunk or a gambler? And what else could explain his long absences? Like father, like son. When the O'Connors asked him if he wanted in, he did not hesitate.

The bell rang in a distant present. Henry opened his eyes. Bang-up time was over and he was ready to seek his latest target, the Jihadi Kamal.

* * *

"She was very keen to speak with us," Pole said leaning against the coffee machine. "She works at the National Portrait Gallery so it's close but, still, she really wants to tell you what happened to Felipe, her boyfriend two years ago – I mean according to her." Andy nodded.

Pole entered the room and the young woman stood up nervously. Her face looked swollen. The tea in front of her had not been touched. Pole smiled kindly and put down a fresh cup.

"I am DCI Jonathan Pole. You have spoken to DC Todd. Thank you for coming at such short notice and I am sorry we have to speak to you about Mr Martinez again."

Anna-Maria Sanchez shook her head, a few curls had escaped her tight bun, but she did not bother to replace them. "It's fine Inspector. I would do anything for the Met to reopen the file." Her voice was firm and had an edge, someone used to speaking in public perhaps, Pole thought.

"I am afraid I can't promise anything."

"But if something new comes up?"

"You have my word. I will look into this again."

Anna-Maria breathed deeply and held the air in for a few seconds. She took a sip of tea and started. "This position at GL had been a dream come true for Felipe. No one in his family had ever gone to uni before him, let alone land a job in the City at one of the largest banks. And before you ask, yes he was stressed, but he had been under no illusions when he got the job. These guys were never going to make it easy for a poor kid to join their ranks." Her fist clenched the plastic cup she was holding even tighter.

"You mean he was..." Pole thought about the right word. "– mentally prepared."

She nodded.

"How about the nootropics?"

"He said they would help his brain. We argued and after that he never mentioned them again."

"But?" Pole asked kindly.

Anna-Maria sighed. "He slept less and less. He said he had to keep up with the demands of his bosses."

"You know I have to ask my next question, don't you?"

"Any other drugs?" Her eyes narrowed and she clenched her fist again. "I am not going to lie to you," Anna-Maria said avoiding Pole's eyes. "We smoked a bit of weed but I swear to you, Inspector, I swear to you, we never did anything else." The despair in her eyes rattled Pole. She believed it, whether she was right or not.

"But a toxicology report does not lie," Pole spoke without pushing. "And I can't explain why or how. But Felipe would never have taken LSD, never."

Pole's mobile buzzed in his pocket "Would you like to take a moment?"

Anna-Maria opened her bag to fish out a tissue.

Pole took his mobile out of his pocket and read his message, keeping the phone underneath the table – one line from Nancy.

The room disappeared around him. An eerie silence surrounded him. He must not yield. He must finish the interview. He must take the risk of losing her.

* * *

The prison-standard shirt was still hanging on the back of his chair. Henry slipped it on and was already opening the door of his cell when a familiar silhouette walked past. Three guards were following the new con who was replacing the Cell 10 suicide. The slow walk, the bulk of the body, made Henry freeze. Ronnie Kray was moving to 10.

He steeled himself and stopped inside his own door. Henry rolled his shoulders, moved his head around. The palms of his hands had become moist. He rubbed them on his trousers. He walked out of his cell a full six foot three tall. Big K was out as well, his body leaning against the corridor's balustrade. Everybody on the wing had slowed their pace and everyone was watching the well-rehearsed ritual. Kray had put his box down. He was waiting, arms crossed over his chest, legs apart, a man who would not be dislodged that easily. One of the guards was doing a final check of the cell whilst the other two waited.

Kray was moving his head around, taking his time to survey his surroundings.

"Come on Ronnie, in you go," said one of the guards.

Ronnie ignored him for long enough to create what he wanted amongst the three guards.

Restlessness – no, fear.

Kray slowly bent down and picked his box up. His head turned as he did so to meet Henry's eyes. He kept looking into them until he had reached the door and as he was about to disappear, he winked. And there was nothing friendly about it.

* * *

Nancy was facing Victoria Embankment when she spotted the image of Pole's tall frame appear as a reflection in the bay window of Scotland Yard's foyer. In the reflection of her own face, she saw anger and pain. A sight she did not want anyone to see except perhaps Pole. His hand landed cautiously on her shoulder and when she turned Pole's expression changed, his face dropped slightly, his eyes searching her features.

"I know I am mighty pissed off with you, Jonathan Pole, but I am also too sad to take it out on you."

"What you need is a very large cup of good honest tea and a proper talk," was all Pole could say.

"No, what I need is you answering your bloody phone when I leave umpteen messages or even a reply to my texts."

"I know – point taken, and I do apologise," Pole's shoulders had dropped forward slightly. Not a sign of contrition but that of a tall man eager to listen and share the burden of pain.

They reached his office in silence, and he opened the door, making way for her to enter first. Pole moved the pile of documents sitting on the only chair facing his desk, but Nancy chose the window.

"You do remember William, don't you?"

Pole nodded.

"I have known William Noble since my King's College London days."

"Not Sorbonne then?"

"Not Sorbonne. I did a Law Masters at KCL." Nancy shivered, still facing the window. "As you might recall, William is a very senior civil servant, works at the Treasury," Nancy's voice trailed. She thought of Paula. Nancy turned back to face Pole. "He has been hit by a van."

Pole remained silent. The connection to his case would be made shortly but the word Treasury had already created a link for Pole to ponder on. Pole took a seat and invited Nancy to do so. She hesitated as small bubbles of anger still shook her slender frame. Pole took it in. He understood pain. A lifetime at the Met showed you an endless supply of it. Nancy moved slowly to the empty chair, drawn to the comfort Pole's presence was offering.

"Let me get us some tea. I think this is going to take some time."

Her cup of tea was empty. Nancy had finished telling Pole about her conversation with William. Pole had not interrupted and had been taking copious notes. Pole clenched his fist a few times. Something was troubling him.

"Without wanting to state the obvious, William's story validates Henry's hunch regarding LIBOR." Nancy said.

"I have not been idle and have done a bit of digging myself," said Pole lifting a file stuffed with press articles and other research documents. He carefully extracted a piece. "There was an article published in *The Wall Street Journal* in 2008. It was largely ignored by pretty much everybody that should have taken notice. A very good piece of investigatory journalism."

Pole handed it over to Nancy. She read without stopping and at the end released a small sigh. Pole was finally considering the impact of a large-scale manipulation of the LIBOR benchmark on Gary Cook and Tom Hardy's strange suicides. She straightened up a little, ready to deliver her understanding of the situation.

"Anything new on your side then? The tox reports? The background checks?"

Pole smiled perhaps a little too broadly. She had turned on the charm, a sharp mind in an attractive woman – irresistible. The unhappy meeting seemed a distant memory now. Nancy had been wounded by the attempt on her friend's life and Pole's silence.

"On the ball as ever. Gary Cook was certainly taking a lot of little pills: mostly good old-fashioned amphetamines though, for performance enhancement. The guy was obsessed with boxing and no longer a spring chicken. But more interestingly he was also into something called nootropics. I gather it was the latest addition to his performance enhancement programme."

"Nootropics. You mean the drugs used by some of the Silicon Valley app developers to enhance their brain function? It's not so new by the way."

Pole raised an impressed eyebrow.

"No, Jonathan, I do not need any form of drug to enhance an already more than highly performing brain."

"Yep, I can vouch for that," Pole said wryly. "I am in conversation with the Drug Squad; we need to find the supplier. Both Cook and Hardy used nootropics, from the same batch. Can't be a coincidence."

"Hang on, what are you saying?" Nancy frowned. "Are you saying the pills killed Gary? Or that they pushed him to jump and Tom to commit suicide too?"

"Not really but I need to be sure we are not missing anything. For a start, poisoning takes time to prove unless it's a very high dose and a very well-known substance. More importantly, the background checks have thrown us some curveballs."

Nancy clenched her jaw. "It had better be good, otherwise..."

Pole interrupted by extending his hand and taking Nancy's. His touch was warm and firm, yet soothing. "Let me finish. Then you can get mad at me – again."

Pole told Nancy all he knew about the unlikely suicide of Felipe Martinez at the fateful GL party, and the interview of his girlfriend. "She is adamant," Pole finished. "Felipe would never have used hard drugs – certainly not LSD."

Nancy frowned. "LSD? The Martinez tox report showed a high dose?"

"Enough to be detected and deemed the key factor, why?"

"Before nootropics were invented, the start-ups tech gurus used LSD as a mind-enhancing substance. I am talking over twenty years ago and am also talking very small doses. But in a small quantity LSD is supposed to have the same effect as nootropics, according to these techies – enhanced creativity, focus."

"How small is small?" Pole asked dubious.

"Maybe one tenth of a recreational dose, and not every day – and how do I know about it? One of my clients was a user – got him to become an excellent hacker."

They both paused. Pole slowly released Nancy's hand and she slumped back into the chair.

"Fine, I follow, but Gary's tox report, even in prelim form, would have spotted LSD, I presume, and anyway why would Gary go for an illicit drug when he can have access to legal nootropics?" Pole said breaking the silence.

"And you said Edwina was at this party?"

"She was, although I am not yet sure how relevant that is."

Nancy inhaled deeply. "And what is your view, Jonathan? Does it introduce another lead?"

Pole smiled. "Thank you for keeping an open mind. We may be looking at a drug deal gone wrong although…"

Nancy closed her eyes, her eyebrows strained and almost touching. "You mean someone flogging LSD rather than nootropics?"

"That would fit the Martinez case and perhaps that of Cook. No, I have just made one assumption which I need to check."

"In any case all this does not fit so well with Tom Hardy," Nancy cut in.

"And it does not explain William," finished Pole. He too could keep an open mind.

Nancy opened her eyes and stood up, moving towards the window once more.

"We are missing something."

"We are missing the supplier."

Nancy moved back to Pole's desk.

"But if we abandon the suicide theory, replacing nootropics with LSD might work well. Taking too many nootropics might not agree with you but it's not going to have the same effect as forcing the dose on LSD."

"That's an interesting idea but we still don't know whether the increased dose is accidental or criminal," Pole said. "Assuming I go along with criminal intent, Gary gets supplied with a new performance little pill that is a low dosage LSD and…" Pole waited.

"And it provides an opportunity for control either by creating addiction or…" Nancy stalled. "Perhaps worse?"

"But—" Pole leant forward against his desk. "Gary must have trusted the person who fed him this new drug, and if it is his regular supplier he would have had a whole batch to sell – the drug squad might have had wind of this. I'll check."

Nancy remained silent.

"You don't agree?"

"Oh, I do. Gary is not going to buy his drugs from a kid out of a North London estate. He buys quality consistently if he is going down that route."

Pole pursed his lips. Good point.

"I think he knows the supplier of the LSD really well and I think this supplier has not told him about the content of this new drug."

"Something he has not tried before but that he is willing to try because it's supposed to give much better performance?" Pole asked. "Gary is not the sort of man that is going to risk damaging his mind. He is after maximum effect to increase his potential, if he has just lost his job. He wants to remain top dog. So, he seeks something that supposedly will work better for him."

"Or he spirals downwards and takes one little pill too many," Pole said.

"If he does not know it is LSD light, maybe. And yet that would make him very reckless with his health. Not in character and, as you may recall, I know what he is capable of at my own expense. Remember, I lost a case against him."

"People change," Pole tried, fidgeting with a small elastic band that was lying on his desk.

"Not Gary."

"Are you trying to lead me where I am not yet prepared to go?" Nancy nodded.

"What is still a leap of faith – from suicide to homicide, with intent."

"You mean murder – a completely plausible line of enquiry that you should not discard."

"Because now we have a motive," Pole added drumming his fingers on his desk. "The manipulation of LIBOR."

"Correct." Nancy's voice had an irritated edge she could not control. Pole was pulling a piece of paper from underneath another precariously balanced pile of documents when his phone rang. His face darkened – Marsh was calling, not via his PA but directly. He hesitated but let the voicemail kick in.

Nancy read his face. "Is it?"

"Marsh? Yes, he will want an update," Pole said, dismissive. "I'll go when I am ready." Pole drummed his fingers on the side of his desk. "What is your take on Tom Hardy then?"

"Collusion. I think Tom was the intermediary or one of the intermediaries between William and Gary."

"William speaks to Tom Hardy, Head of the BBA, because the BBA fixes, I mean establishes, LIBOR daily. It's his role. Tom Hardy finds a trusted trader who can follow through because..."

"He has already done it on a much smaller scale and he is one of the submitters of LIBOR quotes at his bank GL."

"Speculation on the first assumption but correct on the second," Pole said with an approving nod. "And, more importantly, because Gary and Tom have both worked at GL. Tom would want to speak to someone he trusts."

"That's right and someone who has the ear of senior management at the bank too."

"OK," Pole said. "But from what I remember. LIBOR calculation involves quite a few banks."

"True, but if Gary has already moved the benchmark in the past, he will know who to speak to and how it can be done."

Pole waited a moment. He was wavering whether he was willing to follow Nancy along her train of thoughts, Henry would be the surest expert.

"Jonathan."

"OK, but where is the evidence?"

"You know who can help you with this don't you?"

Pole gave a short grunt. "But who truly benefits?"

"You mean in whose interest is it to see these two dead?"

"Two bankers dead. I am sure I can line up a number of willing participants."

"Very funny. Besides, you don't really mean that," Nancy replied casting a dark eye towards Pole.

"I don't mean it but I still have a point. My reading leads me to believe that billions of dollars, or even sterling, are at stake. People will lose their businesses, their homes – the usual abomination."

Nancy paused. "I am not so sure. Because we speak of a low-bowling of LIBOR, so it means the rate of interest that LIBOR represents becomes cheaper for the banks." Nancy let the question hang in the air – only one person could answer with confidence, and it was Henry. "But whatever the outcome, I don't think it will be coming from one of the people ultimately affected."

"Why the hell not?"

"Because it's too soon, because it's targeting a small number of people at the highest of levels. The people who usually get away with it. My intuition tells me it is all about keeping that story quiet rather than a punishment for the damage it might create."

"I do trust that intuition of yours, Nancy, but I can't bring it as evidence," Pole said kindly.

"Targeting Gary for manipulating the benchmark, OK. Possibly Tom because he heads the BBA that accepted underestimated numbers without exercising due care, maybe. But William? No one could have suspected Whitehall."

"That's more like it. And why do I need Henry when I have you?" Pole asked, attempting to tease.

"Jonathan, I am not in the mood."

Pole's reply was silenced by the sound of Nancy's phone, indicating there was a text waiting. "It's Paula." Nancy snatched her mobile. "William is out of surgery and in intensive care." She read aloud. "The prognosis is bleak, but he is alive." Pole stood up and reached Nancy. He put a comforting hand on her shoulder. Nancy laid her hand on his and squeezed hard. Her elegant almond eyes had lost a little of their spark.

"I am going to… powder my nose. I won't be a moment."

Nancy soon reappeared with two cups of tea. A drop of water had landed on her jet- black hair. It coursed down her face. She walked to the window once more and leaned against it. Pole's office was high enough to make out the line of trees in St James's Park.

Pole joined her at the window, their reflections distinct in he glass. She handed him his cup. They drank in silence, appreciating this simple moment of peace. No need to speak to feel at ease. Nancy looked at her watch. It was nearly midday.

"How about Henry?" Nancy asked finally turning an exhausted face to Pole.

"Let me do a little more digging and I will also keep William's story in mind," Pole added.

Nancy's face relaxed a little. "Good, because William certainly believed LIBOR was the reason why something may happen to him." Pole reached out for Nancy's arm. "I know William is not paranoid. I take him seriously." Pole squeezed gently and let go. "And to prove that I do I will send a couple of armed guards to look after him."

Nancy managed a smile and moved to leave. She stopped before reaching the door that Pole was about to open.

"What did you mean a moment ago when you said you had to check on one of your assumptions?"

"Let me come back to you when I have thought about it a little more. It's all about what goes into a routine tox report and what does not. You have enough on your plate though."

Nancy did not protest. Pole gathered she too had a little more digging to do.

Chapter Fourteen

Nancy haled a cab on her way to meet Eddie. She was at the centre of a hurricane and the eye of the storm was only a brief reprieve before it lashed out again. Everything was still in a state of flux. She took her BlackBerry out of her bag, made sure she had not missed a call.

Nothing. She pushed her head against the headrest of the vehicle – unbearable. She lifted her BlackBerry from her lap and scrolled mechanically through some of her old messages.

Nancy stopped on the other text Edwina had sent and that Nancy had only spotted late in the morning.

Breakfast, 8.00am?

She pondered on the intention behind the meeting and why the hurry.

She didn't need to be suspicious about everyone, but Nancy also knew better. Her strength, the quality that had propelled her to the pinnacle of her legal career so fast was just that, the ability to ask the harsh question that even she did not want an answer to.

Sorry to have missed breakfast. Couldn't do breakfast but could do lunch at Nelly... make it 12.00?

Perfect, make it Barbican. The reply was instant.

Nancy raised an eyebrow. Nelly had been a favourite for years and so much closer to work for Eddie. She wondered why the favourite place had lost its appeal.

Nancy wished she was sat back on the sofa of her lounge. She had created warm and peaceful surroundings with the understated aesthetic that so characterised her. Henry had succumbed to the atmosphere too, him usually so guarded had finally spoken to her about Belfast and his childhood there.

The large abstract paintings that hung on the walls retained their fascination. They could still uplift her even after all these years. She had bought her first Rothko years ago. A present to herself to celebrate her elevation – Silk at the age of thirty-five. The youngest barrister ever to have been made QC. She was not living in her penthouse then. In fact, the painting she had bought was so large that it would hardly fit on the wall of her very small flat.

"What a ride it's been so far," Nancy murmured.

Her home was her sanctuary. She absent-mindedly moved her focus towards a piece of paper that looked out of place on her coffee table. The letter she had received from Hong Kong was still open, carelessly marked by the stain from one of Nancy's mugs.

It was unanswered as yet, begging to be dealt with. Was it too much to be delving into the past today? The letter had curled up slightly, an attempt to fold itself back, to mask the message that had woken her distant past up. The nagging memories had resurfaced not because of the letter but because of a taste, that of pepper. Of course, the letter had been a trigger. She couldn't deny it.

Nancy had ordered peppercorns from the Sichuan province in China and they had been delivered on the same day as the letter. Her father used to tell stories about their provenance, and she loved the way he spoke about the most beautiful city on earth, Chengdu, and how the Chinese Emperor prized this extraordinary spice way before black pepper overtook the world.

She is sitting in his artist's studio – large pots of paints, traditional brushes and ink challenged by the more contemporary look of hardened brushes, sticks or simple rags to apply colour. She is only seven ,, crossed-legged on the floor, elbows on knees and hands supporting her head. She is looking up at him, her father, this tall and elegant man in his Mao collared shirt, unbuttoned and covered in paint.

"Not now," Nancy moaned. She opened her eyes and turned her face ever so slightly to see where she was. The cab was stuck at Smithfield Market. She stopped it and got out. A short walk to reach the Barbican would do her good.

* * *

He had not been followed to his Club; Brett was sure of it. Last night's tail must have been sufficient. He had led the young man straight to his Belgravia apartment. The Sheik knew where he lived. This was the way they would do business, once in – never out.

Breakfast was being served late for the members requesting it and his MI6 contact was keen to meet again.

Unusual, Steve liked to space his visits to remain unnoticed.

Brett did not feel *well over his head* as MI6-Steve had put to him in their late-night conversation, but Brett feared the moment was arriving faster than he had anticipated. It was fine to inform and be used as a data mule. He knew the drill. He knew the pitfalls. But people trafficking for the Jihadis was another ball game altogether.

Brett looked at his watch. He had arrived early, and his contact was now late. Unusual too. He was tired of waiting and raised his hand to order. The waiter was arranging Brett's breakfast on the table when Steve arrived. Steve asked for tea and a full English breakfast. The waiter disappeared promptly.

Steve looked tired, bloodshot eyes, hair not quite managing to look tidy. Brett could have sworn he had not changed his shirt.

"Any news?" Brett asked, not hiding his displeasure.

"Yes. You've hit the jackpot. Well done," Steve answered.

"Is that supposed to be funny?"

"Nope, just fact. By the way, you did the right thing last night. Got the tail to follow you to your flat. Good man." Steve grabbed a piece of toast as the waiter arranged breakfast on their table and wolfed it down. By the look of it he had not had dinner either.

"Uncomfortable, but I assume that is what you meant when you said I had to let them come close to me."

"Correct. Now your next move. You'll be asked to facilitate the transfer into the UK of one of their high-ranking operatives. We want him to come in."

"Do you know why?"

"Not your problem at this stage. You get him in. We do the rest."

"And what if there is more?"

"Such as?"

"Armaments, logistics. I don't know."

"We talk – at this stage nothing is off limits."

Brett's spoon stopped in mid-air. The boiled egg the waiter had brought to the table remained intact. "Are you serious? Nuclear? Sarin gas?"

"Absolutely." Steve was tucking into his sausages with gusto.

"As long as I inform you."

"As long as you inform me."

"Can we stop playing silly arses for now?" Brett asked, cracking his egg open with lethal precision.

"I've never been more serious." Steve answered. Brett eyed him closely. He was indeed serious.

"You know and I know how this is going to end up," Brett said, without waiting for Steve to protest. "This guy is going to place a bomb somewhere high profile or people are going to get shot. It would be good if you were to indulge me for once. I'm the one risking my skin here."

"Brett, you know the rules. The less you know the better it is. Precisely because you are putting your neck on the line. If these guys decide to ruffle you up a little, trust me, you don't want to have anything to say to them."

Brett finished buttering his toast and took a bite. The toast was a little hard to swallow. He wiped his mouth ostentatiously with his napkin, took a sip of tea.

"That's a lot of bull – if I may say so."

Steve attacked a second piece of bacon. He chewed thoughtfully. "Very nice bacon."

Steve took a mouthful of tea, sat back and crossed his legs. "Do you know Henry Crowne?"

Brett's fair complexion turned a little paler. "What has he got to do with this? You know full well I once was his art dealer and lost a lot of money because of him. And for the record, I obviously despise this individual, this—"

"Northern Irish peasant," Steve completed, holding his cup of tea on the arm of the chair in which he sat. "But there is a connection."

"Oooh, I see. The IRA connection."

"For a toff, you have got some brains, you know." Steve moved forward to finish his breakfast. And Brett took no offence. He did not care. He needed more information. Question was how to get it? "Why the IRA connection?"

"Now Brett, you're gonna have to let those little grey cells of yours work doubly hard."

"Have they selected me because I know Crowne?"

"That *is* a much better question – possibly."

Brett finished his cup of tea. Poured a second cup, a splash of milk. "But surely they must know that Crowne and I—"

"Never hit it off. Don't think they care. You know him and for their purposes that's all they want. You know how to approach him. You know what makes him tick."

This time Brett's face remained blank.

"You sold him the best part of his antiques collection – despite the fact you hated each other's guts. That takes some doing."

Brett noticed the pool of tea in his saucer. One of the waiters had also noticed and his cup was replaced immediately.

"What do you anticipate they want to do with Crowne?" Brett's voice wobbled almost imperceptively; being part of Henry Crowne's future demise had a delicious appeal.

"Not sure yet. I spent last night going through some fresh transcripts of comms exchanges. His name popped up a few times."

Brett straightened up. His mind was racing. He sat back again and felt a patch of sweat between his shoulders.

"You wondering whether you can deliver?"

"I presume I can if you're asking me," Brett replied sharply.

"Wrong answer. *They* think you can deliver. We are simply happy to tag along. Don't disappoint *them*," Steve said with a grin. "I don't intend to."

Brett turned around, attracting the attention of a waiter. He would sign the bill to his Club account. Breakfast was over whether Steve liked it or not.

* * *

On my way. Pole pressed the send button to warn Marsh's PA as he headed for Marsh's office. He did not need his boss barging onto his floor again, disrupting his investigation.

Marsh's stocky frame overshadowed Denise as he was standing behind her, his index finger following a line written on the screen and not to his liking by the sound of it. Pole stalled a little and coughed discreetly.

"Pole – finally." Marsh narrowed his eyes and moved into his office without another word.

"Sorry sir, new evidence in the double-suicide case," Pole replied as he closed the door behind him.

"It'd better be good." Marsh sat heavily in his large leather chair and waved for Pole to sit at the desk. No comfy armchair in the corner of the office as was usual for more relaxed conversations. Marsh was playing it very formal, and Pole did not care.

Pole launched into the Martinez case, the LSD angle, the search for a possible link between the two cases using the Met's latest CCTV face-recognition software.

"You think of a drug deal gone wrong then?" Marsh interrupted. "A possible lead that can't be ignored, sir." Pole enjoyed the moment. He had Marsh where he wanted him

"What does Ms Wu think?" Marsh had moved his chair forward, his forearms resting now on his desk.

"She is also keeping an open mind."

Marsh nodded. "Anything else I should be aware of ?"

"Nothing that is demonstrably relevant." Pole winced inside. If Whitehall was involved the pressure on the enquiry would reach a completely new level. And if he needed Henry out of HSU Belmarsh that needed to take precedent over the political elite seeking to cover their arses.

Pole rose slowly from his chair. Marsh's fingers fidgeted with the different Montblanc pens on his desk. He wanted Pole to stay but why?

"I am expecting a more prompt response next time." Marsh replaced the pens in their holders. "If you need me to support you, I need to anticipate."

"Absolutely understood, sir."

* * *

The Barbican cafeteria was buzzing. The smell of coffee and baked food made Nancy's mouth water. She had not eaten a decent meal since she last saw her friend. Their leisurely lunch felt so far away and yet the very same Eddie was waving at her from a corner table well situated near the bay window.

Nancy waved back, avoiding the suited men and women who were negotiating their way to their own tables laden with their lunch trays.

"I hope I am not imposing. You look tired." Edwina said, moving forward to kiss Nancy's cheek. "There was quite a queue, so I bought something for both of us."

"Nonsense. I have had a rather unpleasant couple of days. A spot of lunch with a friend is exactly what I need, *n'est ce pas*?"

Nancy sat in front of Edwina, poured some tea and took a bite. The hot baguette was warm and tasty, the sweetness of its ingredients gave her a little taste of hope. But Edwina also looked unusually pale. Her make-up could no longer conceal the dark blue rings under her eyes.

Nancy made idle chit-chat, reluctant to engage her friend on the thorny issue of the Governor's succession. Edwina listened to Nancy, opened her sandwich, spread some mustard on the first piece. Distracted, she let it reach her fingertips. She swore silently, getting up abruptly to find spare napkins. The scene was out of kilter: the Barbican cafeteria, Edwina's awkwardness, Nancy's own uneasiness. The sudden shift was palpable. Nancy took note.

Edwina apologised as she sat back down.

"How is your plan going, *ma chére amie*?" Nancy volunteered. "On track, of course. I had another chat with the Chancellor of the Exchequer."

So their conversation was not about succession – intriguing. "Good. How about the markets?"

"Working on the next round of QE. Mervin is such a pussy footer," Edwina embarked on a passionate description of the process, her eyes shifting though, never quite making contact with Nancy's. She had picked up her BlackBerry several times, putting it down without looking at it. Nancy slowly put a hand on herso make her stop. She smiled a reassuring smile – tell me what is wrong it said in her most persuasive manner.

"What does Gabs think about this?" A question that always reminded Edwina herself she was not alone. But not today. Gabriel's name shocked. She clenched her fist, tried to grab her BlackBerry again, stopped.

"I don't know," she said. "He is acting strange."

"What do you mean?" Nancy frowned. "Do you think he no longer supports you?"

Edwina shook her head. She took a sip of tea, preparing to formulate her answer with caution.

"He sounds *too* keen?"

Nancy was taken aback by this unexpected statement, "It's an odd thing to say, Eddie..."

She did not have time to further query this most unexpected statement.

Her phone was ringing.

"Paula." Nancy's eyes shifted away from the room and Edwina. "They are moving him. He is conscious. He asked for you." Paula said.

"I am on my way." Nancy inhaled deep, closing her eyes for an instant.

"I am so sorry Eddie, but a very good friend of mine is in hospital. He was hit by a van yesterday. Anyway, I am not sure he is out of danger, yet. You will understand. I must go. He's asked to speak to me."

"Anybody I know?" Edwina asked without thinking.

"William Noble," Nancy said whilst rising to leave.

Edwina's face drained of colour. She dashed out of the door, just in time to be sick on the terrace.

Nancy grabbed a handful of paper napkins and rushed after her friend.

She guided Edwina to one of the chairs outside and helped her to sit down.

"Thank you." Edwina managed to articulate. "I didn't feel well this morning but thought I'd shaken it off."

"Shall I call a cab to take you home and call your husband?" Nancy asked.

Edwina shook her head vigorously. “No need, Nancy. I’m already feeling better, and I have too much to do. I’ll be fine.”

“If you are certain.”

“I am… just a stomach bug. Nothing more.”

Chapter Fifteen

Pole's half-eaten piece of sandwich had leaked a butter stain on the paper that contained it. It would soon reach one of the documents it lay on. Pole finished the unappetising bread. He would soon have to speak to Marsh about William before Nancy did. He had seen the determination in her eyes. And yet he could not ignore the Martinez lead.

Pole left his office and reached Andy's desk. He had been running the new identification software. A way of comparing and identifying faces from a large quantity of images.

"I got the software to run the images I was sent of the party where Martinez went to and that of the party at which Cook jumped... and I have a number of hits: a few women and one man."

"Who are they?"

"Not sure yet, Guv. I have just got the answer."

"Come on, you're the tech genius around here," Pole said with an encouraging nudge.

"Will be on your desk within the hour." Andy adjusted his thick glasses and smiled.

"And have you finished the report you were writing with Nurani on the use of nootropics? She said you had discovered evidence some could cause psychopathic episodes."

Andy fumbled with his glasses once more.

"That's OK. I don't need it in full just yet. Just want your verdict."

"Well, I extended the search to include LSD as we discussed and it is possible to achieve an enhanced cognitive state with a small amount of LSD. You've got to be careful of course but the effects would be similar, except that with the nootropics you sort of can exceed the dose without too much damage. With LSD – well you know."

"Yep, I am old enough to know enough about LSD," Pole said, prompting a wide-eyed Andy to fumble even more with his glasses.

"Not as a user, if that's what's worrying you," Pole replied tersely. Andy opened his mouth but thought better of it.

"Come on – spit it out."

"Guv, it's hypothetical and all."

"And?" Pole gestured, unusually impatient. "Unless the user did not know it was LSD." Pole was listening.

"If someone wanted to get a person to switch to LSD to mimic the effect of nootropic drugs that would work in small doses. Then it would be much easier to convince that person to increase the dosage. LSD is addictive. It's a typical addiction progression. And on a particular day, if that someone needed to be given a push. They just need to be encouraged to take a little extra or—"

"Hang on, Mister," Pole said putting his hands up to stop the flow.

Andy stopped dead, a rush of red that had started forming around his neck reached his entire face.

"So, it is true. LSD does work like a nootropic – at least in small quantities. Because it does 'feel' like a nootropic." Pole had not doubted Nancy but an unprompted confirmation by his team gave the idea more credibility.

Andy nodded.

"If I want to control someone or even get rid of someone and I know they are taking this LSD-substitute I do what?" Pole was moving his hand in a circle, as though kickstarting a process. "I increase the dose by putting that someone in a position where he might need a boost. Like an important event, with tough competitors or people you want to impress – and if that event is on a rooftop..."

Andy had just made the point Nancy was trying to make. Pole returned to his desk. "Hold on."

He yanked Cook's preliminary Toxicology Report from a pile of documents, found the page he wanted and ran his finger alongside the long list of drugs included in routine post-mortem toxicology. He came to the part he urgently wanted to consult – Cannabis, Cocaine, Narcotic analgesics (including morphine); no LSD testing.

He returned to Andy's desk, still holding Cook's report open. "Show me Hardy's tox report again." Andy called the report on screen and Pole scanned the report.

"No LSD testing either but surely it would have been identified, as a foreign substance sloshing around their bloodstream?"

"Not necessarily," Andy said slowly. "LSD is one of the most difficult drugs to detect in blood. It stays there two, three hours at most."

"You mean you can't trace it after that at all?"

"Not quite; it stays longer in urine samples."

"How much longer?" Pole said as he was already preparing to dial a number from his mobile.

"Three days, tops."

"Shit," Pole blurted. "Get to the lab now and speak to Yvonne. Ask her for a retest. Both Gary Cook and Tom Hardy. I'm calling her too."

Andy stood up like a jack-in-the-box, grabbed his mobile and started running. Yvonne's mobile was going to voicemail. Pole left an urgent message.

"Shit," Pole said again. He'd started writing a text to Yvonne when his mobile rang. Nancy's name came up on screen. This time he would take the call.

* * *

"Has he regained consciousness?" Pole was walking back to his office in long strides.

"Yes, for a short moment, and he asked to speak to me." Nancy replied.

"I see. But has he been transferred out of intensive care into a single room?"

Nancy's voice was muffled. He could hear she was trying to shelter it.

"He has and I fear he needs protection, Jonathan."

"And you know I agree so you should have a couple of armed officers on the premises very shortly."

"I don't want anything happening to him. He knows so much more than he let on and he is in real danger."

"I realise this, Nancy. I won't let you down." Pole scanned the open-plan office he was crossing for a sign of the person he now so wanted to speak to. Unsurprisingly, Nurani was not around.

"I am also sending you one of my team, young Andy."

"The young man who was working on Henry's case."

"The very same. Glad you remember him."

Pole walked into his office and started moving files around, his shoulder keeping his mobile stuck to his ear.

"Can you spare him?"

"I want him there when William wakes up. I need the name of the caller. And Nancy, don't go and do something daring."

"I am not a little wall flower, Jonathan. But I know my limits."

Pole smiled at the sound of indignation coming from the other end of the line.

"Tut, tut, tut. I know you too well. You might decide to tackle anyone who tries to get to William and that would not be a good idea."

"I'm sure I can find an implement or two to dissuade any intruder."

Pole's smile widened. She was responding to his tease, a good sign.

"In any case should you not be focusing on more important things, such as breaking the good news to Henry? I am ready to speak to him." Pole enjoyed Nancy's stunned silence, bade her goodbye and retrieved the file he was looking for from the pile of documents stashed on his desk. His LIBOR file was now impressive: news articles, extracts from financial publications, expert advice, searches on a number of relevant individuals involved in the calibration of the benchmark in London.

He had a solid case to present to the Home Secretary requesting Henry's temporary exeat from Belmarsh. How far he would involve him in the case was still largely undecided. Pole would not pre-judge. But having worked Henry's case a few years back he was in no doubt that if Henry put his formidable mind to work, he would bring the pieces of this financial puzzle together before anybody else could.

Pole found the form he needed online and started the request process. Marsh would back him up. At least one positive. Pole could have delegated but knew the pitfalls from having successfully extracted a convicted killer out to assist with another case.

He had received a lot of flak for it at the time. Another high-profile case in human trafficking that had left people dead. A case he reopened after establishing a connection between the trafficking of young Eastern European women and a string of suspicious property deals. Both cases had started with the discovery of a body, same MO and yet a man had confessed to the first murder. Marsh predecessor had been sceptical at the time, but the man Pole had trusted to do the right thing had come through and Pole had been vindicated.

Pole had the same the same hunch with Henry – atonement. It happened, more often than expected and Pole was willing to bet he was right.

His phone rang and Marsh's PA's name flashed on the screen.

"Denise, a good afternoon to you... Marsh not in a good mood."

"Well, do bring my email to his attention. It might cheer him up."

"I'll tell him to read it before he descends upon you."

Pole read his submission one last time. He was about to press the send button when a figure caught his eye. Nurani had just dropped by her desk. She still had her light mac on and was looking for Andy. She spoke to another colleague avoiding looking in Pole's direction.

Pole stared at her. She would notice his gaze in a minute. Time to have the conversation he had been waiting to have since yesterday.

Chapter Sixteen

Big K sat his massive body on the puny chair. His arms looked like a map of his personal history, tattoo after tattoo relating a story. Henry searched for his name amongst the cards stacked up in the box at his side.

"What are you gonna do about this Kamal bloke? You can't do nothing – right?" Big K whispered.

"I have a plan. I'm going to find out what he wants," Henry replied as he took the return book from Big K's hands.

Big K shook his head.

"Man, this is not wise."

"Why is that?" Henry wrote 'returned' in the ledger of the library card delivered to Kevin Kenneth Kendal. Henry was impressed by Big K's appetite for reading, from classics to sci-fi. "Anything else for you this time?"

"I mean it, man – if you get involved with these guys, there won't be any turning back."

Henry smiled and pushed a pen into Big K's hand. He signed the register and walked away still shaking his head.

Henry mechanically consulted the clock on the wall, subtracted five hours to calculate the time in New York, an old habit he found hard to lose. The trading floor had shaped who he was, had been part of him for far too long. It was ironic that what had put him in jail was a good old-fashioned money laundering scam. Granted, money laundering for the IRA. Still, none of the subprime rubbish that all large investment banks were peddling. He almost felt pride at the assured stance he had taken on the subject. How could he have been so right and yet so wrong about what mattered most to him?

Henry remembered with absolute clarity the first time Liam had asked him to help. Setting up a new vehicle, offshore, making the structure untraceable, a platform the IRA would use to route the funds they received from outside Ireland in particular the US and the UK.

The soft cap that was circulated in the pubs of Kilburn, gathering donations, was not meant for the Red Cross. Henry had not even questioned the request; of course, he would help. It had been what he had been waiting for. A way to belong, finally; a way to repay his best pals for years of friendship – he was part of that family.

A narrow figure sat in front of Henry, in the chair that Big K had just left and for a short moment Henry lost track of where he was.

Kamal was sitting still. His intense dark eyes blinked softly, and he moved forward slowly to ask his question.

"Which book do you recommend?"

"What makes you tick?" Henry replied, his blue eyes locking with Kamal's for an instant.

"The delivery of a perfectly elaborated idea."

Henry waited.

"The beauty of solving a complex equation and admiring the geometrical mosaics of the Grand Mosque of Mecca."

Henry's body tensed slightly, a muscle in his neck twitched, reminding him of the pain he had felt when the Paddington bomb exploded. The images Kamal was summoning had nothing to do with beauty; they spoke of hatred. The urge to grab Kamal's head and smash it onto the desk almost overwhelmed him. But Kamal had become part of a bigger plan. Henry had known the temptation would arise and he had prepared for it.

"Not a believer, mate," Henry replied sinking his nails into his left thigh with ferocity.

"I don't think it is true my friend. You are." Kamal's quiet determination sobered up Henry. Kamal was right. Henry had believed and despite all that had happened – the deceit, the sacrifice of all that had mattered to him – Henry still had hope.

"So, you are looking for a book about the philosophy of faith?" Henry said, sarcastic. Kamal smiled. The airy calm he displayed propelled Henry back to the Belfast of his youth when he had met the same sort of radical believer. Nothing would detract them from their missions. He had Liam and Bobby at his side then: Liam the pragmatist; Bobby the believer, the zealot.

"I have all I need for faith. Allah provides for those who seek. The Jihad is a way of life that needs to express—"

"You mean you need a way out of here," Henry interrupted. No speaking in riddles; they would come straight to the point or else Henry had no use for him.

"You like plain speaking, Henry?"

"Goes with my territory; your brother who worked at GL would understand."

"Plain speaking requires trust. Can you be trusted, Henry?"

Henry gave a short laugh. The prison officer looked in their direction. For the first time Kamal's composure floundered, a flash of anger showed in his eyes, receding abruptly to be replaced by the same inscrutable gaze.

"Look. You don't know me. I don't know you. I don't trust easily and I presume neither do you. But I think we both want the same thing. And you now need to choose a book, or the prison officer will start asking questions."

"I will take a book on the philosophy of faith then," Kamal replied with confident humour, "a little Nietzsche perhaps?"

"This is Belmarsh library, not Oxford," Henry replied. Kamal had scored unexpectedly a point.

"Well, Henry. What else do you have to offer?"

Henry plucked a small card from inside the index box and handed it over to Kamal.

"Please sign before you leave," Henry said a little louder than usual. The prison officer had materialised dangerously close to their table. Kamal looked at the title and a faint smile brushed his lips. He disappeared amongst the bookshelves.

Henry rearranged the cards again. A surge of energy ripped through his body, a sudden burst familiar and yet forgotten. He had felt it on the trading floor in times of turbulent markets, on the eve of closing the ridiculously large deals that had become his trademark.

The excitement of the chase, the taking of risk, the ruthless and clever assessment of who the opposition was. The certainty that he would, no matter what, win.

Henry's heart had started racing again yet his head remained cool. When Kamal reappeared, to sign the ledger, Henry hardly acknowledged him.

* * *

Edwina looked at her face in the mirror; she was still ashen white. She had splashed some water on her cheeks. Part of her make-up had rubbed off on the cuffs of her shirt. She looked a mess. What was happening to her? Like Alice in Wonderland, she was falling down a rabbit hole, but this time there appeared to be no bottom.

Nancy had left after Edwina had convinced her it was nothing, a stomach bug as she'd claimed. Nancy had accepted the explanation as she was on her way to St Thomas's Hospital. Her mind was racing thankfully in another direction. Edwina was still holding on to the sink. She thought of William and her stomach lurched again. She just managed to stop herself from throwing up again. It could no longer be a coincidence: Gary, Tom and now William.

She would be next. But why? And who would or could have known about the LIBOR manipulation? Tom and William would never blab, of that she was certain. Gary had always been the weak link, sacked from his job in the most unceremonious of fashions. The most stupid of mistakes – GL management must have known what Gary was up to. Then again, the takeover had diluted their influence. HXBK, the buyer of GL, had not discovered yet that Gary's desk was manipulating LIBOR. The questions why and who remained intact.

Edwina shook her head. It did not make sense. She straightened her skirt, rearranged her shirt and reapplied her make-up. It would have to do.

She had nearly reached her office when a hand on her shoulder startled her. Gabriel had materialised at her side without her noticing. "My God, Eddie. I hope you don't mind me saying, but you look dreadful," Gabriel said, his face showing genuine concern. Edwina rushed into her office, Gabriel in tow, He closed the door quickly.

"Something terrible happened. William, William Noble, has been run over." She tore at her jacket, shoving her bag underneath her desk. She ran a shaking hand through her short blonde hair. "This cannot be a coincidence. It's too much, too close, too..." Edwina was pacing down the length of her office. Her hands clasping the sides of her face, in a pose that closely resembled Munch's *The Scream*.

"Hang on, hang on," Gabriel replied. He walked over to her and grabbed her shoulders, forcing her to stop and face him. "Sit down, tell me what it's all about."

Edwina gave a disjointed account of the hit and run, the emergency operation, Nancy at St Thomas's.

"What do you mean, Nancy is involved?"

"She knows William very well – friends, old friends."

"Has he said anything then?"

"What do you mean?" Edwina sensed Gabriel's anxiety.

"Do you think he has said anything about...?" Gabriel's voice trailed.

"I don't know. If he has she's said nothing. She simply said he had been hit by a van."

"So, it could be an accident?"

"How can you say that?" Edwina shouted, shaking off Gabriel's grip and resuming her pacing. "It's impossible; don't you get it yet? Gary, Tom and now William. It's gonna be me next."

Gabriel stood still in amazement, a strange smile ran over his lips and then disappeared.

"It won't happen."

"Why?" Edwina felt her stomach churn again.

"OK. Sit down," Gabriel moved her to her desk. "Let's look at this rationally." He held his hand up before she could protest. "I know, not easy for you but easier for me. Still, by all accounts, I could also be in the frame, right?"

Edwina slumped in her chair.

"Who is... was the weakest link of all? Gary?" Edwina nodded, exhausted.

"Tom had contacted Gary?" Gabriel carried on without waiting for an answer. "Tom spoke to you, but why would he have disclosed your name to Gary? No reason and William spoke to you and Tom – but not to Gary."

"Wait. You're losing me," Edwina said, her face on fire. "Are you implying that Gary, who is the most obvious leak, would not have known I was involved?"

"Correct," Gabriel replied, clicking his fingers. "But so what? Explain."

"Well, if someone – and it is frankly a very big *if* – is after you because of – Gabriel was looking for the words – The market arrangement we facilitated, it would have had to be leaked to that someone and Gary is the most obvious person so..." Gabriel said slowly, allowing Edwina to gather her thoughts.

"I still don't buy it. There are quite a few people who need to be involved to alter LIBOR in the way we discussed. Gary would have had to speak to his regular brokers and other traders. You don't decrease your LIBOR quote by 50bps without a backup story. And we are the backup story."

Gabriel's face reddened a little. He mechanically touched the scar on his face that looked angrier than usual. Edwina sagged back in her chair. Why did he act so pig-headed today? They both were a target, as simple as that.

"But Gary is not an idiot. He would have selected the right people, maybe not even mentioned us." Gabriel objected.

"How can you say that? Gary would have mentioned he was low-bowling LIBOR because the Bank of England had asked him to. And he would have also let his CEO know. This is too big to carry on your own, even for a tough guy like Gary."

Gabriel's silence was ominous. He knew she was right.

"Anyway, I really must consider whether I need to go to the police."

"No don't." Gabriel jumped towards her desk.

"I know Gabs. You're worried about your reputation, but no one needs to know you were involved. If I go down, I go down on my own."

"Eddie, Eddie – slow down, will you? You are so goddamn close to getting the big job. I just can't bear the thought of you throwing it away."

Edwina remained silent. Gabriel had as ever pressed the right button. Ambition swelled in her chest, a warm glow that could dissolve even the best resolution. Edwina James-Jones, Governor of the Bank of England. It had a certain ring to it.

She dropped her head in her hands. Raised it after a couple of minutes, looking at Gabriel with sudden suspicion.

"Why are you so sure it won't be me next?"

"Because it does not make sense. You're two steps removed."

"I don't know. I don't know," Edwina said mechanically.

Gabriel shrugged. "Just don't make any rash decision without telling me, OK?" Gabriel insisted. "OK?"

"Fine, I will."

Gabriel left and closed the door of her office. Edwina felt a bead of sweat rolling down her face. She grabbed a tissue and dabbed her forehead. For the first time since she'd started working with Gabriel she felt out of sync with him. She was on her own.

* * *

"He only regained consciousness briefly," Nancy said softly. Pole and she were in the corridor outside William's room. Her voice trembled and she grabbed Pole's arm to steady herself. The shock of seeing William's body hooked up to so many monitors that beeped and hummed, tubes sticking in and out of his body, feeding, extracting, keeping him alive – it had almost been too much.

"And when he wakes up again he may be able to tell us who called him. Paula and Andy are at his side. He *is* well looked after.

Nancy nodded. The deep lines etched on her forehead seemed permanently frozen there. She walked a few paces to find a seat. Pole wondered whether he should send her home but recalled the Nancy who had so vigorously defended Henry a few years ago. She would see this through.

"Don't you have someone to visit, *ma chére amie*?" Pole said with a smile.

"I know. I have missed the morning visits. But I will manage one in the afternoon. The good part of being Henry's legal adviser."

"Is he expecting you?"

"He knows I am coming but not why."

"He knows. My request was sent an hour ago. Belmarsh will organise a bit of a surprise visit. You don't get out of Belmarsh for a jolly that easily." Pole was allowing Henry a little rope for his trip outside prison, but it would be very little rope. Pole understood why Henry had argued that carrying out controversial research on LIBOR manipulation inside Belmarsh was not a good idea, but he also suspected there was an agenda. "One condition to Henry's trip into the free world."

"Which I am not going to like, *n'est-ce pas*?" Nancy replied with a fatigued yet attractive smile.

"*Peut-être pas.* I need to be absolutely certain Henry is not going to do something stupid." Pole put his hands up before Nancy could reply. "Do not tell me his escape has not crossed your mind. Charlie, his former driver, visits him regularly; Charlie has contacts. Promise me you will let me know if you suspect anything."

"You'll be the first one to know. The one thing Henry is not going to do is escape, for as long as I am his legal adviser it won't happen." Nancy's verve surprised Pole. Good to know she was on his side. "You're surprised, I can see it, but really you shouldn't be. Henry being on the loose with a number of IRA connections is not what anybody needs, including Henry himself, although he probably doesn't see it that way."

They had walked away and found a few free seats in a waiting area. The faces around them spoke of anxiety and pain. Nancy turned paler again and she locked her arm into Pole's, moving him along a little more.

"And what made you change your mind if I may ask?"

Pole looked surprised but understood almost instantly it was not a trick question.

"Andy came up with some interesting details about the use of LSD and—"

"It confirmed what I was saying," Nancy added without joy.

This was not a point-scoring exercise. Pole tightened his arm around hers. "The problem with LSD is that it does not stay in the blood for very long, but we might get there in some other ways."

Nancy nodded. "What about Felipe Martinez?"

"There is perhaps a connection but not yet sure what." Nancy stopped and sat down.

Pole's phone was on silent, but the buzz indicated that someone was trying to reach him. He cast an eye at the screen. Superintendent Marsh's PA was calling him. The big man wanted a word, again. Was Marsh getting cold feet about Henry?

Chapter Seventeen

The morning visit started at 9.15am. Henry expected Charlie would be as always punctual as long as the prison officers did not exercise extra zeal. Charlie had done time and once relied on visits to keep him sane too. He had not been in Henry's league of course, never a Cat A prisoner, but still an armed robbery that had gone wrong and turned bloody. He had not killed the woman, but his brother had. He was driving the car. How stupid. He had barely turned eighteen.

Henry heard the third prison officer call his name. Yet another set of doors to go through, yet another check. Seven in all.

Charlie was already sitting at the table when Henry arrived. He rose. Henry smiled his crooked carefree smile, all for show of course. Charlie had guessed it and that made it somehow acceptable. Both men chatted for a while: the jazz club, Charlie's favourite topic; the fallout from GL's botched takeover, Henry's favourite topic. Charlie knew so many of the senior management team from having chauffeured them around from one meeting to another, most of them to be told they would not be joining the combined bank.

Henry relaxed in the chair as Charlie fed him some tasty morsels. Ted Barnes, the useless little prick who had dared succeed him at the head of his team, had finally met an inevitable fate – the dreaded black bin bag treatment. Five minutes to clear his desk, escorted by HR and some security guards: just enough time to dump his gym kit into it and the Hermes scent his wife had bought him for his promotion. Henry's pulse was on a rollercoaster, triggered by the names of the bankers who would be meeting their sorry end next.

His breathing finally eased off. Reconnecting with the outside world proved complicated. Charlie had warned him. Prison was a slow alienator. It removed people from the reality of the outside world. And Henry was no longer at the centre of City news. How much had changed in his absence? A lot he suspected.

Charlie returned to the subject of the Vortex Jazz Club and Henry seized the opportunity.

"Do you remember what you said to me the evening we both spent at the club before my arrest?"

Charlie's face went blank for a moment. His hand moved naturally in front of his mouth to shield a cough.

"You mean – leave the country?" Charlie's hand stayed in place.

His voice had changed to a low, steady tone that punched guts.

"You said you had contacts." Henry rubbed his chin, using a similar masking technique.

Charlie's eyes searched Henry's, an uncomfortable gaze that evaluated the weight of a man. He kept drilling slowly. "I know it's tough in here for a man like you, but you really have to think this through. It will pass."

"I know you did your time and have done brilliantly well at putting it all behind you, Charlie." Henry meant it. Charlie nodded. He was proud of that.

"But something has happened inside, and I need to be ready for what comes next," Henry continued with confidence.

"You've lost me there," Charlie replied, focused on the prison officer who was looking their way.

"I need to understand what it takes to leave Belmarsh."

"Look," Charlie said trying not to lose his cool. "For starters we are talking Belmarsh. And second, Belmarsh is bad enough but the HSU... No one has ever escaped, let alone tried as far as I recall." Charlie hesitated.

"I am not going to ask you to organise it, Charlie. I could never put you in that situation – never," Henry looked him in the eyes with what he hoped was the utmost sincerity. Charlie nodded.

"But I need to understand whether it could be done." Henry's voice was pressing. His jaws had clenched and released. He had to have this information.

Charlie's cold scrutiny resumed. His smooth, close-shaven face had lost some of its energy. But his eyes had an intensity Henry had rarely witnessed. He must have thought Henry was mad.

"Just the background info, Charlie – you don't need to know the rest."

"OK. I'll see what I can do," Charlie said pushing himself away from the table slowly. "But as a friend, I can only say this, reconsider."

Henry nodded, lowering his eyes to regain composure. "Thank you."

The visit had another half hour to run but both men had fallen into a strained silence. Henry rose slowly. No point in pretending or making Charlie feel awkward. If he had offended him or, worse, lost a friend, he would have to bear the weight of that mistake for the next twenty-five years. Henry had made his choice. He would run with it.

* * *

Nurani had finally arrived, from where, Pole didn't know. Pole had left a vague voicemail that showed little of what he wanted to discuss. It was all about the case, the witness statements, the gym. Pole felt certain the gym would prove fruitful beyond the discovery of the drugs: gossip, bits of info that taken together may give them what they needed – the supplier.

Pole waved to her as soon as she looked his way. His phone rang, Superintendent Marsh's PA was not giving up on him. He grabbed the phone with a swift irritated movement.

"Pole."

"He is on his way. I thought I'd give you the heads up."

"Much appreciated, Denise."

There could only be one reason The Super wanted to speak again. He put the phone down and moved to the door. Nurani had acknowledged him briefly and started making phone calls again. Marsh would try to get more from Nurani, and he was certain she would indulge him, an excellent way for Pole to provoke a much-needed conversation about her promotion. He walked to her desk and asked her to join him in his office for the overdue update.

"So, Nurani what's new in the big bad world of investment banking?"

Nurani smiled and sat herself comfortably in the only free chair in Pole's office. The very chair Nancy had sat in only a few hours ago. Pole's pulse quickened a little.

"The gym was a great idea, Jon," Nurani said, praise or flattery? The latter it seemed. Praise had not been forthcoming of late, not that Pole cared for either.

"Do tell," Pole replied, his lean body well ensconced in his chair. He was, for once, enjoying the game of cat and mouse he had started. "I've been going through a list of the members. A lot of high- profile bods there. Bankers of course but also Bank of England senior staff and people from the BBA."

"BBA!" Pole said. "You mean Gary Cook and Tom Hardy shared the same gym?"

"Correct, sir," Nurani said emboldened. "Turns out Tom was also a gym fanatic – more a cyclist than a boxer, but still. I'm checking the CCTV cameras at the gym in case something comes up: a familiar face." Pole remained silent. Andy would not be going through that alone for her. This time she would be on the front line, nose to her screen, doing the checking too.

"Bank of England's angle could be interesting," Nurani continued. "Have you checked the list of guests at the Women in Enterprise Conference and compared it to that of the gym members?" Nurani shook her head.

"You should. It might be a good way to establish a list of connections," Pole said. And Andy would certainly not be doing that for her either, if Pole had his way.

"Possibly," Nurani made a face., not complex enough for her it seemed. "Andy can do that."

Pole sat up straight in his chair.

"Keep going – how about the various tox reports?" Pole needed a little more from his DI before setting the record straight.

"Not yet received the final report on Hardy, a little too early. With Cook we're done and dusted: lots of nootropics and amphetamines. But nothing that may have pushed him over the edge."

"Nothing in the batch found in Cook's locker?"

"According to the lab that batch was of poor quality; would have underperformed if anything." There was no doubt in Nurani's voice. She was convinced it *was* suicide.

The word "underperformed" registered with Pole – an underperforming drug needed a replacement.

The ideal ambush to provide Gary with a lethal substitute.

"So far so very good," Pole smiled. Nurani looked confused for an instant then matched his smile. She must have thought he was coming around to her theory and had certainly not noticed she had missed the latest toxicology report.

"Still looking for the replacement drug – if there is any of course," she added.

Marsh would appear any minute. Pole stretched. "I fancy a coffee – want one?"

"I'll get it," Nurani volunteered eagerly.

"Nope, my turn to get it. You know me. I don't like abusing my extreme seniority." Pole smiled again and stood up. "Black, two sugars – strong and yet sweet, as ever." Pole was giving Nurani all the room she needed to expose her theory to Marsh. He gathered LSD would not be part of it.

"Yep, Jon. That's me."

Pole took his mobile out of his pocket. No call. He looked disappointed. He opened his desk drawer and took out some coins. He moved swiftly through the door.

"Back in two ticks," Pole said, not turning back.

Marsh was walking with his imperious stride in the direction of Pole's office. From the recess in which the coffee machine stood, he could see the back of Marsh's body. Always in full uniform but this time no idle chit-chat with the troops. Pole turned to face the grinding noise of the coffee machine, taking his time to complete the second selection. He turned his head a fraction. Nurani had stood up and she was chatting to Marsh, confident.

Pole headed back to his office with the two coffees, exchanged a few words with a colleague on his way and entered the room.

"Sir, I did not expect another visit."

"What's this story about a bad batch of pills? I thought we had agreed—" Marsh's nostrils had flared but Pole interrupted.

"We have indeed, sir – to limit ourselves in our search to things of relevance," Pole said. "Here you are." Pole handed Nurani her cup. "And we have found the substitute drug, in the revised tox reports I ordered - LSD - Unquestionable in the case of Hardy, traces for Cook, but explainable due to the time lapse."

Marsh turned towards Nurani with a quizzical eye. His disappointed glance did not last, soon replaced with the greedy look of an animal on the prowl.

"Do tell," Marsh said settling into the chair Nurani had just vacated.

Pole recapped for Marsh who was nodding repeatedly. Nurani retreated from Pole's office, moving backwards slowly in disbelief. She stopped at the door no longer certain what she wanted to do. Pole noticed more concern than resentment on her face this time. She could have followed the tox reports from close up but hadn't.

Pole told Marsh all he needed to know.

"And you think it is worth bringing Crowne in?" Marsh asked. "We need to dig around the LIBOR idea seriously."

"And Ms Wu will be facilitating?" Marsh asked nonchalantly, brushing an imaginary piece of fluff from his trouser leg.

"She will." Pole would not say more. If Marsh wanted to hit on Nancy, he would have to do better than that.

* * *

The letter was still on her coffee table. Its content had been festering there ever since she had read it. Nancy checked her watch yet again, pushed the cushion that she had propped behind her back. She had returned to her flat for a few moments' rest and to change for her Belmarsh meeting.

She grunted and threw the cushion on the sofa, grabbed another one and tried again – a little better. This new case had pulled at her in a way she was not expecting. It had given Henry what she feared might be false hopes of freedom, possibly even, much worse, desires.

William had regained consciousness for a few minutes during which he had called for her but had fallen unconscious again before she got to the hospital. She moved the cushion a little again. The case had become personal on so many levels, a minefield she could barely avoid. She had never won or even lost a case where she had suffered such an emotional rollercoaster. Being detached but never remote and aware of her client's manipulations were her core work principles.

But principles always suffer exceptions and her last case at the Bar had been such an extraordinary departure from what a strict code of conduct had been. The call that had followed from French barrister Jacques Vergés was a bolt out of the blue and yet so predictable. She had considered his offer, she had seen the possibility the case offered, defending Saddam Hussein. Nancy stood up and walked to her designer kitchen: steel, stone and wood, a balance of simplicity, elegance and warmth. She put a piece of cherry clafoutis on a plate, one minute in the microwave – perfect: the slight acidity of the fruit softened by the vanilla sweetness of the flan. She moved to the large window overlooking the garden to enjoy the treat.

She stayed with the moment, looking out of and refusing to consider the task that still lay ahead: to gather her thoughts and make a decision.

She returned to her lounge. She lifted the letter she'd received a couple of days ago from the Hong Kong gallery. The invitation was designed to be attractive to collectors like her. Hong Kong was still safe enough for the daughter of a political dissident, no need to travel to mainland China.

"Serves you right for telling Henry he must come to terms with the past," Nancy said aloud. The sound of her own voice made her uneasy. She had not heard it for a while: cultured, assured, sometimes biting, sometimes cajoling – the voice of an exceptional QC.

And what did she have to say in her own defence?

She had ignored China and the past for so long. The place where her parents had met, the place where she was born and the place she had fled during the Cultural Revolution. To this day she still did not understand why her father had wanted to go back. After all they had endured and all they had seen. Did art matter so much more than his wife and daughter?

Her mobile buzzed.

Received OK from HMP Belmarsh and Superintendent Marsh. Prep up Henry! Jon

Nancy gave a sigh of relief. The letter from Hong Kong would have to wait a little longer. She was still holding the paper in her hand, the quality of which was rarely produced in the West, its resistance and yet lightness, its softness to the touch. She remembered the Ai Weiwei pieces she had seen at the Lisson Gallery, the attention to detail, the flawless production process. Surely this was in keeping with Ai's own practice, a most excellent way to honour him. She assembled the documents she had received from Hong Kong in a neat pile. She would answer – perhaps.

For now, her priorities were William and Henry. William was secure, guarded by some of Pole's men and Paula – the fiercest of them all. Henry was about to get what he wanted, a way to prove he too could contribute. There was more to it, of course, and she would do what she did best, observe and ask at the right time the question that no one wanted to ask let alone answer. She had an hour or so to spare before meeting Henry, giving her time to put her thoughts in some order. he pulled her yellow notepad out of her satchel.

Nancy sat down, read the notes she had already jotted down, and completed them by recording what she had learned from William.

There was no doubt in her mind that both Gary and Tom had been murdered ingeniously. Even Pole was coming around to the idea. The SOCO team and the toxicology report must have turned up more evidence. She stopped writing and bent sideways to reach for her bag. She fumbled around and finally found what she wanted, the business card of Yvonne Butler, the pathologist she had met at Tom Hardy's crime scene.

"Maybe I will call after all," Nancy murmured. Whether it had been a little curiosity that had pushed Yvonne to hand Nancy her card or simple courtesy, Nancy did not care. Yvonne answered her phone promptly, surprised but pleased to hear from Nancy. Was she free for coffee? Certainly.

Nancy thought again about Henry's theory. Henry had been convinced from the very beginning that the deaths of Gary Cook and Tom Hardy could not be suicide. Something would have alerted Henry though to the connection. Something he had seen, read or heard in his previous life.

She opened up the laptop she had brought from her office and searched LIBOR. A little refresher on how the benchmark was calculated would give her more to go on when she met Henry. LIBOR was fixed by the BBA on the basis of submissions given by eighteen banks: before the average was calculated, the lowest and highest quotes were eliminated. The remaining submissions formed the base of the averaging.

In other words, a number of banks and hence people in management, working for these banks had to be involved. Nancy paused. Was it conceivable that someone had decided to systematically eliminate all those people? She estimated that four or five banks had to be involved for a wide manipulation to work. Henry would confirm of course, or maybe she was wrong.

Then a number of traders would have to be involved in each bank as well. This was ridiculous: a bankers' cleansing on a large scale did not make sense. No one would feel sorry for these people, but still. Was she going in the right direction?

"This is the next question for you Henry. If LIBOR manipulation is at the centre of all this, is it the only reason?"

Nancy pulled her papers together, meticulously arranging them, slid them in their file and placed the file in her satchel. She moved to her bedroom to change into a suitable dress. Belmarsh visits warranted a business suit, but she would allow herself a little eccentricity. She pulled out a pair of immaculately cut trousers, a black jacket with bold white stitching around the collar and cuffs and found her designer black pearl earrings from her dressing room. Black did not have to be boring. She sprayed a little Issey Miyake at the nape of her neck. She was ready to do battle.

The Perspex glass that separated the mortuary from the visitors' gallery left nothing to the imagination. Yvonne was running late and had invited Nancy to the finishing touches on Tom Hardy's post-mortem. "I hope you're not squeamish and you're not going to faint on me, are you?"

Yvonne's voice sounded muffled through the intercom.

"If I faint, I will be discreet." Nancy would not disappoint Yvonne and had seen her fair share of gore. She would rather have had Gary Cook on the slab though.

Yvonne was still in her blue overalls and looked on as one of her interns finished the sewing up the body. She waved at Nancy and indicated five minutes with her hand. She moved around the body, inspected the work and moved away towards the intercom again.

"Pole asked me for a revision of both tox reports. Did he tell you?" Nancy old her what she knew. Yvonne moved back to Tom's body and gave the young woman a nod. She could finish without her. Yvonne walked towards the door, removed her gloves meticulously. Nancy left the visitors' gallery and grabbed the door frame for support before walking towards the lab door. Yvonne was changing into fresh clothes. Her blonde hair, spiky and rebellious, gave her the air of a reformed punk.

"Thank you for taking the time," Nancy said stretching out her elegant hand.

"Nonsense – us girls need to stick together."

"I could not agree more."

"Are you not the current Chair of Women in Enterprise?"

"I am indeed. We would have had an excellent conference were it not for the unfortunate suicide of Gary Cook."

Yvonne moved her towards the exit. She was still questioning Nancy about the WIE when they entered a Latino coffee shop. Yvonne placed their order, and they found a table near the shop window to sit down.

"Coffee and Pastel de Nata." Yvonne sampled her coffee and pastry. Her face broke into a large smile. "As good as ever. But you don't believe it is suicide," she said, her spoon stirring in sugar in her triple espresso macchiato.

She lifted her questioning eyes to meet Nancy's. Why would Nancy have called her otherwise? Nancy appreciated the sharpness of her mind.

"I am not denying it but my opinion is neither here nor there. What do you say?"

"Why don't you ask, and I will see how best I can reply?"

"Inspector Pole seems to have come round to my view that it is not suicide. I expect something helped him to decide besides the attempt on William Noble's life."

"I am sorry about William by the way. Pole told me," Yvonne said with genuine regret. "Yes, the revised tox reports have shown some interesting results."

"More than simple nootropics?"

"You're right there. Traces of another substance – five days have passed but we still managed to find it. I am running tests again to be absolutely sure but it is there."

"Can I hazard a guess?"

Yvonne nodded. Her eyes creased slightly. She was enjoying the quiz. "LSD?"

"Now, I am impressed. How did you know?"

"One of my former Silicon Valley clients became a user before nootropics became popular. A story for another time."

"LSD is clever. In small doses it acts like a nootropic, a capacity enhancer, but also it does not stay in the blood for very long. Hard to ID if you're not looking for it. And of course, it is extremely addictive."

"Gary took a larger quantity and that sent him over the edge – literally."

"Almost certainly. The question remains. How?"

"Perhaps the suggestion of someone he trusted. Someone would told him it would boost his performance – a man preferably. In a conference full of women, he might have felt he needed to."

"One of the guests?"

"One of the male guests, possibly." Nancy recalled the list. There were maybe forty men in attendance.

"Then of course, there is the story of the bad batch," Yvonne volunteered.

"Bad batch of nootropics? How bad is bad?"

"That is the intriguing thing – useless. I mean this defective batch would have produced sweet FA, zip."

"Really?" Nancy frowned. She reached for another Pastel; she took a bite. "It must be important, but I don't yet see why."

Yvonne nodded. She caught Nancy's eye and smiled.

"Now Yvonne, would I be wrong in thinking you have a question for me?"

"Am I that transparent?"

"This is – or rather was – my job." Nancy grinned.

The Pole–Wu double-act intrigued his colleagues and her friends. Yvonne probed a little and Nancy delivered her answer back to Yvonne convincingly enough she thought.

"Jonathan is such a special guy. I hope he has found '*l'âme soeur*'," Yvonne said, her voice genuinely kind.

"Another Francophile – *bienvenue*."

"Nice of you to say so but not really. I expect you know Jon's family history?"

"I saw the art collection his grandmother left him. The pieces she bought after running an art gallery in Paris and London."

Yvonne's BlackBerry buzzed. She reached into her bag and checked it.

"Ah, something that may interest you, Nancy." She opened the email. Her head moved as she read softly. "Faint traces of LSD confirmed on second reading."

"Which still begs the question – how? LSD does not come in liquid form, correct?"

"Usually tablets – but it can also come in liquid form when the LSD crystals are dissolved. Someone could have spiked his drink."

Nancy paused, dabbed her lips with her napkin and bent forward slightly.

"I have a theory."

"I'm listening," Yvonne replied, bending forward in turn.

"First, Gary's murder must have been premeditated." She carried on. "Whoever decided to eliminate him knew he was going to be at the venue – ideal for a jump. That person also knew Gary well enough not only to know his drug habits but also to convince him to try something new."

"Pop one and you're already pepped up, a little more and you're on the path to losing control," Yvonne said.

"And it's going to be so much easier to push Gary over the parapet at 1 Poultry if he is out of it on LSD."

"Which means…"

"That Gary Cook must have been invited to the event by his murderer."

"Or he knew he was going to be there," Yvonne rectified.

"Not so – a chauvinist like Gary would never have gone on his own. Someone got him there – and he would have wanted to be on top intellectual form."

Yvonne raised her coffee cup. "Pole could not have done better." Nancy raised her cup in return. "To a fruitful collaboration."

Chapter Eighteen

The rhythmic shuffle of feet, men moving to take a tray, the sound of plates banging on the cheap Formica tables irritated Henry. He should have gone earlier to the canteen but he had been too busy recapping on what he had learned so far. Nancy was coming today for a visit. He had more arguments to feed to Pole if he was not yet willing to budge on Henry's involvement with the Cook-Hardy case. The queue stalled. Henry was holding his tray in front of his chest, the fingers of each hand drumming on the cheap plastic.

Lost in his thoughts, Henry did not immediately notice voices rising. The shouting started when the pushing began. The young man with a long fraying beard was already on the floor, his face covered in blood. He kicked the short stocky man in the groin who groaned in pain, his hands reaching down to protect himself from another kick.

The siren sounded. The canteen was already swarming with guards. Henry fought the mass of bodies that pushed and shoved. He ignored the grumbles that told him to move his arse. The men were still fighting. The unmistakable sound of blows crashing into flesh, the muffled cries of two men who did not want to let go. Henry twisted his neck to see, struggling to stand his ground.

More prison officers arrived with anti-riot equipment. Henry surrendered to the crowd that bore him away before he could see the outcome of the fight.

"Fucking idiots," Henry swore. He would have to make do with biscuits until dinner tonight.

"OK, OK, I am moving," he said holding his hands up. As he hurried up towards his cell, he saw Kamal. Already at the top of the stairs, he was observing the commotion. He was looking for something, or someone. He locked eyes with Henry and a faint smile brushed his face.

Not accidental, Henry thought. He accelerated, this time gaining ground on the inmates swarming around him, his tall body ducking, pushing, ducking. This was not the time to piss off another inmate he had learned. Nerves were often frayed at the prospect of going with little food for almost a day.

Another fight could erupt any moment. But the benefit of the gym was paying off. For the first time since he had entered Belmarsh, a sense of purpose was moving him. His heart was beating a little faster, not from the accelerated pace but from something he had not felt for a long time, excitement. Kamal started to move again at a slow pace. Henry caught up with him, walking alongside.

"I am in," Henry said looking ahead.

"This fills me with joy my brother," Kamal replied, his eyes shifting quickly towards Henry.

"I am not your brother."

"Not yet," Kamal replied. There was unexpected kindness in Kamal's voice that shook Henry to the core. Words he had heard before, words that belonged to his past in Northern Ireland. He knew this voice and for an instant he felt like Odysseus, chained to the mast of his ship, yearning to yield to the song of the sirens.

Henry clenched his fists and kept walking without another word until he had reached his cell. It was only a few metres away, up one more flight of stairs: three doors to go. Henry raised his eyes as he was turning into the staircase. But the distorted face of a man stopped him in his tracks.

He was trying to cry but with no result Blood was already dripping onto the landing below. The other inmates had stopped walking. And as the noise of their feet subsided, Henry heard them. The ferocious blows that were ravaging the other man's face, rhythmic, yet muffled. The guards would soon notice that they were not moving.

Whoever was doing the beating knew it; he finished with a vicious blow and threw the limp body down the stairs. The body landed with a crash of bones, barely missing Henry. The guards were coming. Henry hesitated but he could not risk it. He moved with the crowd. Walking past Kray's cell, Henry saw him leaning against the door frame. He was slowly removing bloodied bandages from his hands. His foot moved onto the landing almost tripping Henry up.

"You're next pretty boy and so is your girlfriend," Kray whispered.

Henry closed his cell door with a thud and pressed his back against it.

"I know what you are trying to do." Henry said aloud, his head tipped back against the cold metal. "I know what you are trying to do." Henry slid slowly to the floor. He sat, head on knees, his hands on his head massaging his scalp. He could not afford to let a fight get the better of him, not now. And what was this shit about a girlfriend? There hadn't been a woman in his life he could call a girlfriend for a while even before he was sentenced to prison.

Henry stood up suddenly. There was only one person he could have mistaken to be his woman. His jaw was clenched. No, this is what Kray wanted – a fight. He would alert Nancy as soon as he could.

* * *

Edwina threw her file on the desk. She leaned against it, arms stretched, head bowed forward.

"Another bloody useless meeting – fuck," she said shaking her head, her neat bob rolling from side to side. "I wonder why we employ economists?"

"In the hope they might tell us something we don't already know." Gabriel was standing in the doorway, his gym bag slung over his shoulder, his light-brown eyes showing amusement.

"Does anything ever faze you?" Edwina asked.

"Not much, that's why we work well together." Gabriel winked. The scar over his eye pulled at his face a little. He mechanically brought his hand to it but stopped abruptly before his fingers could reach it. "I'll be back in an hour."

"Maybe I should go to the gym too, get that crap out of my system" Edwina said. No matter how angry she might be with Gabriel she did not want to remind him of how his face had been damaged so many years ago.

"Yep – go and unleash some of that frustration; use some of the punchbags, clip a photo of The Oracle on it." Gabriel was already moving away, punching the air with his fist.

"Is that what you're gonna do?"

"Yep. I've booked an excellent boxing class today – just what the doctor ordered."

"Enjoy," Edwina forced her voice to sound cheerful. She watched Gabriel disappear along the corridor, heard the lift's doors click open, then shut. She moved to the window and saw Gabriel cross the street. Saw him disappear down Threadneedle. She hesitated. Gabriel's office was empty. She swiftly moved to his desk, tried the drawers but they were locked on both sides. Gabriel was a fan of the latest clean desk policy: no documents were to be left on desks, under any circumstances. Edwina swore underneath her breath. There was no obvious place he would have left a spare key and yet a spare key there was. She had left hers with the team PA. He might have done the same.

"Clara," Edwina stood over her PA's desk. "You have a spare set of keys for our desks, don't you?"

"Of course, Eddie, all of them," Clara looked bemused. "Any problem?"

"No, I just wanted to make sure. We are all very twitchy at the moment. I'd rather have you keep our spares than having spares floating around and unaccounted for." Convincing, she thought.

"They're all here," Clara opened a little box she kept on her desk. "Colour coded: you're red, Gabriel blue, Adrian yellow and Ken green."

"Perfect, as ever," Edwina delivered one of her best smiles, the one that showed a perfect set of teeth and accentuated the little dimple she bore on her chin. "Very clever."

Clara nodded a thank you and stood up. "I'm getting myself a sandwich. Shall I get you anything?"

"That would be great please. Something fishy – in keeping with the current mood and crisis." Clara gave her a wry smile.

A few seconds later the doors of the lift clicked again. Open–Close.

Edwina's fingers reached nervously for the box. She fumbled through the tangle of keys, bit her lips and tried to pull free the blue one. It was caught with hers, red and blue entwined. Ominous, maybe? Edwina had no time to consider it. She grabbed both keys and moved back to Gabriel's office.

The inside of each drawer was meticulously organised, unlike hers. She did not know what she was looking for, or even why she was taking such a risk, but she needed something, anything, to help her understand the growing unease that had settled in the pit of her stomach and would not go away.

Stationery was organised by categories and size. Ridiculous. Files ordered by date and urgency.

The bottom drawer had more personal items: comb, deodorant, Kleenex (man size). She was about to shut it when a rattling sound attracted her attention. She knelt on the floor, bent forward and extended her arm to reach the back of the desk. Her fingers were moving around, feeling anxiously for the source of the noise. She retrieved a large bottle full of pills, no name. She hesitated, opened the container and tried to ease one into her hand. The pills were stuck together. Edwina bit her lips again and shook the bottle a little harder. An entire pool of them tumbled into her hand, some dropping to the floor.

"Bugger!"

She quickly poured back the contents of her hand into the bottle, dropping more pills on the floor. She was desperately picking them up, with shaky fingers, kneeling further underneath Gabriel's desk, ramming the blue pills as quickly as she could into the bottle. Clara would be on her way back by now. Edwina took a final look around her, shoved the bottle in the bottom drawer where it belonged. Pushed the key into the lock. It did not go in. She tried again, realised she was using her own key.

Come on. Come on.

Locked the drawer. Sprinted across to her PA's desk. She could hear the doors of the lift.

Open–Close.

Edwina dropped the keys into the box and turned around. Clara was turning the corner and looked a little surprised.

"You did not need to wait. I would have brought the sandwich to you."

"I just heard the lift. I am famished," Edwina replied flustered. Clara smiled and handed over a smoked salmon and watercress on brown. "Perfect," Edwina said with a little too much enthusiasm. She disappeared into her office clutching her sandwich in her right hand and a little blue pill in her left.

* * *

Sotheby's was preparing yet another exceptional contemporary art auction. How many exceptional art auctions could there be in one lifetime let alone a year? None, Brett estimated. But by his former employer's standards there was one blockbuster sale at least once a year. October would soon be upon them and with it the beginning of the Art Fairs season. It started right here in London with Frieze, then moved to Paris and New York. Antiquities were doing fine but were dwarfed by the magnitude of the sums that changed hands for modern and contemporary art. Brett sighed. No matter how much he tried, nothing attracted him in this contemporary gobbledygook. He did not understand the mania for conceptual art, had no time for abstraction. He could just about see the skill in early Picassos.

Walking back from his Club, he cut through Burlington Arcade and strolled down Cork Street. He stopped, looking into the windows of the better galleries. He could not see the fuss. His phone rang. He reached into his pocket, noticing the reflection of his face in the window, tired and – well – concerned.

"Antonio. What can I do for you?" Brett had called his Italian smuggler on the night he had met with his new client, The Sheik. He had put the deal to him, sparing him the details. Still, he had volunteered the transaction was unusual, and possibly riskier too, but the price was also fair. The eye-wateringly large figure Brett had offered Antonio had struck the right chord.

"Yes, it is a one-off," Brett replied stopping walking altogether. His voice had stayed remarkably courteous. He had no time for Antonio to wobble. Brett listened to the habitual ranting, the lengthy description of what had been done to prepare the transfer. He was nodding as if Antonio could see him from the few thousand miles that separated them. Brett would not push back with his usual impatience this time. MI6 had been very clear. Facilitation. This Middle Eastern clandestine had to arrive on UK soil.

Brett retraced his steps and found a little alcove from which he could speak securely.

"I don't want to hear the T word, Antonio. And anyway we deal with these people when we move art pieces around. None of our business," Brett added.

Antonio became even more animated on the other end of the phone. Brett changed ear and started walking again.

"That is why you are paid a six-figure sum of money." Brett pulled at his well-trimmed moustache. The conversation made him sick. How much more sucking up to this Italian riffraff would he have to put up with? The six-figure sum that had suddenly pacified Antonio reminded Brett of the equally large sum of cash he was about to bank. He managed a smile. Yes, he could endure a lot more of this after all. Brett arrived on Hanover Square, still in conversation with his smuggler. He was moving slowly towards a line of trees. The summer luxuriant greens distracted him for a moment. He entered the square and found a suitable place to sit. The timing of the clandestine transfer had to be impeccable.

Clandestine X would arrive by sea from Libya. Antonio had a consignment due to leave on that same day for Europe. He used a number of points of departure from the Libyan coast. But it was always a night crossing. The route into the UK would then be a tried and tested one.

Switzerland via Lugano on a truck that would cross the Italian border there. A change of truck again with another consignment, crossing into France at one of the busiest checkpoints, counterintuitive but very effective. A change again across France, a smaller van taking the deserted B roads. The final crossing from Le Havre to the UK. Two days in total.

There was no equipment. If this chappie needed it, it was travelling through a different channel. Or maybe it had reached the UK already.

MI6-Steve was only concerned about Clandestine X. Brett had not asked. Antonio had fretted about the issue of armaments but the absence of any had made the mapping of the route so much easier. Antonio had almost been cheerful that day. Brett had insisted on understanding the details of the transfer and for once Antonio had not minded. Antonio was most anxious when it came to crossing into the UK, although Brett suspected that border control would be asked to facilitate. He had communicated the details to Steve and, for once, Steve had sounded mildly impressed.

"You might even pull it off," Steve had conceded.

"When the package arrives, I don't have to deliver it anywhere in particular. You're OK with that?"

"We'll take it from there."

"You know where Clandestine X is going, don't you?" Brett asked not expecting an answer.

"What do you expect me to say?"

"That he is a Brit returning from the war zone. Then again, as you've told me so many times not my problem."

"That's my man." Steve sounded relieved.

"As soon as Clandestine X has arrived in Italy, I will transfer thirty per cent of the sum to my smuggler. Then another twenty per cent when he crosses into France. The rest when he has entered the UK."

Antonio had not even negotiated.

Brett terminated the call. There would be many more before the deal was done. He leaned against the backrest of the bench, his fingers drumming a nervous tune on the worn-out part of the wood. He breathed in the fresh air. It was time to resume his day job as an independent art consultant. Sotheby's liked punctuality.

He reached into the inside pocket of his jacket for a packet of Benson & Hedges. One last cigarette would probably make him five minutes late. A small amount of subversion, how pleasant. He took out from another pocket an elegant lighter that had belonged to his great-grandfather, nothing ostentatious except perhaps the engraving *With Gratitude, Victoria.* He pulled on the cigarette and inhaled deeply. The nicotine did its trick and his jaw relaxed. He took another drag and closed his eyes.

When he opened his eyes he noticed him, a small figure hunched on a bench at the far side of the square. Brett shrugged.

Still tailing me? Ridiculous.

Brett took a final pull and flicked the cigarette away. They did not want to be subtle. That much was now obvious. He was safe until Clandestine X was delivered. But maybe the delivery of this man would only be the beginning. Henry Crowne's name popped back into his mind. Why had The Sheik chosen him? He hated Crowne with a passion and for good reasons he thought. Had Crowne not reneged on their *Ur artefacts* deal he would not had fallen into the claws of MI6. Brett pulled the gate of the square open.

"One thing at a time, old boy," he muttered. "One thing at a time."

* * *

Henry's face changed in an instant at the news, his blue eyes turning a shade lighter and the deep furrows that defined his face smoothed over. He had braced himself for it but the knowledge that he would be allowed to leave the Belmarsh HSU compound overjoyed Henry.

Nancy had smiled kindly and yet her gaze had delved into his eyes so deep that he thought she might have guessed. There was no time for questions. Only facts regarding the process. She would not be there to accompany him when he came out; there was no need.

The Belmarsh Governor had been informed. Henry would be taken to New Scotland Yard the following morning. He would be leaving before the other inmates were allowed out. The moment of joy had quickly been replaced by the intense focus that so characterised Henry.

He had taken all the details in. No need for notes; he would remember. Nancy was as prepared as he was. Her eyes rested on him, friendly, and yet for an infinitesimal moment he thought he had detected something he had never seen before, suspicion. It had vanished as fast as it had come. Nancy had defended enough high-profile criminals to know how to get to the truth. Henry was in no doubt that one day she would; it just couldn't be yet.

"One final thing before I go; they will be searching your cell," Nancy said somewhat anxious.

Henry's mouth pursed in return, almost arrogant. "Anticipation at what may lie ahead is one of the things I do best. And I know the guards will look at all I own thoroughly."

"Glad to hear and I hope you are right."

Nancy's irritation surprised Henry. He shook his head. No time to be an arrogant arse. "Do you know what Epiphany is?"

"The visit of the Magi to the child Jesus. What of it?" Nancy inhaled a little Henry noticed, enough so as not to lose her cool.

"Bear with me. You know that the French eat *la Galette de Rois* – yes?"

Nancy rolled her eyes.

"And you know that they put a little token in the cake; the one who finds it is King or Queen – right?"

Nancy's eyes widened. "You haven't?"

"Yup. A little piece of my Japanese art collection called a Netsuke has ended up inside my lunchtime bread roll. It makes it one of the most expensive buns in the world."

Nancy moved forward, her hand clenched against her mouth, hardly containing an incredulous laugh. "You hid the Netsuke into a bread roll?"

Henry raised his eyebrows in quick succession – who was a smart-arse after all: his netsuke in a bun – genius.

Back in his cell Henry slumped onto his bed. His body was shaking, a small rumble almost delicious. He had not felt this alive for years – before the death of Anthony Albert and his arrest for murder, before the GL takeover. He rubbed his face gently. It was only the beginning. But at present, he suspected that the entire prison service was going after him. By now the Governor had been fully briefed. He was instructing the prison officers to carry out a full-blown search of Henry's cell. This was an exceptional situation that would warrant exceptional measures.

Henry stood up. A last-minute check before they arrived, he thought. He looked at the papers he had squirrelled away, notes he had not yet destroyed. He had thought he could save them in his legal file. A file that should never be opened by any guard, prison officer, even the Governor himself but why take unnecessary risks? He tore them into small pieces and flushed them down the toilet.

He picked up the pad he had used to take the notes, tore the last pages on which these had left an imprint. He flushed these too down the toilet. He looked around.

His uneaten bread roll was convincingly squirrelled away with a piece of cheese inside a paper napkin. He unfolded the paper carefully, inspected the bun. He had removed a piece of crust, eaten some of the inside and replaced it by his precious netsuke, secured the crust back. He shook the bread a little, the crust hardly moved. He closed the bundle again. He was in the clear.

Henry sat down at his small desk and started a new letter to Nancy. The perfect way of creating a fresh set of prints on the pad and an equally good way of calming his nerves as the inspection was approaching.

He was still writing when the key turned in the lock. He turned towards the door and suppressed a smile.

There were three of them. The tallest of the lot, John he knew well. Never trust the screws was Charlie's motto. Still Henry had to admit the prison officers of the Cat A wing were more decent than he had expected.

"You're taking a little trip, I gather?"

"If you say so," Henry replied, still seated. Henry eyed the other two quickly: an Asian chap, small but muscular, and a bald guy in his fifties. He had seen him before handling an inmate who had pushed his luck too far with a mobile phone – not a pretty sight.

"We need to do a search before you're allowed out. You won't mind will you Henry?" The guard sneered.

Henry shrugged. He stood up, mentally checking that all was in order. He was about to reach for his legal file when the bald guy stopped him dead. Henry turned abruptly towards him. Within a second the atmosphere changed; everybody froze. Henry clenched and released his fist.

Calm.

"This is my legal file, privileged as you know."

"Something in there I need to know?" The bald guy was still standing between Henry and the file.

"Well, all of it – that's the idea of a privileged file."

The prison officer turned to John

"Let it go," John said.

Henry grabbed the file and moved to the side wall. Papers were dropped on the floor. His bed turned upside down and the flimsy sheets left on the ground. The few bits of food he had stashed away were thoroughly fingered, including his bun and cheese. Henry forced himself not to budge.

"In case you're peckish later, then." the bald guy said. He pushed the bun around to the edge of the desk. One more move and it would drop onto the floor. Henry squeezed his file tight against his chest, his eyes riveted on the piece of bread.

The prison officer lost interest in his desk and moved to his shelf. Still not quite out of the woods yet. Henry had been subjected to these intrusions regularly since he had been incarcerated. They had become less frequent until today, when he had become a high-profile con again.

"We'll pick you up during bang-up time. Be ready," John said as he closed the door with a thud. It had hardly closed before Henry jumped forward and caught the bread roll before it hit the floor.

No one would beat Henry at his own game of hide and seek. The file would prove a useful decoy for what came next.

Chapter Nineteen

The room was small and smelt of sweat and cheap coffee. But the four plasma screens Henry had requested had been installed on the table at the centre of it.

Henry entered, still rubbing his wrists where the handcuffs had clasped his hands together. Pole was already there waiting for him and the two men greeted each other briefly.

The buzz Henry had felt when he'd stepped into the anonymised police car went up a notch. Someone had done a good job, tested the screens and some of the familiar trading market charts and colour-coded displays were already flickering.

He walked to the monitors and started typing rapidly on the keyboard, his fingers dancing to a tune he knew so well. The tingle extended to his hands, his arms. It had been almost four years since he had last sat at a Bloomberg keyboard, so distinctive with its yellow, green and red keys. He pressed the enter button and memories of the trading floor at GL flooded his mind, unstoppable. He closed his eyes for a moment. This was not the time. He keyed in more instructions and the screens came to life.

Henry turned to Pole with a grin he could no longer suppress.

"You did good. Who set this up – someone from your team?"

"They have. Not rocket science despite what you lot would like us to believe," Pole replied.

"You're right, it's quantum physics actually." Henry was still grinning.

Pole rolled his eyes. "Do you have all you need?"

"Give me five to run a few checks." Henry's long hands were running across the keys, elegantly. The screens changed again. The data mining had begun.

"Is Nancy joining us? She couldn't pick me up but still," Henry said, a little put out.

"She's on her way."

"From seeing William?" Henry said, configuring yet another Bloomberg screen.

"That's right." Pole had moved closer to the desk, standing now at the back of Henry, his tall body casting a shadow over Henry's desk.

"Sorry, I don't like people standing behind my back when I'm on my screens," Henry said half-turning towards Pole, his hands frozen in mid-air.

"Certainly," Pole replied clearly amused by the request.

Henry faced the monitors again. "You probably think it's a little OTT but I have my reasons."

Pole's eyes rested on Henry, light but observing. "Care to elaborate?"

"The chap who ran the investment bank at GL used to walk the trading floor nearly every day when he was in London. He would stay there at the back of your desk – saying nothing, just watching."

"Good bullying technique. Did he get away with it?"

"Yep – for a very long time. I never took any notice, although I could quite happily have clocked him one."

Pole laughed. "And your guys?"

"I trained my team well. Polite but cool. Of course, there is always a smart-arse on the trading floor who thinks he knows best and starts talking too much. That never ended well."

Henry pressed the enter button with a flourish. "I am ready to roll." Pole's phone rang.

"Nancy is on her way. You've got an hour, Henry."

"Before you go Inspector…" Henry turned towards Pole, hesitating "It has to do with Belmarsh."

"What now?" Pole was not indulging any demand.

"I'm not trying to be difficult, But I'm concerned about one of the inmate. A guy who calls himself Ronnie Kray."

"Are you serious?"

"Very. He had I don't see eye to eye for reasons I won't bore you with but he seem to think that Nancy and I are..."

Pole frowned. "...together?"

"And he has bee making stupid threats... I'm not sure whether he could get to her but I'm not taking any chances."

Concern flashed on Pole's face. "I'll deal with it."

Henry nodded and returned to his screens.

"Have a good time with Nancy," Henry said, waving Pole away with a renewed grin.

* * *

Henry was tilting his chair, one arm resting on the desk turning a pen across the back of his thumb in a hypnotic motion, listening to Pole's recap.

Pole and Nancy had joined him in the same meeting room Henry had occupied since he'd arrived. Nancy, focused as ever, was taking notes on her yellow pad.

"On what basis have you conceded that both Gary and Tom were murdered?" Henry interrupted.

"I don't see why that matters to you," Pole pushed back.

"It might be relevant. I need to get the full MO of the guy or gal you are looking for."

"Since I'm the detective here why don't you just let me do that – detect. You're the banker so why don't you unravel the mysteries of LIBOR for us. Then we talk."

"OK, your call," Henry replied putting his hands up.

A stack of printed documents sat on the printer specially set up in the room. Henry stood up and distributed them to Pole and Nancy. She had been uncommonly silent until the wad of paper placed in her hand brought her back to life. She smiled to both and shook her head. "Sorry gentlemen, I was back at St Thomas's. But here I am back and ready to go."

Henry smiled a kind smile and Pole squeezed her shoulder. There was only goodwill in the room borne out of love and friendship. Nancy sighed. Pole sat down, and Henry started.

"First of all, three documents to consider: a superb article written in *The Wall Street Journal* relating to LIBOR manipulation, note the date, suggesting that LIBOR has been rigged by the banks for years. Then a rebuttal from the International Monetary Fund insisting that there was no such thing as LIBOR fixing - no pun intended - and finally a rather recent but potent analysis of LIBOR by two well-known economists corroborating the *WSJ* findings."

"The *WSJ* thinks it is an attempt by the banks to look stronger; the two economists – Connan Snider, UCLA and Thomas Youle, Minnesota - conclude that it was more a way to increase profits," Nancy said licking through the documents.

"So, whatever the reason, there was manipulation," Pole said. "But that is a US analysis, right?" Pole lifted a quizzical eyebrow. "And you got that info Henry in under one hour?"

"Inspector! I don't have the reputation of being a smart-arse for nothing. I was approached by MENSA you know," Henry kept rocking on the back of his chair, a faint smile on his face.

Pole grunted but let it go. No time to deflate Henry's ego. At least not yet.

"How large are the stakes?" Nancy asked oblivious to the banter going on between them.

"Trillions." Henry answered without hesitation. "You mean billions?" Pole frowned.

"Trillions. You are thinking purely about the mortgages. And they are real money of course, but you also need to think about the derivatives."

"You mean interest rate swaps and the like?" Nancy asked. She sat back in her chair, slowly replacing a strand of jet-black hair that had escaped from her hairclip.

"That's my girl," Henry replied winking at Nancy. Pole cast a dark lookin his direction.

"*Je ne suis pas ta cocotte*," Nancy replied almost amused.

Pole nodded in agreement that Nancy was *not* Henry's girl.

"I had a look at the audited accounts filed by some of the banks that submit quotes for LIBOR fixing – I mean the actual process." Henry paused, waiting for the question that never came.

"Yeah, yeah. I know the process is actually called *fixing*," Pole waved away Henry. "With eighteen banks submitting their quotes daily as part of this *fixing* process," Pole emphasised the word fixing with a air quotations.

"Hey, Inspector Pole you're not just a pretty face." Henry grinned.

"What? An olive branch from you, Henry?"

"Do I need to extend one?"

"As far as I am concerned you need to extend the whole goddamn tree."

"Ça *suffit vous deux*," Nancy snapped. "You, Henry, think that either way there was manipulation."

"Yes, I am positive. On Dollar LIBOR, I'd say I am ninety-nine per cent certain but on Sterling LIBOR I need to do a bit more work. The reason why I really need to do the work out of Belmarsh is that I may be able to determine what is really going on."

"You mean you can determine whether LIBOR manipulation is simply to make money or to save their banks' credentials in the marketplace?" Pole asked, dubious.

"I understand you're sceptical Inspector, but I know a particular program that I can use to detect irregularities in trading patterns. If I use it and apply it to the quotes made by the eighteen banks that submit on LIBOR, I'll have a pattern," Henry said enthusiastically. He had turned away from his audience and was already finding information on the net. "Then, I will look at the level of derivatives like interest rate swaps these banks have traded."

"Why not mortgages?" Pole asked.

"Because these instruments, unlike mortgages, are not based on hard cash but on notional amounts."

"The notional amount is not cash that moves from hand to hand but a number on which the results of the transaction are calculated," Nancy added.

"You mean it does not exist?" Pole said with knitted eyebrows.

"Well, you could say that. There is no cash changing hands on the notional, only on the outcome. Say your swap has a notional of £200 million, that amount does not change hands, but the net movements of rates on that amount will be the outcome payable," Henry explained further.

"But why?" Pole still looked puzzled.

"Because it is a risk management instrument. If I want to protect myself against a negative outcome on the £200 million, I just spoke about, I enter into a swap and change the outcome – hence the term swap. I literally swap the negative outcome for a positive outcome."

Pole nodded. "Let's do apples and oranges example to help a simple copper like me."

Nancy shook her head, but Henry grinned.

"I grow oranges and you, Henry, grow apples." Pole said.

"Sounds good to me."

"I want apples because I am growing too many oranges, but I don't want to plant apple trees." Pole said slowly stroking his goatee. "So, if you want oranges and are ready to swap your apples for my oranges we are in business, right?" Pole said waving a finger at Henry – a eureka moment.

"And as long as I don't want to plant orange trees either we are definitely in business," Henry replied impressed.

"But how many apples do I receive?"

"Very good question, Inspector," Henry nodded. "Say today an orange is worth an apple; tomorrow however the price may change. We agree that we are going to look at these prices every three months and then we agree who gets what. If oranges go up, you get more apples. If apples go up I get more oranges."

"And ultimately you and I do that because I think oranges are going to go up and I will get more apples and I have an apple-pie factory." Pole grinned.

"Damn – you could have been a mean trader," Henry teased.

"Only now you're telling me."

"Never too late to learn."

"Back to the case Henry."

"Yes, Inspector – so for the banks the choice is between different types of interest rates, say fixed against floating," Henry said.

"LIBOR is the floating part because it resets regularly," Pole added energised by understanding what the financial markets represented.

"Correct and I think I can estimate what was happening as long as I can get to the right data."

"Do you need something else from me," Pole offered.

"Not yet. I'll see how much I can gather from Bloomberg and the audited financial reports of the banks I have in mind. I have to say though, I am not surprised it has happened. It was such an easy way of making a bit more money – this LIBOR fixing."

"But what's changed?"

"If William Noble had not been involved, I would have gone straight for the money-making angle, but his involvement changes everything."

"Unfortunately, I must say I agree." Nancy sighed.

"If you combine the financial crisis and William's involvement, you end up with a level of manipulation of LIBOR that is much more structural, probably geared at saving the banks and ultimately saving the financial system from collapse." Henry's face had grown serious. "I know this is not acceptable, but I understand why a man like William may think it's necessary."

All three fell silent, each measuring in their own way the impact of Henry's findings.

"But William would not have spoken to the banks directly, perhaps the BBA?" Nancy broke the silence.

"Did he say anything that could help us?" Pole asked.

"Nothing, he was keen to protect his contact." Nancy replied.

Henry hesitated. Should he break the news now?

But Nancy was following her train of thought.

"What do we know about the various protagonists and their connections?"

"Gary Cook worked at GL until very recently. He was the LIBOR submitter for them. Been in the market forever. He can call his pals at Barclays, RBS, Lloyds etc. But he also knows Tom Hardy, CEO of the BBA very well," Pole said.

"The very same BBA whose job it is to publish LIBOR," Nancy added.

"My guess is that Tom and Gary have spoken. We still don't know who initiated what," Pole said.

"I think we do," Henry said. "If this is a request from on high to ensure that the banks start lending to each other in order to save the financial system, then Tom reaches out to Gary. If Gary has ever been a naughty boy, it was on a small scale – maybe half a bp."

Before Pole could ask, Henry explained. "A basis point or bp is 0.01 per cent."

"That sounds very small."

"Yes, but on a very large notional – remember what we discussed earlier. These banks trade billions in notional."

"Understood, but you say it's different from what Gary would then have been asked to do."

"Absolutely, if Gary was seeking to alter the LIBOR benchmark altogether, he would need to move his submission by a substantial amount to make a difference. He no longer seeks to go under the radar; he is the radar."

"I see what you mean. So now the changes are much more visible," Pole said slowly to convince himself – it sounded so impossible.

"Besides, if Gary had simply sought to improve his P&L he would have remained well under that radar and avoided Tom like the plague."

"That sounds right. So, Tom initiates the conversation with Gary because he has been contacted by...?" Nancy said, thinking aloud.

"William?" Pole said turning to Henry for confirmation.

"Don't think so." Henry shook his head with the beginning of a smile that gave his face a much younger look, the look of mischief from someone who has the answer.

"All right, genius, do tell us," Pole stood up and placed himself in front of Henry's screens.

"There is a little word missing, Inspector."

"What! I can't believe you. No actually I can believe you, *please*," Pole said pressing two fingers into his eyes to make the pain of the word disappear.

"The Bank of England," Nancy spoke the word slowly and Pole suppressed a smile. She had robbed Henry of his thunder.

"Spot on – wow, Nancy. I am impressed," Henry's face had lifted. His light-blue eyes flickering with admiration. No hard feelings amongst friends. "It's the only possible explanation."

"William, being a Whitehall mandarin, would have floated the idea with the Bank of England first, to see whether it would stick?" Pole said.

"Discussing options – all done behind closed doors. No trace of the conversation. After all there was an unprecedented crisis to manage." Henry moved away from his screens. His face lost its slight carefree expression, a deep line etched on his forehead had grown deeper.

"This is the sequence of events, I think. William is kept informed by his contacts at the various large banks, CEOs, Heads of Risks as well as the Bank of England that the pressure on the financial markets is about to create the biggest crisis since 1930. One of the main issues is that all the banks are so worried they have stopped lending not only to Joe Bloggs on the street but also to each other. The reason: they are too shit scared about the exposure they all have to the subprime market. Banks not lending to banks: unsustainable."

"Agreed, that was all over the news," Pole said.

"If the banks stop lending to one another, this ripples down the whole market and the financial system collapses. So the government wants, actually needs, to reintroduce some stability. William who is at the forefront of the effort has a conversation with the Bank of England. The Bank of England somehow accepts in order to preserve the integrity of the system: – needs must. Only one or two people are involved, no more."

"Agreed again. William himself wants one contact and one contact only to ensure maximum discretion," Pole said.

"The Bank of England in turn needs to test the plan with a trusted chum, om Hardy at the BBA." Henry nodded.

"Did they really need the BBA involved?" Nancy asked. "The Bank of England knows exactly who submits in each bank, don't they?"

"Not necessarily all of them," Henry replied. "And you probably want the BBA to be picking the best candidates for the task."

"But surely top management is also involved somehow?" Pole was now leaning against the wall still in front of Henry's screens.

"Absolutely. The BBA can test the idea with a couple of traders, and they will be able to tell the Bank of England whether Management may buy the idea. Then the Bank of England makes the call – to the CEO. And the instructions start coming from on high."

"But LIBOR can't be manipulated in that way only by one bank, right?" Pole frowned.

"Right again. LIBOR is calculated on a basket of submissions, so other banks have to be involved."

"Let me see whether I've got this right," Pole moved towards Henry's desk and started leafing through a file. "Tom Hardy, BBA's director, calls his pal Gary Cook, head trader at GL. Gary tells him he thinks GL might be up for it but, at that level of alteration, top Management needs to give the OK. Tom relays that to the Bank of England, the Bank of England calls the CEO and makes a direct request."

"Uh-huh." Henry nodded.

"Tom and Gary have worked together before: same brokerage firm, then same bank," Pole was reading from a typed note. He put the file down, one hand still resting on its cover. "They can go straight to the point without worrying about the consequences of talking openly about LIBOR fixing. Gary starts calling his mates in other banks."

Pole was about to let go when he opened the file again and frowned. "And they belong to the same gym."

Nancy looked at him quizzically. Was it not time to put all his cards on the table?

"You mean the Embody Fitness Club?" Henry asked

Pole's jaws clenched.

"Showing off, are you ?"

Henry shook his head "That's unfair. If it was Nancy, you would be impressed."

"I doubt Nancy feels the need to outsmart everyone all the time."

"*Vraiment, vous deux* êtes *incorrigibles*," Nancy said standing up to stretch a little.

Pole looked at her miffed. How could she compare him to Henry?
"Let's talk about the gym," Nancy said.

"Fine," Pole replied reluctantly. "Some of the nootropics that Gary took were stored there. Although the owners had no idea that something dodgy was going on."

"And Tom?" Nancy asked.

"There were plenty of painkillers in his blood. Some opiate medication used to relieve extreme pain: – post-op injuries or very strong chronic pain."

"You know that Olympic athletes train at Embody, don't you?"

"Make your point," Pole said.

"Athletes at that level do incur severe injuries that need pretty strong drugs."

"Was it your gym when you worked in the City?" Pole asked

"Of course, you wouldn't believe what people talk about when they are training together – a gold mine of info."

"And how does Belmarsh compare? Pole said closing the file with a snap.

"A gold mine too." Henry grinned, placing his crossed arms behind his head.

"Anybody from the Bank of England?" Nancy asked. The shadows underneath her eyes had deepened suddenly. Henry and Pole slowed down, concerned.

"It's already 7pm. You need to be on your way back, Henry." Henry face tightened. "Tomorrow?"

"I've asked for a couple of days. You're back at the same time tomorrow morning."

Henry turned towards the screens still flickering, scrolling down information. "Thank you."

Pole called for the guards. The cuffs were put on Henry without much consideration. He disappeared down the long corridors of Scotland Yard.

Nancy had hardly winced at the sight of Henry being taken away. Pole and Nancy walked the same long corridors without saying much.

"Something on your mind?" Pole asked as they stood in front of the lifts.

Nancy sighed. "I can't hide very well from you, not that I would want to, Jonathan. But allow me a little time to think it through. I need to get this right."

The lift doors pinged open. They pushed their way into the crowd.

Pole would have to wait until the morning.

Chapter Twenty

"He is crossing tonight," Brett said, his mobile stuck to his ear. He was finishing his cigarette, inhaling deeply. The nicotine kicked in, a welcome light-headedness and feeling it would be all right on the day. Information was strictly on a need-to-know basis and Brett had so far felt that his need to know was reduced to three words *Not Your Problem*. But today MI6-Steve was precise, perhaps even helpful.

"I hear you, but until the Merchant of Venice calls me, I am in the dark." Another apt code name for Antonio; Brett managed a smile.

"Well, it's not reassuring to be reassured, especially by you," Brett took his last drag and crushed his cigarette under his shoe. If only it could be Steve's head.

Brett crossed Piccadilly over to the Ritz. He turned right towards Belgravia. A little walk would clear his brain. The young Middle Eastern man who was tailing him this morning had disappeared. If they were still following him, they were getting better at it. His new burner phone rang. Brett stopped dead. A woman with her dog almost bumped into him, barely apologising.

"The Sheik wants to speak to you," Mohammed's voice was strained.

"When?" Brett reached for his Benson & Hedges in his inner jacket pocket. He pulled the pack out, flicked the top flap open.

Empty.

"What do you mean now?" Brett looked at the empty pack and crushed it in anger; a cold sweat covered the back of his neck. This was definitely not part of the deal. "I need to be careful, Goddamn it. I can't just make my way every five minutes to your neck of the woods."

Brett heard the intake of air at the other end of the phone. "Sorry, not your choice. I know." Brett never apologised as a rule – aristocratic upbringing. Today, however Brett felt for his contact. "Fine, fine. I'm on my way home. I need to change. I will be there in a couple of hours – yes, same place."

No point in calling Steve. Bringing Clandestine X into the country had just been an appetiser, he feared. He was about to be served the main course and was not going to like the taste of it.

* * *

Her footsteps pounded the pavement in anger. Nancy was beating the concrete slabs with her heels, releasing with each kick the searing sensation in her belly.

Betrayed.

Not only as a friend but also in the cause she so passionately believed in. Thousands of women, good honest women, fighting the harsh battle of equality and recognition would suffer. What had Edwina been thinking of? She was not even yet in the Governor's seat and she was already playing God.

Nancy had left Scotland Yard abruptly. Her departure would not fool Pole. She had not even wanted to hide her discomfort. But Edwina deserved to be heard. She was not, or at least not yet, one of the unsavoury clients Nancy had defended during her eminent career as QC. Edwina was her protégée. Only a few hours ago she would also have called her a friend.

Nancy reached The Mall. Plenty of cabs if she wanted to hit the City quickly. She stuck her hand in her pocket to avoid temptation. Getting to the Bank, demanding to see Edwina and savaging her was not a solution. She reached Trafalgar Square. The constant flow of cars, buses and bikes forced her to stop and wait. Today the National Portrait Gallery restaurant would be open late; she would probably not get a table for one but it was worth a try.

Sitting at the small comfortable bar, Nancy was sipping a soft Chilean Merlot. She stabbed an olive with conviction and crunched it with one bite. Deliciously spicy and garlicky. She had not touched her

BlackBerry since she had taken it out of her bag. She had checked on William as she had settled down at the bar – no change.

The restaurant was filling up quickly; fewer tourists than expected but many regulars – artists, art critics, a couple of TV personalities. She could still call Pole to tell him what she knew. But no, Edwina deserved the benefit of the doubt. Was it not the way she had been trained? She was not yet sure and would not rush to conclusions. Nancy closed her almond-shaped eyes in a slow, calming movement. She inhaled deeply and released.

In a moment she would reach this place of peace and quiet that she had learned to create so many years ago. The buzz of the bar had become less distracting. She breathed in again, letting the old habit kick in. Her mind had slowed a little more. She was reaching that space where her intuition could speak unencumbered and where she was free to consider all options.

Nancy opened her eyes. The barman was looking at her with a mixture of concern and surprise. She smiled comfortably and took another sip of wine. The young man blushed, attempted a smile, and turned to serve the next customer.

She had an hour to decide.

* * *

The police van was rocking uncomfortably over the potholes of East London. Henry sat silently at the back, locked in his cubicle. The two guards sat near the door, engrossed in a low-voiced conversation. A few words drifted towards Henry – pay rise, bloody bad, prison officer badly injured. Henry had started taking mental notes of the process of transfer the second he had been on his way to central London. What would happen if the van broke down? In his last two years at HMP Belmarsh nothing of the routine followed by cons and guards had escaped him. He knew how the prison worked in all its minutiae, who the prison officers were, their habits, what made them tick or flare up. He knew the layout of the Cat A wing, the number of steps between each security lock and to the other main parts of the building. He could have walked around Belmarsh blindfolded and not tripped once. It had started as a way to reassure himself, a way of focusing the mind and conquer a new hostile environment. Now it was feeding the project that had been gnawing at him relentlessly.

Escape.

He could count on Charlie to come up with the information he needed. What had been tried before and had, so far, never succeeded. Inmates were receiving drugs and mobile phones through drones – several drops every night in the main prison. But what could be shipped into HSU Belmarsh?

The trip to Scotland Yard had provided Henry with exceptional information. Something he would trade with Kamal, if he needed to. The plan had started to evolve slowly and was gaining momentum. So long as he behaved and gave the guards no bother, he might be allowed out again.

Henry looked at his hands in cuffs. He clenched and opened his fists a few times. He had so feared his mind would be dulled by the routine of prison life. His talent had sprung to life again after only a few lapses around the Bloomberg terminal. The flow between his deep analytical skills and the ability to synthetise a large amount of data had resurfaced almost intact and the joy had almost been overwhelming.

A shiver moved down his back, rippling deliciously into his entire body. He muffled a groan. The guards had not noticed. The conversation they were having over pay and working conditions was still occupying their minds. Henry relaxed against the cool surface of metal. His mind had been freed and was feeding into a single purpose.

* * *

Need to see you urgently. Nancy pressed the send button and put her BlackBerry down next to her wine glass. She would give Edwina five minutes to reply and then call her. Implicating her without having a conversation was tempting but unfair.

Once Pole knew, there would be no turning back. And he would know, either today or tomorrow. Edwina had the choice. Speak to Pole herself or Nancy would do so. Pole did not care about market manipulation, but he had a double murder to solve. Edwina's career was on a knife edge. Nancy sighed. So much talent and hard work, swept away. Did she really need to go down that path? Her BlackBerry buzzed, reverberating on the counter with small jumps.

Fiendishly busy with next round of QE. Can it wait?

No.

Nancy went outside and hailed a cab. Edwina would meet her tonight.

* * *

Cook's revised toxicology report had been neatly placed on Pole's desk. A collection of coloured stickers indicated key findings. Pole smiled. Andy had as ever done a Sterling job. Nurani was nowhere to be seen. Out and about, checking on the leads they had gathered through Gary's gym and nursing her wounded pride. Caught short of the latest information on the case in front of Marsh – not the desired effect for someone nursing high ambition.

And yet Pole did not mind her desire to succeed. If she could only overcome her deeply entrenched self-doubts, she could be one day the finest of detectives.

Pole closed his door. A clear sign that no one should cross the threshold until he was ready to be interrupted. He read the file cover to cover, ignoring Andy's tabs, comfortable in his old armchair and a hand playing with an elastic band he had found on the floor. He stopped the repetitive movement and straightened up. His hand hovered over his phone. He called Yvonne.

"Don't give me an earful. I know it's late." Pole pulled the phone away from his ear.

"I bloody well will give you an earful, I was about to *finally* leave this goddamn place." Yvonne was not in the mood.

"I owe you, I know."

"The list is too long for me to enumerate them all, but recently getting two tox report in record time, with some extra profiling on LSD. Analysing all the bloody pill you lot found in the Lockers of the two vics..."

Pole was nodding away, waiting until Yvonne was done with all the things, he owed her for whilst calling her at 9pm.

"I can't thank you enough for all you do. But if you could still bear with me."

Yvonne grunted. "You're going to ask me about the traces of LSD, despite a five-day lapse between Cook's death and the latest tox report, right?"

"Yup – and the answer is?"

"No idea, but I can hypothesise."

"Hypothesise away," Pole said, firing the elastic band across the room.

"We put the guy on ice; this slows the process of decomposition. And before you ask why I didn't find it to start with?"

"You said it, not me."

"I used an advanced testing method this time round, not the standard method as with any routine tox screen. So I was confident but the other drugs sloshing around his blood overwhelmed the initial test. This time I used a urine sample"

"And that will hold up in court?"

"What do you take me for?"

"The best of the best, of course," Pole replied "And Hardy? No fingerprints on the hose that connected the exhaust to the car?"

"None. Hardy had no gloves on when we found him, but we did find an old pair in the car."

"He stays strapped in with his seat belt on but puts his gloves back in the side pocket of the car?"

"Strange but correct."

"Final tox report on Hardy?"

"It will be on your desk tomorrow, but he took some pretty strong painkillers Prescription drug only. The sort of stuff you take after an op or a very bad injury."

"Sporting injury for example?"

"If severe enough, yes – nerve pain in particular."

"Anything new on Felipe Martinez?"

"Nope, the Martinez tox report is clear. High dose of LSD, no question. But, the hair sample analysis indicates it was a new habit. Not sure it's relevant."

"You mean he was not a habitual user?" Pole said, not waiting for the answer he knew. "That corroborates what his girlfriend said to us."

Pole and Yvonne fell silent.

"Jon, are great minds about to think alike? Jon, are you still there?"

"Sorry Yvonne, not sure. I mean I am here. That was great." He thanked Yvonne once more and put the phone down.

Pole stretched in his chair and looked around his office. The desk was a mess, nothing new in this.

The latest news gave him a good reason to call Nancy. It was only 9.30pm and she would still be up. He rolled the BlackBerry in his hand a couple of times. Not a good idea though. Nancy was following her intuition and he had learned not to interrupt the workings of her remarkable mind. She would call when ready.

His phone rang. Pole ignored it until he cast an eye on the screen that showed Superintendent Marsh's name. His boss was calling at this time of night – not good. Marsh had fretted about Henry. He only needed half an excuse to cancel Henry's second visit to the Yard. Pole picked up the call and was asked to make his way to Marsh's office – not good at all.

Marsh was on another call when Pole entered. He waved him in. His monosyllabic replies gave Pole an inkling about the identity of the caller. If he was a betting man, he would have put his money on the Governor of HMP Belmarsh. Marsh terminated the call too courteously for Pole's liking. Marsh sat back in his chair and fired a volley of questions about the case. Pole batted them back with the coolness of a man in control.

"Crowne is delivering – was worth twisting Belmarsh's Governor's arm, I suppose," Marsh said rearranging his Montblanc pens on his desk with a meticulous gesture. "And Ms Wu was there to assist?"

Was The Super disappointed that the delightful Ms Wu had not visited him?

Pole had taken a seat and crossed his long legs, pushing his back comfortably into the chair. He straightened up a little and raised a quizzical eyebrow. "She was indeed. As ever, very much on the ball."

"And you are certain she is not too close to Crowne? Are you not sailing close to the wind a bit on this?"

Pole's gut tightened. He felt the blow he had not anticipated. The Super had not been indulged as quickly as he might have expected, and he was flexing the muscles of his authority. Pole's light-grey eyes drilled into Marsh and retreated. A confrontation would be of no use. "That is precisely what I want. If Henry tries to find a way to escape Ms Wu will be well placed to detect."

"But she was part of his legal team when he went to trial. Correct?" Pole nodded.

"And she visits him regularly – still. Correct?"

"A lot of briefs do." Pole's focus changed. He was losing the argument that had not been made yet but would soon come. "Frankly, this is not a reason to stop Henry coming back tomorrow. Belmarsh's governor has organised the trip with prison officers who know how to transport high-profile prisoners. I am not worried about Henry escaping. However, I need the intel now or I fear there might be another victim."

Marsh shifted in his chair. He had not anticipated Pole's challenge to be so well-targeted. Marsh rearranged his pens once more. "Who do you have in mind?"

It was Pole's turn to switch position in their cat and mouse game. "We are speaking to contacts at the Bank of England, Edwina James- Jones." Pole was rehearsing his arguments quickly: LIBOR, the BBA – no Whitehall for the moment. "Is she credible?" Marsh asked.

"You mean as the next governor of the Bank of England?"

"Well, yes. You must know she is very close. First woman to be appointed," Marsh said with a small sigh. The next thing would be the appointment of a woman as the Commissioner – unthinkable.

Pole seized the opportunity; this was why they needed Henry. He kept going with details of LIBOR, enough to make it sound as complicated as it was. Marsh nodded. Pole pushed his body out of the chair and was halfway to standing up.

"And Ms Wu also knows Ms James-Jones. Correct?"

Pole collapsed back into the seat. He had been a fool not to see this coming. Nancy was connected to Henry and Edwina, and Marsh was minded to be suspicious.

* * *

The Barbican Members' Room was remarkably quiet. It was gone 10pm and the intervals for both concert hall and theatre were long over. Nancy had chosen to sit in a secluded corner from where she could see the entrance. She sat in a comfortable armchair. Edwina would be here any minute. The knot in Nancy's stomach had tightened a little more. More difficult to control was the anger that made her right hand twitch ever so slightly. She had known the anger of the rebellious when she was a student in Paris. She had known the anger that came with fear when she had left China as it became clear to her parents that the Cultural Revolution had veered off course to the detriment of artists of any value. She had become an angry young barrister, schooled at the Sorbonne and King's College London.

Criminal law had seemed apt for channelling her permanent sense of injustice. She had worked hard at understanding why and finally at letting go. But it had meant leaving the Bar, transforming radically the way she lived – and she loved it. Occasionally the beast would be summoned, and Nancy resented anyone who asked her to call upon its power.

Nancy glanced at her watch. Edwina had no more than five minutes to appear, then she would call Pole. She was browsing through her call history when a swift hand stopped her. Edwina was standing at her side, arm outstretched, a desperate look etched on her tired face. Her voice sounded strangely raw. "What is so urgent? Is William…?"

"Still unconscious," Nancy replied sharply. "Drink?"

"Yes, anything."

Nancy ordered and pointed at the seat next to her. "Tell me all you know about LIBOR fixing."

Edwina's blue eyes widened; the colour drained from her face. "You mean, the process of setting LIBOR?"

Nancy smiled thinly – was Edwina still hoping she wouldn't be found out? "You and I know this is not what I am asking, Eddie." She could savage Edwina here and now, but it would not help. "Let's not lose time. There is a murderer on the loose."

The drinks arrived and Edwina clung to her glass, undecided it seemed whether she should stay or flee. She took a gulp of wine. Her eyes had not met Nancy's yet.

"I hear you," she murmured.

"When I say fixing, I mean manipulation: fraud, lies – and in general the type of crappy behaviour that caused the crisis in the first place."

Edwina dropped her head in her hands.

"Oh God." She rubbed her nose with the back of her hand. "Nancy, I am scared."

Nancy gave Edwina a dispassionate look. Was it an act? She scrutinised her face, the clasped hands, the dark rings underneath her eyes.

"Speak to me," Nancy said in a softer tone.

"How much do you know?"

"Not the right question, Eddie. I know enough to have gathered you're involved. If you want my help, I want the unabbreviated version of events. Gary and Tom are dead. William is breathing through a ventilator. The choice is yours."

Edwina drew the light pashmina she wore more closely around her shoulders.

"I had a meeting with William a few months back. We had been talking QE…" her voice trailed. "I don't know how we came to it. I suppose it is the skill of a high-calibre civil servant to ask without saying."

Nancy nodded. William had spoken to her when the crisis started biting – he was there to save the UK financial system come what may. "After that we spoke of hypothetical ways, and it seemed to eventually all into place."

"Who else knows?" Nancy asked.

Edwina looked up and anger flashed in her eyes. "This is not a police interrogation you know."

"I am well aware of this, my dear, and believe you me I have attended more than I care to remember." Nancy paused.

The pressure of silence, always a powerful tool. "Who else?"

"Gabriel is aware."

Nancy waited. It was not enough.

"He knows I spoke to Tom at the BBA and William, but he does not know who Tom contacted within the banks." Edwina looked drained. She sat back, holding her pashmina even tighter.

"Only you and Gabriel?"

Edwina nodded. "We had to do something."

"As much as I would love to spend time arguing whether any form of manipulation is justified – pre- or post-crisis, What I really need from you are all the names..." Nancy said with a hint of sarcasm. "People in the US are getting agitated and they have started talking."

Edwina opened her mouth, but nothing came out. Nancy had found the angle of attack once more and hit hard. She sat back to see the result unfold.

"Geithner, US treasury knows," Edwina volunteered.

"I bet he does," Nancy replied. "Who else in his team across the pond?"

"Not sure:, a couple more," Edwina's hand moved blindly to her glass. It was almost empty.

Nancy looked at Eddie with a sudden deep sense of sorrow. So much talent and hard work. Nancy hid her disappointment. "You must speak to Inspector Pole."

Edwina closed her eyes. Tears had gathered underneath her blonde lashes. She cleared her throat.

"You're right. I must – and I will – but I'd like to prepare the final papers for the next QE round. My legacy. And a better outcome than the current LIBOR mess." Edwina stopped. She met Nancy's eyes. "Give me until tomorrow morning. After that I'll speak to Scotland Yard."

"Why should I trust you?"

"Because you know that William and I shared the same view – we needed to save the system and so needs must."

Nancy gave Edwina a long hard look. "The greater good?" Edwina gave a feeble smile. It sounded so arrogant now that Nancy had laid down the consequences of Edwina's actions. .

"I will be at Scotland Yard tomorrow at 8am. I hope Inspector Pole will have heard from you by then."

"He will," Edwina replied. She stood up slowly, gathered her belongings and left without another word. Tomorrow Edwina James-Jones would be history; today though she had a job to finish.

Nancy followed Edwina's silhouette. It disappeared through the doors of the Members' Room. She waved to the waitress; another glass of wine would help to dull the pain a little. She mechanically reached for her phone inside her bag. Pole had called, then left a hurried text.

Marsh on the warpath – call me PLEASE. Jonathan

Chapter Twenty-One

The Tube was not moving. Defective train on the line, the announcement had said. Brett cursed. He was late. Mohammed may not wait. No, he would. He was too scared of the small man in his white robe, The Sheik. Brett looked around the carriage. He had squeezed his lanky body in the last seat in the row. The space was packed. The old gentleman next to him was fingering prayer beads. His tatty clothes smelt of spices and his lips kept moving noiselessly to words he knew by heart.

The train jolted into action again and Brett breathed in. He looked at his burner mobile. No signal yet. The train stopped at Highbury and Islington. A group of women in full niqab walked on. Sweat had started to gather on his forehead. The temperature was suffocating. He stood up and pushed his way towards the opening doors.

The SUV was parked on the opposite side of the road. Mohammed had disappeared swiftly leaving Brett on his own to board the car. The same Middle Eastern man who had taken him the last time was driving. He shrugged his head towards the back door. Brett got into the SUV, tied the cloth around his eyes. The drive seemed to take less time than before. Were they more relaxed about him?

Unlikely.

He left his mobile in the back of the car. Stepped out to be frisked and stepped forward into a different house. The man pushed the door open, removed his blindfold and waited for him to go in. The smell made Brett's skin crawl: chemicals – weed killer, ammonia? A hand guided him towards the smell. Brett's stomach lurched. The man jerked his head in the direction of a small stairwell. Brett climbed up moving away from the acrid vapours. He wiped his forehead before knocking at the door. No response. He tried again and the door opened ajar. He was alone.

Brett stepped into a large room, a couple of different armchairs had been gathered in its centre, with a coffee table before it, and a low couch stuck against the wall. He moved towards the coffee table and spotted three photos, arranged at an equal distance face down. Brett moved closer, his mind racing through the various possibilities. Had they followed him to his club? Did they know of his MI6 involvement despite Steve's assurances?

The soft draught of an opening door and the sound of the floor creaking told him his host had arrived. Brett tried to compose himself and turned around slowly.

The Sheik signalled him to sit down. He moved to the couch and tea appeared poured by a slim young woman wearing the full burqa, her hands were gloved, and Brett could see she was struggling to move around.

"You did well. I hear my Mujahidin is crossing the Channel tonight."

"Then you know more than I do," Brett replied taking a sip of tea.

A slim smile came to The Sheik's face. "I have another deal for you."

"Look, I only do art," Brett said without conviction. He would say no only if MI6 allowed him to.

"Is the remuneration not adequate?" The look was amused but the tone cruel.

Brett fretted for a moment. Some semblance of opposition, deliberation then acceptance.

"Take a look at the first photo."

Brett slid the picture towards him, still face down. He turned it over and looked at the face closely. A man, in his thirties, light-brown hair and distinct light-brown eyes, he might have been handsome had his face not been marked by some ugly scarring. Brett gathered by his countenance that he was well educated, even polished – government, Army?

"I don't know him."

"Good." The Sheik took a sip of tea and gestured. "Next picture." Brett slid the second picture down the table, a building, The Royal

Exchange. He slowly put down the photo on the table and waited. "Now, you must know this building?"

Brett nodded.

"You work for some of the companies that rent offices there?" The man finished his tea.

"I advise on what art they put on their walls." Brett just managed to steady his voice as the unthinkable started unfolding in front of him. Beads of sweat had started to collect on his forehead. He kept his eyes fixed on the photo. If he moved them, he would meet The Sheik's eyes and the man might see fear.

"I want access to this building," the voice was relaxed. He could have been asking for Brett's favourite Renaissance artist.

"Why?" Brett lifted his face and met the dark-brown eyes that had not left him since he had come in.

"It won't be a bomb."

Brett took in a short breath, surprised at the frankness of the answer. He was still dubious.

"The price will be right."

"When?" Brett swallowed some tea, the burning liquid dispersing the feeling of nausea.

"Monday, perhaps earlier—"

Brett put down his glass noisily. "Impossible."

"Monday."

Brett ran his bony hand through his thinning hair. "I need to think."

The Sheik nodded, took out his mobile. Brett's minder appeared at the door.

"Mohammed will contact you." The Sheik said, not bothering to stand.

Brett cast on eye towards the third photo on the table. "Some other time," came the answer.

* * *

His thumb was drumming some complex rhythm on the wheel. Pole glanced in his rear mirror, indicated and switched lane. The traffic was light. He would be at Scotland Yard before 7am. Nurani had done enough damage with Marsh, a good old-fashioned talking to was what she needed. Pole kept drumming the tune. Jazz FM was playing one of his favourite pieces by Didier Lockwood. His head started moving with a saxophone solo.

Nancy had called Pole back to discuss her early meeting with Marsh. She would seek to appease the great man and Pole was convinced she would succeed. And Pole would certainly not work with Henry from Belmarsh. He had managed to lose Marsh with the complexity of LIBOR. His superior would never admit to not understanding an issue, especially one that was at the centre of a high-profile case.

Still Marsh would do his research too and it wouldn't be long before he caught up. Using Nancy to gain time was not his preferred choice but she had volunteered. A small pang of doubt hit him: Marsh–Nancy, nah, never.

He cranked up the radio, seeking to chase away the small bubble of anger that was threatening to burst. Jazz was the least recommended music to listen while driving, too intellectual and demanding. Pole shrugged, so what, much better than Techno – No Thank You. His mind concentrated on the improvisation for a short moment. But last night's conversation would not go away.

Some idiot tried to squeeze in front of him. Pole looked at the blue light he used in an emergency. Taking out his wrath on some stupid driver would not do. He would square the impact of Nurani's conversation with Marsh with the lady herself. Nurani was unquestionably an excellent cop, resourceful and dedicated. She could not let the pressure of promotion send her off course though. She was better than that. Pole relaxed as the next tune started, confident he had found the right tone for speaking to his DI.

Pole's mobile started buzzing, a text had been sent to him. He pulled off the road and read the content. Edwina James-Jones was calling him in a couple of minutes. He recognised the name immediately, the first woman tipped to become Governor of the Bank of England but also the star guest of the Women in Enterprise

Conference at which Gary had been murdered and of course, a good friend to Nancy. Still the early morning call surprised Pole.

The conversation was short. She would come to the Yard and speak to him today about the LIBOR matter. She wanted to deliver a major report to Mervyn King this morning. Would 10am therefore do? Pole was on his way to episode two of the Henry Crowne Show. He had to reluctantly admit he was looking forward to Henry's incisive way of dealing with the case. And yes, 10am would do.

Pole resumed his driving, stuck the blue flashing light to his roof and accelerated across a red light. He would be at the office before Nancy arrived for her power breakfast with his boss. She might even have time for a quick tea with him beforehand.

Henry was already working at his Bloomberg terminals when Pole entered the room. The same dingy place, four plasma screens gave it a surreal look but Henry was smiling.

"Morning Inspector. I have pulled up all the stocks and delivered a cracking model that will speed up the investigation."

Henry faced Pole. Deep circles had appeared underneath his eyes and his paler face told Pole he had not had much sleep.

"Morning Henry. Care to elaborate?" Pole placed a Caffè Nero double macchiato he'd grab before coming into work on Henry's desk, pulled up a chair and sat next to him.

"Ta. I am not trying to be a pompous arse. You may not agree, of course, but I spent the night reading a couple of books about this new financial model. It enabled me to spot any substantial variations in the LIBOR quotes of the banks who submit to the LIBOR panel."

"You mean that your model can detect the magnitude and time of any manipulation of the LIBOR benchmark by the banks that submitted?"

"In a nutshell," Henry said disappointed. No need to further elaborate on his brilliant idea – sulk.

"Good man," Pole replied, amused. "Although—"

"We still don't have a real motive. I know."

Pole grunted. His mobile buzzed. Nancy was at reception.

* * *

"We still don't have a motive. LIBOR manipulation is what links these guys together but that's all," Pole said putting a fresh cup of tea in front of Nancy. She gave it a questioning look.

"Builder's tea, *ma chère*; nothing else will do in the morning for a good old-fashioned copper like me."

"I know but it depends on which builder's tea we are talking about," Nancy said. She took a sip, and looked surprisingly content. She leaned back in her chair. She looked around at the room they were in. Pole caught her inquisitive look.

"Superintendent Marsh is taking a keen interest in the investigation."

"And he thinks you are sailing a little too close to the wind by involving too many *outsiders*, unless the said *outsider* pays more attention to the very large—" Nancy took a sip, "ego of the said gentleman."

"In a nutshell," Pole said stiffly.

"Are you?"

"You mean do I need to be more cautious? Probably, but I won't be. Not the way I work, and no one will make me change that."

"Does he know about William?"

"No, and please don't think I don't care," Pole interrupted advancing a hand kindly. "I can't have him making a number of calls to the Chancellor. It will stop this investigation dead."

Nancy nodded. "Yes, that is wise. I don't think William would want Osborne to be involved in any case." She took another sip of tea to steady her nerves. "I'll be as brief as I can."

"I need you to help with Edwina too," Pole said, a way to keep Nancy close perhaps.

"That I can do. I think the conversation with Edwina will be a turning point."

"Why don't you give me a preview?"

"I won't put words into her mouth, but you may find your motive to be a major cover-up involving very senior people."

Pole raised an eyebrow. "You think that Henry's list of banks that have manipulated LIBOR will give us nothing?"

"Not nothing. It will confirm our thinking," Nancy was enjoying her tea. "If my theory is right, it will show you that no one working in the banks that have manipulated LIBOR has died."

"Righto, I see where you are going. If it had been an exercise to eradicate the traders who have moved the benchmark, we would have more dead bodies on our hands. And it has not happened." Pole pursed his lips in agreement.

"*Absolument, vous avez tout compris.* Hence we need to look into the top government institutions."

"You suspect Edwina?" Pole asked bluntly.

Nancy's jaw clenched and released. "It did cross my mind, but no is the short answer."

Pole stood up, still holding his cup, and moved to the window. The sun was playing hide and seek with some large ominous clouds. He turned around.

"You need more evidence. I understand, Jonathan, but hear me out. Two questions intrigue me."

"Pray tell," Pole asked with a flourish of his hand.

"We have had two murders and one attempt," Nancy said. She straightened herself up and carried on. "In quick succession – then nothing. Why no attempt on Edwina's life? And yet looked worried when I last saw her."

"She is putting on an act? She realises what she's done and is frightened of being caught?"

"Edwina is a smart woman. I can't believe she would have let us come so close to her in the first instance. The Women in Enterprise Conference? Far too obvious."

"She could have an accomplice?"

"She could, but here again why the conference?" Nancy's mind had become alert to a change, thoughts that were slowly gathering and ready to surface. Something important lay below that surface; she just had to stretch to grab it.

"Anything you'd like to share?" Pole asked, knowing the answer might be no.

"You must be impartial when you hear Edwina."

"That is not an answer. I am not some rookie detective." Pole gave her a charming smile.

Nancy hesitated.

"Come on, just a little clue?" Pole held his thumb and index finger apart.

"We need to think laterally. If not Edwina. Then who and why?"

"You mean who could benefit from her involvement not being discovered?"

"*Exactement.*"

Pole's mobile rang. He gave it a dark look and was about to ignore it when he noticed the name on the screen. Yvonne was calling. "Why did you not call the landline?"

"And good morning to you too Inspector."

"And good morning to you Yvonne – sorry, you're on loudspeaker."

"Good morning, Nancy; making sense of this case yet?" Yvonne said with a smile in her voice.

"Morning Yvonne – any clue from you would be most helpful."

"Well, I have something for you." She heard the muffled sound of paper. "Here we are. Working on Hardy's forensic for the final tox report. I promised Pole it would be on his desk asap. You recall that the passenger door was taped with some heavy-duty parcel tape, right?"

"All around the window to seal any gap that the hose pipe carrying the exhaust's fumes had created." Pole said. He could see it clearly. "And the same tape was used to fix the hose to the exhaust."

"Spot on. Well, I noticed that the tape was jagged and therefore had not been cut with a sharp instrument. That got me thinking," Yvonne waited. "Anyone with a view – no?"

"Someone cut it with their teeth," Pole said snapping his fingers.

"Hey, don't burst my bubble," Yvonne said playfully. "But correct – and I found saliva which gave me DNA but—"

"Not the DNA of the victim," Pole finished. "He never taped that tape to the hose."

"Nope. And before you ask there is zero match on the database, nothing on NOMAD."

"You're a star." Pole said.

"I know – only to be eclipsed by dear Nancy of course." Yvonne was enjoying the tease. "I will leave you guys *alone*." She hung up with a naughty smile in her voice.

Pole tried to ignore the slight blush on Nancy's face. "Let's see what Ms James-Jones has in store for us then."

"Enjoy. Let's see what Superintendent of Police Timothy Marsh has to say for himself then," Nancy said.

Her eyes met Pole's. There was only defiance and humour in them – somewhat reassuring to Pole.

* * *

Henry was sitting back in his uncomfortable chair, rocking on its back legs. He had finished his coffee long ago and he was craving more. He had completed the financial model that was about to reveal which banks had moved their LIBOR submission artificially. It had started to churn from live data at 9.17am. Henry looked around the room for the first time, a drab little place not so dissimilar to the cell he occupied at HMP Belmarsh, apart from the larger size and the lack of a window. Pole could have at least provided him with a coffee machine; he was not asking for The Ritz.

The door opened, letting in a draught of much needed fresh air. Henry did not bother to look at who had come in. He wanted to strike the right note and was still appraising his handiwork. Pole had been daring in choosing Nancy as a consultant when Henry's case had turned nasty. Granted, he evidently had a soft spot for the lady but this was not the sole reason. Nancy had proved to be an asset to The Yard. If Henry could prove to be an asset too, the plan would work.

A cup of fresh coffee materialised on his desk and the refined scent of Nancy's perfume announced his friend. Her face looked even more tired than his own.

"I know what you are going to say. I should have thought twice before stepping into the world of crime again." Nancy sighed.

Henry stood up and brought a second chair close to his. Nancy deserved more attention than he had given her recently. He could never take her for granted. He had not seen the deep lines etched on her forehead since the days of his trial.

Henry's prosecution had been more than just facing accusations that made him a monster. He had had to face the consequences of his friend's betrayal. Yet, she had never shied away from her commitment to helping him.

"I would never criticise you for believing in someone, perhaps too much," Henry said as she sat next to him.

"You don't have to do it, Henry. I am quite capable of doing this to myself."

Henry took his cup of coffee and stirred in some sugar. "Friendship takes two things to be called just that – time and obstacles, I discovered at my own expense."

"You are so right, and I know this too. I even take pride at being a good judge of characters but this time, well..." Nancy pulled a face.

"You shouldn't regret fighting for the causes you believe in."

"Perhaps, but I will not advance the female cause by backing the wrong sort. It will do ten times more damage."

"Still, damn sight nobler than the IRA. Although of course, when I supported them, iit never felt that way."

The door banged open, interrupting their conversation. Pole walked in, took a chair, turned it around and straddled it to sit down.

"Your friend's almost certainly in the clear," he said, crossing his legs underneath his seat.

Nancy's body straightened up a little. "James-Jones not in the frame then?" Henry said surprised.

"Don't rub it in Henry, please," Nancy said with a mix of impatience and tiredness.

Henry's face dropped. "Sorry, I did not mean it that way."

"How did you get that name anyway, Henry?" Pole asked, pleased at the rebuff.

"The Bank of England is involved, Edwina was the main speaker at the conference where Gary was killed and," Henry hesitated. "Nancy is upset, so

"How do you know she is not involved?" Nancy asked.

"Her alibi stacks up for Gary. Still need to check CCTV cameras but she was speaking to a lot of people, so we'll get there. For Tom, she was working until late with one of the sub-committees she chairs. Again, we'll check but there are CCTV cameras everywhere around the Bank of England, so difficult to slip out without being seen."

"Accomplice?" Nancy forced herself to ask. Her hand slightly clenched.

"Don't think so," Pole said. "She is scared, not of being caught but because she thinks she is next."

"I know you are going to tell me I am a smart-arse, but don't you think she would have been done in by now?" Henry ventured.

"Your point?" Pole shot back.

"What if someone is trying to save Edwina's bacon?"

"Henry has a point." Nancy nodded.

Pole stood up slowly. "Right. Let's have a final chat with Ms James-Jones. Nancy, care to join?"

* * *

Pole and Nancy were retracing their steps towards the rooms on the upper floors.

"Whether we like it or not, Henry has a point." Nancy said.

Pole grunted. "How was your pow-wow with Marsh?"

"Predictable – a lot of ego management; I'm not sure I delivered."

"I sincerely hope we can nail this one before he knows about William."

Nancy kneaded her shoulders, keen to relieve some of the accumulated tension there. "I'll be fine," she said anticipating Pole's concern.

Pole nodded, looking unconvinced.

"You should speak to Gabriel, her number two. He understands better than anybody the politics around Edwina's job at the Bank of England, perhaps even better than Eddie herself," Nancy said still massaging her neck.

"We did speak to him after Gary's jump. Remind me. What does he do exactly?"

"He has been working with her for over ten years. His father was a diplomat with, I believe, a long stint in the Middle East. He speaks quite a few foreign languages – Arabic, Farsi as well. Very bright young man."

"Why is he so faithful to her?" Pole had stopped walking.

"I can only guess but his appearance makes him a little shy of crowds."

"He is the guy with a scar on his face," Pole said, his memory jolted. "What happened?"

"No idea. You need to ask Edwina. She knows and yet never speaks about it at his behest."

They started walking in silence again.

"If she gets the job, he gets a boost to his career too?" Pole asked one hand on the door handle.

"*Absolument*," Nancy said.

"*Compris*." Pole eyes had lit up with the bright spark of realisation.

* * *

Her friend looked bewildered. Edwina had aged ten years in one hour. She answered Pole's questions in half-disjointed sentences. The ceaseless pressure to reach the top, the financial crisis and now Pole's interrogation had broken down Edwina's resilience. She would soon have to salvage what she could of her career in the LIBOR manipulation scandal that was about to explode.

Nancy sat on the other side of the tinted glass, anger gradually replaced by sympathy.

What a fool. Yet Nancy still felt raw, disappointed not so much for herself but for all the other women who had taken Eddie for the perfect role model.

Some of Edwina's answers drew Nancy back to the room in which she was sitting. Of course, her elevation benefited Gabriel. Of course, he was at the conference, he is her right-hand man and, yes, he has the same alibi as her on the day of Tom's murder.

"Could he have left for a few hours?" Pole was prodding.

Edwina seemed less shocked than Nancy would have expected by the implications of the question. She was thinking hard. Yet she seemed unwilling to give up on Gabriel just to keep Pole at bay.

"We worked separately on certain issues." Edwina hesitated.

Pole was on the attack again. "Why is Gabriel not in the running for the Governor's job?"

Nancy winced. It was a slap in the face.

"You mean because he is a bloke?" Edwina blue eyes had turned dark, her brows were knitted so tight they almost touched one another.

"No," Pole was not letting go. "Because he is just as good as you are."

"Point taken," Nancy murmured.

"He is not comfortable with large audiences and certainly not with the prospect of fielding press conferences."

She had refused so far to talk about the scar, a pledge to him Nancy wondered. "But if you're sacked because of LIBOR, he goes down with you?" Edwina's face changed once more. Reality had sunk in – hard, raw, unbearable. Her hand travelled to her stomach. For a moment Nancy thought Edwina was going to be sick.

"Yes, if I go, he goes." It had been softly spoken, a whisper.

Pole had stopped the savaging. He pushed the untouched glass of water towards her. Edwina took a sip and put it down with a trembling hand. She now knew. It was over for her.

"But he can get a job anywhere." Edwina protested.

Pole had sat back in his chair, considering. Nancy saw from the tilt of his head she knew so well that he was running with a new line of thought.

He terminated the interview and let one of his team process Edwina. "She is not telling me everything." Pole had joined Nancy in the viewing room. "Stay with her but don't do anything—"

"Silly." Nancy managed a faint smile.

Pole was so close. He could put his arms around her and pull her to his chest. But Nancy knew he shouldn't.

"I'll get to the truth," Nancy nodded, breaking the moment. She too never took no for an answer.

Pole had no time to reply. His mobile was buzzing urgently. His face said it all – Emergency.

"St Thomas's – Is he all right?"

Nancy sat down abruptly, her eyes wide with worry. William had been targeted again.

"He is fine but whoever has targeted him has given my guys the slip. I'm going." Pole squeezed her shoulder with all the affection he could muster.

"Careful too," she managed to articulate.

"Always – you need to go to Edwina."

"Yes, of course."

Pole disappeared but Nancy was still sitting. She shook herself out of her slumber. Edwina would be out soon.

Nancy retraced her steps and entered the room in which Henry was still working.

"Don't ask please, no time, but can you find all you can on Gabriel Steel?"

Henry nodded and moved to his computer screens without hesitation.

Nancy was already on her way. She stopped, turned back, and laid a burner phone on his desk.

"Call me – my number is there under my name. The phone won't lock."

Henry gave her an approving look. This woman was the business.

Chapter Twenty-Two

Brett reread the text.

This morning He threw the mobile on the sofa. It had spoilt a perfectly good breakfast – full English this Saturday morning accompanied by an excellent cup of Jamaican Blue Mountain coffee.

MI6-Steve had been *crystal clear*, as he put it. Do whatever they ask you to do – sound reluctant if you think it will work better but facilitate. Brett had given up asking why.

Yet today he felt he deserved a bit more of an explanation. The Sheik had proven to be an unexpected cross between Jihadist and shrewd businessman. He almost certainly despised Brett and would eventually seek to do away with him.

9am

Brett texted back. He would walk towards Harrods at nine this morning, a man would bump into him, lift his wallet and escape on a scooter with his accomplice. Brett would report it two hours later. The card he used to enter The Royal Exchange building would be in his wallet.

He would also leave a message with the firm that employed him as an art consultant but, because today was a Saturday, they would not pick up the message until Monday morning. Credible enough, he thought. Brett sent a message to Steve from his other mobile. He took his cup of coffee and looked through the window of his lounge. He was high enough to see the treetops of Eaton Square. A name entered his mind and he smiled. One thing was certain. Unlike Brett, Crowne would not be enjoying a leisurely breakfast this morning. Brett moved from the window to his kitchen and poured the last of the coffee into his cup. That thought made his final cuppa delicious.

* * *

They had not exchanged a word. Edwina collected her personal effects and Nancy waited with an odd sense of déjà vu. She had waited at this exact same desk for Henry after his first interrogation. But this time she hoped she would not have to assemble a defence team for Edwina.

Edwina averted her gaze. Slinging her small rucksack over her shoulder she spoke to Nancy in a murmur.

"I must go back to the Bank of England – now."

"Let me come with you."

Edwina hesitated but she did not have the strength to say no. "I need to check on the details I gave you and Inspector Pole – to be sure."

Nancy nodded. They walked out and she hailed a cab. As Edwina entered the cab Nancy felt someone was staring at her but she had no time to look around. Edwina was already telling her her story as they were settling in.

Gabriel had changed, perhaps in small increments she had not noticed until she could not ignore it any longer: a new gym craze she never thought he had, holidays booked at the last minute and not mentioned.

Edwina had found an online airline ticket to Turkey – he always spoke about his holidays: trekking the Himalayas, walking the trail to Machu Picchu. *I live to travel* was his motto.

Edwina's face became animated as she spoke about the details that had been haunting her for days. There was also Gabriel's detachment over the death of Gary and Tom, the lack of concern over her own safety, let alone his.

Nancy and Edwina had arrived at the bank quicker than expected. Edwina had ushered Nancy through security and they'd moved straight to Edwina's office.

The keys jingled in her hand. They never left Edwina's key ring. She fished around for a little parcel in her top drawer. She handed it to

Nancy. Nancy's phone was ringing before she could unfold the paper to reveal its contents. Henry was calling.

"Two things I managed to unearth, but not verified—"

"Never mind that, tell me."

"When his father was UK ambassador to Saudi Arabia, Gabriel got very interested in the Salafist movement – Don't ask me how I got that."

"And number two," Nancy said.

"He and his brother were caught in the 1998 Nairobi attack on the US embassy. His brother lost his life and he got badly injured. Nancy, where are you?"

"Bank of England – will call you later."

Nancy unfolded the scrap of paper Edwina had handed over to her. She carefully retrieved the pill, held it between her thumb and index finger: a little blue pill similar in size and colour to the one Yvonne had shown her.

"Where did you get that from?" Nancy asked.

"Gabriel's desk," Edwina said. "What does that mean Nancy? I can't think anymore."

"One thing I am sure of Eddie. It's time to call Pole." Nancy looked for her phone and spotted its black corner sticking out from underneath a piece of paper on Edwina's desk.

"I think you're…" Edwina stopped dead. Her face etched with terror.

"Good morning, ladies." Gabriel had walked through the door. He had a gun.

* * *

The young policewoman looked exhausted. She was at the end of her shift. Brett couldn't believe his luck. She took his statement. Theft of a wallet.

"Would you be able to recognise the assailant?"

"Not really, they were on a scooter." Brett did not lie. He did not need to.

"Any valuables in the wallet?"

"The usual, credit cards, some cash and – oh yes, my office ID card."

It was all finished in less than fifteen minutes. He texted Mohammed – *Done.* Now the clock was ticking.

* * *

The burner phone rang. Henry cast an eye towards it. Maybe he should let it go to voicemail? Nancy almost hung up on him the last time he phoned her to give her some goddamned good intel.

Still, Henry grabbed the phone with a swift movement and pressed the green button. He was waiting to hear Nancy's voice and had already prepared some flippant comment, but the occasion didn't materialise. There was a rustling noise, paper being moved, then voices two… no three: one man, two women and one of them was Nancy's.

Henry felt a cold sweat coming over him. He had spent enough time in prison, always on the alert for the next challenge, to know that something was badly wrong. He cradled the phone in the palm of his hand. He mustn't hang up.

"Move away from the desk – hands on heads," the man's voice said

"Gabs, what are you doing?"

"That is a really stupid question coming from a top-notch banker like you Eddie," the voice carried on.

Henry made sure the phone was now on mute. He must reach Pole.

* * *

As Gabriel made his grand entrance, Nancy hit the call button. She prayed Gabriel wouldn't find the phone, otherwise…

Gabriel's face was drawn, his eyes glittered with fever – he had not slept for a while. He moved slowly towards the desk so that Edwina and Nancy retreated to the far end of the room. Their hands were resting on their heads.

Nancy was slow and deliberate. She didn't want to stumble. It was not the first time she had had a gun pointed towards her. She gave a discreet look in Edwina's direction. She was doing much better than

Nancy thought she would, struggling between fear and anger. A vein pulsed in her neck and her jaw was clenching so hard, Nancy could almost hear the gritted teeth.

Gabriel was now at the desk, fumbling around the drawers and some of them were shut. His back was turned against the large windows, his face in the shadows.

Nancy's focus had moved from his face to the gun. It glimmered in the sun that had suddenly invaded the room.

"Where is the key to your desk?"

Edwina remained silent. "I will shoot you Eddie if that's what you're wondering – and Nancy. Teach you to be such a nosy bitch."

"Key on my key ring. May I?" Edwina's voice was a little croaky but no longer scared. Gabriel nodded and Edwina bent forward slowly to were she had dumped her keys. She pushed them towards Gabriel.

Gabriel looked at the desk. He was thinking. Nancy measured what it would take to stop him. There was nothing heavy enough. She followed Edwina's glance to a small letter opener on the side of the desk, hardly visible to someone who didn't know it was there.

Gabriel moved towards the door and pointed the gun at Edwina. "Go to my desk, get the black gym bag underneath it – any funny business and I shoot her," his head jerked towards Nancy. Edwina moved slowly, hands still over her head. Nancy moved towards the desk very slowly too, but Gabriel had noticed.

"You stay where you are. You move and you get it in the stomach – very painful I've been told."

"Why?" Nancy put on her you're-so-bright-why-are-you-doing-this look.

"You're not in court any longer. Don't try that lawyer bullshit with me," Gabriel spoke with disdain. He had both women in his firing range. They needed more time.

"I'm not, but if I am going to die, I'd like to know why."

Edwina was back with his gym bag. She dropped it in the centre of the room and moved back to her original position.

"Not so fast – go to your desk, slow and easy," Gabriel was enjoying his moment. "Good girl – open the second drawer on your right. There is an envelope stuck to the inside."

Edwina moved as slow as she possibly could. She sat down, took the key and opened the drawer, dragging every move she made. She too had realised that time was on their side. The envelope was well concealed. She fumbled to get it.

Gabriel was getting impatient, but she looked convincingly clumsy. The packet came loose. She retrieved it, walked slowly to where the sports bag lied and dropped the packet onto it.

"Is it about your brother?" Not Nancy's best-phrased question she knew but she had to try.

Gabriel reached mechanically to his scar. His finger was tight on the trigger.

"How do you know?"

Nancy explained.

A few precious minutes to save their lives?

* * *

The floor on which William was recovering was swarming with police. Pole pushed his way through to find Detective Constable Todd. Andy's face was starting to swell up. He was going to end up with a decent black eye.

"I am impressed," said Pole. "Did you manage to see the guy?"

"He got me from behind and knocked my glasses off," Andy slurred with a pack of ice on his cheek. "But I've got something else for you, Guv."

His laptop was on the chair next to him. Pole sat down and helped his DC by holding it open for him.

"You remember that program – face recognition," Andy mumbled. "I found a match that does not tally."

He got to the image of a young man, medium-build, fair-brown hair and a nasty scar across his face. "He was not on the guest list." And the image showed the man speaking to Felipe Martinez.

"You've done brilliantly," Pole said standing up with a jolt.

"But," Andy struggled. "I don't have his name yet."

"And I do," Pole said already halfway down the corridor. He was calling Nancy, but her phone was engaged. His phone buzzed back, and Pole answered before checking the caller.

“When were you going to tell me about William Noble?” Marsh asked. His voice was calm but the undertone furious.

Pole’s mind went blank for a second – shit; he was not expecting this. He had no time to reply anyway. Marsh wanted him back at The Yard, now – Pole’s phone went dead.

Pole was back in his car, siren screaming, dialling hands free. “Nurani, are you at base?” Pole went through a pedestrian crossing that flashes green. “I know Marsh is looking for me.” He couldn’t get angry with her yet.

He needed her to save time with Marsh. “Check with Crowne. If he has anything good, I will need it. Yep, I need a very large bone to throw Marsh otherwise the suits are going to get involved and it will be the end of this case.”

Nurani didn’t quibble. She must have remembered what had happened last time she tried to be too clever.

The door opened and Henry turned. He recognised Pole’s deputy as she approached his desk. Henry’s face said it all and she froze. She saw the burner phone in Henry’s hand. The phone was on loudspeaker, and she could hear Nancy’s voice.

“She’s at the Bank of England with Edwina. Gabriel – I mean Edwina’s aide, is with them and he has a gun.” Henry spoke in a low voice as though concerned he would be heard.

Nurani blinked… a hostage situation was clearly not what she was expecting. She grabbed her own phone and called Pole. The go-to-man when the going was though.

“Hostage situation?” Pole’s focus was absolute.

“You need me,” Henry snatched Nurani’s phone. “Inspector Pole – I know the bank’s layout. I know where they are.”

“You’re on.”

Pole hang up and was already on the phone to SO19, the Met Specialist Firearms Unit.

Pole ran. He was speaking to Commander Ferguson. He crashed into Scotland Yard whilst agreeing an intervention protocol with Ferguson and met Nurani in the corridor.

“I’ll deal with Marsh,” she said before he had time to ask. “I’ll delay as much as I can so that you can get there before he speaks to Ferguson."

Regret crossed her face and Pole nodded. It was good to have the old Nurani back at last. She disappeared into the lift in the direction of Marsh's office.

Pole ran into Henry's room and signalled Henry to follow him.

"He's with me," Pole said to the bemused prison officers who saw Henry walk free from the room they had guarded all day. One of them tried to protest but Pole was already at the end of the corridor with Henry in tow. He pushed Henry into the lift, both listening to what was being said on the burner phone.

"Nobody moves until I arrive. I'll be there in fifteen minutes," Pole gave his final instruction to Ferguson. Another caller was trying to reach him – Superintendent Marsh. Pole ignored him.

* * *

"How do you know?" Gabriel said.

"I noticed you and was interested to know who Eddie was working with," Nancy lied convincingly. Gabriel thought she was a meddler; let him think that. "You looked so protective of her."

Gabriel ignored the compliment. "What do you know?"

"That your brother died during the US embassy bombing in Nairobi in 1998," Nancy spoke slowly. She was factual. Gabriel did not want pity.

"Is that it?" Gabriel's voice sounded strained, no doubt stirred up by memories that wouldn't go away. "Are you not forgetting something?" Gabriel's face was ashen and the redness of its scar almost unbearably fresh. He was on the brink. Nancy hesitated. "Your face?"

"That – and the rest of my body," he spat out. "Moronic Yanks. They think they know better, can do better than anybody else. Reality is not Hollywood. These fucks think they can blast their way around the world – Vietnam, Somalia, Afghanistan, Iraq…" He was ranting, fact and grudge intricately mixed. "They interfere with people they don't understand. Always more money, more power. And what does our pathetic government do? It follows – because we have a special relationship." Gabriel gestured and for an instant his gun was out of focus.

Nancy saw it now. It was all about revenge – not justice or fairness. She had seen it so often. "You blame the British for what happened?"

"Who else? Who else could be so incompetent?"

Nancy kept talking, kept asking. She had seen Edwina move ever so slightly towards the desk, towards the paper knife.

"You think you can change the course of events if you are at the top of the Bank of England? Economic policy can be a powerful tool."

"Who says I am interested in economics?" Gabriel took a step back. His face had changed again. His eyes bore into Nancy. He had been waiting for this moment since he entered Edwina's office. Edwina grabbed the knife and lunged forward.

The sound of a firearm discharge shattered the entire room.

* * *

The siren was screaming at the traffic. Pole was leaning forward, hoping it would somehow make the car move faster. Henry had cranked up the volume of the phone as high as it would go. He too was bent forward but his ear was to the phone trying to follow the conversation above the noise of the siren.

"What's happening?" Pole asked, eyes rivetted on the road.

"It's difficult to hear… but Nancy is keeping him talking.

Pole forged ahead swearing as he barely avoided cars and cyclists.

Pole turned off the siren as he charged down Poultry. Pole screeched to a stop. Gabriel was still rambling – US embassy, Nairobi…

Keep talking.

Pole entered the main hall. The security guard slowly raised his head from his newspaper. Pole flashed his ID.

"We have a hostage situation, Edwina James-Jones – SO19 on their way."

The guard's face took an extra few seconds to react. It was not the Saturday he was expecting at the Bank.

Pole's phone rang. SO19 ETA, seven minutes.

Henry had been listening to the conversation. He nodded negatively. "I think Nancy is running short of ideas."

"Shit." Pole looked at his watch: seven minutes. Too long.

"Where is Edwina's office?"

"Fifth floor, corner left – lifts very close." Henry said, facing the security guard for confirmation.

"Right," he said, snapping his fingers at the guard.

"Right."

"Is there a service elevator?" Pole was already moving towards the back of the building. The security guard finally sprang into action. "Yes, and you won't be heard when you arrive. You'll need my pass." Pole ran towards the other lift, Henry alongside him. They headed for the fifth floor.

"You should not be here." Pole shook his head.

"No one is going to cry if a terrorist banker gets done trying to stop another terrorist banker."

"Don't be an arse – Nancy will never speak to me again."

Henry had nothing to say to that. Pole had finally shut him up.

The door of the lift opened with a soft ping that sounded deafening to both men. They held their breath. The guard was right – they were at the other end of the building. A couple of doors separated them from Edwina's office.

Nancy had asked another question.

Keep talking please… Pole opened the first door softly, a short walk, the second door. He could hear voices. Henry indicated with his hand a right turn, then a left.

"If the door is open, the corridor will be partially visible – our best bet is to crawl alongside the windows," Henry murmured.

Pole nodded. It was time to switch off the burner phone. Henry hesitated. Pole grabbed it and pressed the red button. He turned away abruptly so Henry couldn't see the dread on his face.

Pole was in front. He could see the door of Edwina's office and movement. Gabriel was well positioned to survey the corridor. They had to crawl their way to the windows. Henry gave Pole the thumbs up. He would do anything now to get to Nancy. So close and yet so far.

Pole was at the window. He could hear Gabriel's voice distinctly. "Eddie, this is a stupid idea," he said, ironic.

The sound of a firearm discharge shattered the entire room.

Pole jumped through the door, ready to slam Gabriel. But the man was already down, half of his skull blown out, the unmistakable smell of blood seeping into the air. Henry was at the door too, frozen by the sight. Pole was about to rush towards Nancy when he noticed a floating red dot that hovered across Gabriel's back.

"Shooter," Pole screamed. He lunged towards Edwina, who was closer to him, and dragged her to the ground. Henry dashed pass Pole. He pulled Nancy behind a filing cabinet and they both dropped to the floor. Pole was on his mobile to the SO19 commander.

"What the fuck are you doing, Ferguson? Who told you to shoot?" Pole was beside himself. He was still sheltering Edwina with his body, but the red dot had disappeared. He turned his head towards Nancy as he spoke to Commander Ferguson. She mouthed *I am OK*.

Pole's attention reverted to the man on the floor. He squeezed his phone between his ear and his shoulder. Pole was about to move forward when he stopped.

"What do you mean your team is not yet in position at The Royal Exchange? Where else would you go, it's right in front of the Bank of England?" Pole signalled everyone to pull back.

"Shit, we have a rogue shooter." Pole moved back against the wall. "Understood, we are not moving until you've secured the area."

Chapter Twenty-Three

Brett picked up the morning papers at his Club, but nothing could distract his mind. Brett had sent a secure email to him reporting the wallet trick as agreed. What else did he want?

Steve materialised in front of his chair forcing him to drop his paper. And his handler finally looked concerned. Brett removed his glasses with a nonchalant hand.

"What's up my dear fellow?" Brett asked, his eyes catching those of one of the butlers.

"Your wallet."

"What about it? I told you I have reported it as agreed."

MI6-Steve plonked himself into an armchair. "The content, I mean your pass, has been used already. Is it too early for a glass of something"

"Never too early." Brett ordered two Glenlivets, no ice.

"The Sheik has used his new operative. The Royal Exchange – this morning."

"You mean?"

"Yes, at least one man – dead."

Brett looked towards the bar. Where was the goddamn whisky? He stuck a finger into his shirt collar and moved the tie away from his neck.

"You're not in the frame, if that is what's worrying you." Steve was also looking at the bar with impatience.

"Really? I'd like to be sure of that. Who is – was this chap anyway?"

"You don't need to know—"

Brett interrupted before Steve gave him more rubbish about the need-to-know basis.

"You don't get it, Steve. I am certain The Sheik showed me his photo when I went to see him."

Two whiskies had materialised. Steve finished his first. "You need to play your cards even closer to your chest."

"Closer than I do already and those cards will be tattooed to this famous chest of mine."

Steve ignored the humour. "You're about to move centre stage according to our latest intel. Don't worry about what you hear or read on the news. We manage the flow of information. Your main concern is to keep The Sheik happy – whatever it takes."

"What's in it for me apart from staying alive?"

Steve paused. He had not expected this. His little beady eyes flashed with amusement. "You pull this one off and you won't have to see me or MI6 ever again."

Brett remained poker-faced. "Righto, and you have the authority?" Brett waved at the butler again. He did not wait for Steve's answer. "One condition – what did the man in the picture do?"

Steve pushed himself back in his armchair, fingertips touching and hands in front of his chin. "He had infiltrated the Bank of England but—"

"He did not quite deliver," Brett finished.

The whiskies arrived and Brett raised his glass to Steve. Something he had thought he would never do.

* * *

The deflated atmosphere was palpable. Henry cast an eye towards Nancy and Pole. All three were holding their cups of tea the way a child might hold his blankie.

A ringing noise came from the computer. Henry cast an eye towards it. There was no point now, but he welcomed the change of subject. "What's the verdict on the banks?" Pole asked.

Henry raised an eyebrow but Pole looked serious. He turned towards the screen and read aloud: Barclays, RBS, Lloyds, Deutsche Bank, UBS, GL.

The last name brought Nancy back to life. "You're sure?"

"Well, this is my first stab at it but I'm pretty certain that those guys have been up to no good. Not that it is relevant now."

"Not so – LIBOR is still at the centre of this investigation. Edwina got far too involved." Pole's voice had an edge even Henry had rarely heard.

"Edwina won't survive that scandal," Henry said. It may not appease Pole, but it might go some way to releasing his anger.

"I wonder whether Gabriel had pushed to get the deal with the banks done too." Nancy asked.

"Ambition always gets out of hand," Henry spoke without resentment. "And I should know."

Nancy managed a smile. She turned towards Pole. "What was in the sports bag?"

"A couple of passports under different names, airline ticket to Turkey—"

"Gabriel was on his way to the Middle East?"

"Almost certainly. I am not yet sure why he was silenced. The team is going through the lot: computer, phone, flat. I have the feeling though that we were not the first ones there to search his place"

They returned to their tea for a short moment, each retreating into their own thoughts. Henry broke the silence.

"It would have been an incredible tool for market manipulation or money laundering if a group had unfettered access to the Bank of England Top Management." Henry's voice trails. The thought is both chilling and exciting.

"You mean a terrorist organisation? It might be far-fetched?" Nancy shrugged.

"No," Pole and Henry reply in unison.

Pole's mobile rang. Belmarsh's van had arrived. Henry's fist tightened around his teacup.

They stood up. Nancy hugged Henry warmly. She didn't care. Henry returned her hug and slipped a small piece of paper in her jacket pocket.

Pole stretched out his hand, "Thank you." Such a small but important phrase. The door opened. It was time.

* * *

Green Park was bustling with activity. A pink fireball, aged six, was on a collision course with Nancy. The future Olympian was not looking where she was going: her head turned back, checking whether her friends were catching up with her. Nancy moved away. The parents apologised. No harm done, not today at least. Nancy was enjoying her walk home. The sun shone through the thickness of the trees. It bounced off the windows of the adjacent building. She fancied an ice cream.

Pole had promised to call in the evening. She suspected it may not be to talk about LIBOR and her pulse quickened ever so slightly. The grass had not yet lost its softness. She removed her shoes and her toes dug into the lawn. An ancient memory was surfacing. Mixed emotions rolled into her chest. If she had had to die on the floor of Edwina's office, she would have regretted not taking Pole's affection seriously.

Memories of China finally broke free: The Cultural Revolution, her father. Not today, she was not ready yet, but soon.

Nancy spotted a bench drenched in sunlight, unexpectedly empty. Not for long no doubt, but presently it offered her the solitude she needed. She plunged her hand in her light mac and fingered a piece of paper. The paper Henry handed her as they said goodbye. She sat down and looked at the sky. Pure blue. The weather may be kind for a while.

Nancy, dearest friend
I could not miss this occasion to write a letter that I know will only be read by you and you alone. Writing to you has been my lifeline; thank you for never giving up on me.

There is not much time and though I feel there is so much I want to say I will have to be brief. I have been restless. Not about my sentence. I deserved it. But it is about going beyond it. If it was right to make me pay for what I did, don't I somehow deserve to be given the chance to show I can change – that despite everything I am redeemable?

You will hear or see things in the next few weeks that might make you doubt me; please give me the benefit of the doubt.

You will be asked to interfere or even stop me – I beg you, don't.

You may even be told that I have killed myself or been killed. I will never let this happen.

Trust has been at the core of our friendship – believe in me one last time.

I know what I must do.

Henry

List of French Expressions with English Translations

French Dialogue	English Translation
absolument	absolutely
bien sur, je n'en ésperais pas moins	of course, I could not have hoped for more
bienvenue	welcome
bonjour mohammed, votre contact anglais á l'appareil	hello Mohammed, your English contact speaking
ça suffit vous deux	enough you two
compris	understood
eh bien	and so
étonnant	astonishing
exactement	exactly
incroyable	unbelievable
l'âme soeur	the perfect match
le capitaine	the captain
les grands esprits se rencontrent	great minds think alike
ma chére	my dear
ma chére amie	my dear friend
mais enfin la voici	but finally, here it is
mon ami	my friend
mon chère ami	my dear
n'est-ce pas	isn't it
peut-être pas	maybe not
peut-être pas mais	perhaps, but
voila. vous avez tout compris, mon cher	here you are, all clear
vraiment, vous deux êtes incorrigibles	really, you two are incorrigible

Acknowledgements

It takes many people to write and publish a book… for their generosity and support I want to say thank you.

Kate Gallagher, my editor and story consultant, for her immense knowledge of good language and of what makes a book great. Ryan O'Hara, for his expertise in design and for producing a super book cover - yet again. Danny Lyle, for his patience and proficiency in typesetting the text! Abbie Headon, for her eagle-eyed proofreading.

To the friends who have patiently read, reread, and advised: Kathy Vanderhook, Alison Thorne, Susan Rosenberg, Helena Halme - author and books marketing coach - and to my very cool ARC team.

Dear Reader,

I hope you have enjoyed BREAKING POINT as much as I have enjoyed writing it!

So, perhaps you would like to know more about Henry Crowne. What are the ghosts that haunt him? What is it in his past that made him who he is?

Delve into HENRY CROWNE PAYING THE PRICE series with

COLLAPSE:
mybook.to/COLLAPSE

NO TURNING BACK:
mybook.to/NOTURNINGBACK

Or

HENRY CROWNE PAYING THE PRICE, BOOKS 1-3:
mybook.to/HCPTPBKS1-3

SPY SHADOWS:
mybook.to/SPYSHADOWS

IMPOSTOR IN CHIEF:
mybook.to/IMPOSTORINCHIEF

Or check out my new series

A NANCY WU CRIME THRILLER:

BLOOD DRAGON:
mybook.to/BLOODDRAGON

It's also time for me to ask you for a small favour...

Please take a few minutes to leave a review either on Amazon.

Reviews are incredibly important to authors like me. They increase the book's visibility and help with promotions. So, if you'd like to spread the word, get writing, or leave a star review.

Thank you so very much.

Finally, don't forget. You can gain FREE access to the backstories that underpin the HENRY CROWNE PAYING THE PRICE series and get to know the author's creative process and how the books are conceived.

Read FREE chapters and the exclusive Prequel to the HENRY CROWNE PAYING THE PRICE series: INSURGENT

Go to https://freddieppeters.com and join Freddie's Book Club now...

Looking forward to connecting with you!

Freddie